NO
EVIDENCE OF A
CRIME

NO
EVIDENCE OF A
CRIME

By
S. Connell Vondrak

Oak Tree Press   Taylorville, IL

Oak Tree Press

Oak Tree Press books may be purchased for educational, business or sales promotional purposes. Contact Publisher for quantity discounts.

First Edition, August 2010

10 9 8 7 6 5 4 3 2 1

Cover by MickADesign.com

ISBN 978-1-61009-000-1
LCCN 2010933218

CHAPTER ONE

THE CHERRY TREES were in bloom, but Kathleen had not noticed them until a plane overhead drew her attention upward. As she looked toward the sky, she saw a cloud of pink petals hovering just over her head. The sky was a perfect crystal blue, flickering through the ceiling of petals above. She breathed deeply and closed her eyes for a moment. She could smell the cool, damp air with a hint of freshly mowed grass overwhelmed by the sweetness of the cherry blossoms. With another breath, she thought the smell alone would lift her ever so slightly off the ground and suspend her, for a moment, away from everything.

Kathleen opened her eyes and looked at the scene before her. A crimson halo of blood framed the face of a young black woman lying on the grass. Occasionally, a petal or two would float down and land in the pool of blood or on the woman's face, as if nature were trying to beautify the gruesome sight.

Kathleen looked over at the thin yellow plastic ribbon that separated her from the growing number of people who had come to watch. Police tape with the words CRIME SCENE – DO NOT CROSS tacked to waist-high stakes was the only barrier separating the horrors of the crime from the rest of the world. But that thin plastic tape seemed to be enough. The onlookers did not want to step into Kathleen's world. They did not want to be standing over a dead woman's body, looking intently at the corpse. They did not want to kneel close enough to smell the blood as they looked for the signs of the body having been moved. They watched from safety, protected by the thin yellow piece of police tape.

Kathleen studied the body. The woman's lips were slightly parted, revealing bright white teeth. She could see the woman's mascara and her curly, black hair carefully tied back with a ribbon. Kathleen could not help but stare. This was not a mock crime scene or a picture in a textbook.

This was not her first murder investigation, Kathleen thought trying to reassure herself, but paused for a moment. Technically, she thought, this may be her first murder case, at least one where she was looking at a dead body. She had only held the rank of detective for a few months, and that meant her assignments had always been as a backup. She had been the officer assigned to check on financial records or to interview the best friend or inventory the evidence. She was called to crime scenes, but only after the body had been sent to the medical examiner's office. Her job was to scour the area for missed items or unknown witnesses. She had been told it was a way to learn the ropes, but there had always been a hint of disappointment with each assignment. She had always thought a job as a homicide detective would be more adventurous.

Kathleen looked at the body once more, wondering what the woman had been like. Did she have friends or family? Were people wondering where she was? She had to have a job or family money. She was too well-dressed to be a prostitute.

Kathleen's thoughts crashed in upon themselves as words broke into her concentration.

"Evidence bag."

She looked over slowly at the man barking the orders. The early morning call to the crime scene did not improve her reaction time and the half-cup of coffee she had on the drive over had not given her its intended jolt of energy.

"KJ, I need an evidence bag." It was Captain Freeman kneeling a few feet away from Kathleen.

"Here you go, Captain." Kathleen watched as her partner, Jim, walked over and handed the captain a bright orange evidence bag.

"Thanks, Jim. I just want to collect some evidence I see here. It's your case," Captain Freeman assured Jim. "I was in the office early, you know, just down the block. When I heard the call, I thought I would try and help out."

"I wouldn't have it any other way, Captain," Jim said with a smile.

Kathleen rubbed her eyes. Jim did not smile much, not at least from what Kathleen had seen, but Jim had a way with his smiles. His thin lips stretched out across a chiseled face, a twinkle of blue from his eyes. When he wanted to, Jim could get a lot with just his smile. Kathleen shrugged away her wandering thoughts knowing her focus needed to be with the crime scene.

The captain looked over at Kathleen. "I don't know where your head is, KJ. But, starting right now, you better start thinking about this case. There is a lot of evidence that needs collecting. There are people waiting for your instructions."

Kathleen watched Captain Freeman kneel next to the young woman's body and slowly pick up what looked like a long blonde hair. It was the first time Kathleen noticed how dark the captain's skin was. It was a deep ebony black. His bushy eyebrows seemed longer than the hair on the top of his head. Across his forehead were deep wrinkle lines made from the years he had spent working homicide cases. The heat of the early sun caused a glistening sheen across his face from the sweat beginning to form. Both his eyebrows and his closely cropped hair were flecked with gray, giving him an air of distinction. He looked like a man of importance, which suited him, because he was.

Captain Freeman was the district Commander in charge of the Crime Scene Bureau for Washington, DC. He looked and dressed the part. Seldom did anyone see Captain Freeman not wearing a suit. Although his job was mostly administrative now and showed in his well-developed jowls and ever-growing waistline, he still commanded great respect from everyone in the department. He spoke with an authority and confidence that only comes with years on the force. Kathleen liked him. It was actually Captain Freeman who had hired her, and she was grateful he had given her the opportunity. Despite his words, Kathleen knew the captain had faith in her abilities. He probably had more faith in her abilities than she did.

"KJ! Come over here," he barked as he walked a few feet away from the body.

"Yes, sir. Don't worry, sir. We're on top of this case, Captain."

"KJ," Freeman said in a whisper, "you know we've been easy on you," he said with a nod. "The cases we've been giving you have been kind of simple. We were hoping to give you and Jim some time to get to know each other, work together as partners. But that just doesn't seem to be working out as well as we thought; nothing to do with you. He lost his partner. When you lose a partner the way he did, it's hard to recover.

"It's hard to bring in a new person and be told they are your partner's replacement. Don't take it personally. I've discussed this with the Deputy Director. We both felt it might be better to put you into the fire. A little pressure is good. This is going to be a big case. I can feel it. We're throwing you into the deep end of the pool. You and Jim are the lead investigators. You can learn a lot from Jim. He and Pete were the best detectives I've ever seen. Too bad you didn't know him then, but now it is up to you to make this work. Are we clear?"

A pat on Kathleen's shoulder before he walked away made it clear his direction had been given and he felt no further discussion was necessary.

Kathleen returned her attention to the young woman's body. The victim rested on her side with her head turned to the right. Her eyes were still open. Kathleen looked into her blankly staring eyes.

"I am going to take scrapings from under her nails," the captain said as he sealed up one evidence bag and marked it with the information of where the evidence was collected and by whom. "Can someone get me another evidence bag?"

Kathleen quickly looked over at Jim. They were thinking the same thing. The captain had not been in the field for years. They were painfully aware of the number of cases in which the investigation was botched or the evidence was inadmissible. More often than not, the foul up was due to someone up the chain of command wanting to be involved in the investigation, wanting to work the evidence, wanting to help with the case when they had been off the street for too many years. They damaged the case beyond repair.

In a whisper barely loud enough for Jim to hear, Kathleen said, "No one collects fingernail scraping at the scene. A wind could blow evidence away. It could get lost in the grass. It could get contaminated. He should know that. Do you think he doesn't trust us?"

Jim whispered back in the captain's defense, "He knows that. He's just not thinking. He trusts us."

Jim walked toward Freeman. "Captain, I think we have this covered," Jim said putting his hand on the captain's shoulder. "We were just about to bag her hands," he said as he snapped open a brown paper bag and placed it over the victim's hand, taping it shut around her wrists. "The area has been secured and we have about half a dozen rookies combing the streets for witnesses. We got officers walking the grounds, looking for any kind of possible evidence. Photographs of the scene have been taken. There's not much left to do but wait until the Medical Examiner's wagon comes. Once we get to the morgue, we'll get her clothes, scrapings, blood standards and the rest of the evidence. When we get everything collected, we'll have it to the crime lab by the end of the day. Promise."

Everyone knew Jim had a way with handling people. He could read their sighs, their gestures, their faces. Most of the time, they couldn't even tell they were being read. It was what had made Jim one of the best detectives in Washington, DC. It was why Kathleen had been assigned to Jim almost six months earlier.

Captain Freeman took a long, deep breath and slowly exhaled. Rising to his feet, he looked apologetic. "Sorry," he said softly. "Collecting scrapings at the scene was probably a pretty bad idea. I know you'll do a good job, Jim, Kathleen." Shaking his head with his noticeable jowls moving back and forth, he repeated sadly, "It's a terrible thing. It's a terrible thing."

"She's about Sarah's age, isn't she?" Jim said, nodding toward the dead woman.

Captain Freeman gave a slow nod as he turned to leave. "Keep me posted on this case. I expect updates."

"Sarah?" Kathleen whispered as she watched the captain walk away.

"His daughter," Jim whispered back.

It took another ten minutes for the police wagon, which would transport the body, to arrive. The flash of a reporter's light bulb punctuated the wagon's arrival. It took another half an hour to carefully load the woman's body into the wagon. To properly preserve all the evidence was always a difficult and time-consuming task. As the blood around the woman's head dried, it became tacky. Care had to be taken to ensure all the important evidence was identified and removed. Everyone at the crime scene knew the ropes. Each officer took the time to do things right. After the body was loaded, Jim and Kathleen followed the wagon to the morgue.

Once at the Medical Examiner's office, things became routine. The processing room where the evidence would be collected prior to the autopsy had bright lights and glass windows surrounding a stainless steel table which had wheels that could be locked when needed. Here, the woman was examined for evidence. All of the victim's clothing was sealed in paper bags. Scrapings from under her nails were taken. Swabs and blood standards, hair samples, and fingerprints were all sealed in separate bags. Once everything was collected, the woman was cleared for autopsy. The autopsy room only had three stations and all of them were currently filled. With a toe tag assigning an ID number and a white sheet covering the naked body, the lonely corpse was left to wait in line for her autopsy.

Seeing the wait, Jim and Kathleen decided to go back to their office and compile the information they had. They loaded the bagged evidence on a metal cart and rolled it to their car. Since the items of clothing were bagged separately, the evidence took a large amount of space. Trying not to crush anything, Jim had to place some of them in the back seat.

"Please make certain anything with wet blood on it gets put in the trunk," Kathleen implored Jim. "I hate that smell."

"Already done," Jim said as he got into the car.

The drive to their office was slow. Tourists always signified the start of springtime, but Kathleen could not fault the influx of people. Spring was a beautiful time in Washington, DC. Green peeked out from the gray and brown silhouettes of the trees. The white marble monuments were at the height of their beauty when accented by the striking fresh greenness of newly sprouting leaves. Spring rains washed away the mud and grime from a late winter snow. Cherry blossoms surrounding the Jefferson Memorial framed it like a painting.

Stopped by a traffic light, Kathleen watched as a class of young children walked in front of their car.

"Kids," Jim laughed.

Kathleen cleared her throat and tried to make conversation.

"I think it's a good sign," Kathleen started.

"What sign?" Jim asked nonchalantly, checking the side street.

"Being put as lead investigators on this murder case," Kathleen explained. "It's a good sign. We will do a great job. Solve the murder. Be the heroes. I think I'll learn a lot, don't you?"

"Sure," Jim said as the light changed color. He paused as the last boy ran across the street in response to the sharp clapping sound of the teacher's hands.

Jim quietly drove on, lost in the thoughts of his own two sons, now teenagers.

"How did you know Captain Freeman had a daughter named Sarah?" Kathleen asked as she glanced out the passenger window of the car.

"When he worked down at Zone Five, he used to talk about her. You know, parents trading stories. We talked about our kids. Things we did on the weekend, how they were doing in school. You get to know one another's family. I think she might be in law school now. Freeman's youngest boy is the same age as my oldest, Robert. Sometimes we went out to the Mall together, to play a little touch football, or throw a Frisbee around," Jim said, thinking back on some very happy days.

Kathleen stared at him for a moment, before saying, "You never talk about your kids."

"I never talk about my kids with you," he corrected her but once he had, he wished he hadn't. He pretended to be intently focusing on driving, but Jim could feel Kathleen's eyes staring at him, trying to decipher what that had meant.

Kathleen didn't want to think about what possible reason Jim would have for not discussing his kids with her. She fixed her gaze on the children who were halfway down the block. It seemed strange to

Kathleen to have children walking so close to a car full of evidence from a murder victim. It seemed strange that the world could be so oblivious to the death of this young woman now, but in a few hours, all would be shocked and horrified when they read about it in the paper or saw it on the news. A young, well-dressed woman found dead on the National Mall would not be overlooked by the press or public.

When they arrived at their office, Kathleen and Jim reviewed the reports of the officers working on the case. Some more senior patrol officers were now tracking down who the woman was, her history, her life. The rookies were given the assignment to find any witnesses to the crime—harder work than one might think. Occasionally, witnesses came forward to give a description of a suspect, but often the witnesses were unaware of the importance of their recollections. A parked car, a loud sound, a dog barking, all could be clues necessary to make the picture complete. Of the two assignments, the rookies had the harder job…walking up and down the streets, checking with the transit system, checking with the people who lived in any nearby apartments. Often people would think they saw something but, eventually, the date or the times or the circumstances didn't match the crime. Kathleen and Jim focused on the reports from the more senior patrol officers. They had found out some basic information.

The dead woman's name was Victoria Young. She was 23 years old and rented a small apartment a few blocks from the Capitol. The estimated time of death was 1 a.m. At the moment, they had not been able to locate any credible witness who had seen or heard anything. A security guard found the body on his way to work at 6:10 a.m. The man had been cleared of any suspicion once his whereabouts were accounted for. He had a second job in a factory, and his supervisor verified the security guard had worked the night before. Victoria Young was currently employed as an aide for a U. S. Representative from Alabama named Philip Thatcher.

Jim raised one of his eyebrows as he read the information. "A U.S. Rep. Well, that puts a bright spot in my day," Jim said, a definite note of sarcasm in his voice. "Things are always more fun when we can mix a little politics in with a murder." Then in a more serious tone, he added, "At least we have a little bit to go on. After we drop off the evidence at the crime lab, we can swing on by and see if Representative Thatcher is available for some questions."

Kathleen had heard all the stories in her time with the department. No one could work as a police officer in Washington, DC and not expect politics to enter the equation at some time. Kathleen had never had the pleasure of working with an elected official, but she knew the minute a senator or representative or their aides became involved in a case, a whole new set of headaches arose.

After giving all the reports a cursory read-through, they started to review and inventory the evidence they brought from the Medical Examiner's office. Using the photos taken, Kathleen reviewed the crime scene. They had been careful, and hopefully that care would pay off with some additional information which might have been lost had they not taken the time to be thorough.

They had a lot of evidence and all the evidence seemed high quality. Everything was labeled correctly. The bags were sealed properly with evidence tape. The chain of custody was clearly marked on the bags and matched the evidence log. They had had no problems with the crime scene being compromised. So far, the case seemed tight. Kathleen knew that this type of case would be highly scrutinized. Every 'T' had to be crossed, every 'I' dotted. If suspects did not develop soon, they would be the two targets for the media. It was the kind of case detectives dreaded, but it was also the kind of case they knew kept them sharp and on top of their game. Kathleen breathed a sigh of relief, knowing the evidence in this case was not going to be an issue.

Kathleen took a break to rest her eyes from the tedious review of evidence and logs. She looked around at their office. It was a large room, quieter than one might imagine. They shared it with six other detectives. Other than using their desks for paperwork, making phone calls, or preparing for court, the desks were seldom used. Detectives would come in and out of the office as needed, but there was generally little need for individual offices. The detectives worked in pairs, usually one more senior than the other. Kathleen and Jim each had their own desk, but someone had pushed the two yellowing oak desks together, probably before Kathleen was born. This meshed the desktops into one large work area. Kathleen looked across her workspace to Jim, as he filled out the paperwork needed to submit the twenty-five bags of evidence to the crime lab.

Jim pulled another form from his desk drawer. It was an evidence inventory log that was required to submit evidence to the crime lab. Jim's taut, square jaw flexed as he chewed a piece of gum and concentrated on the paperwork. His hair was cut short. He had bangs that he combed forward, but their unwillingness to stay flat against his forehead gave an indication of how untamed his hair would be if he allowed it to grow more than an inch in length.

"I think the hair we found on the woman's body was fake hair from a wig," Kathleen said abruptly, thinking about the difference between Jim's hair and the one found at the crime scene.

"Well, that will be an easy call for the lab," Jim said, not looking up. Jim was never one to presume. It was one of his best traits as a detective. He never came up with a theory or a suspect until he had all the information possible. That was one of the traits Kathleen admired about Jim but also drove her crazy. Even when the clue was a neon sign pointing to the suspect, flashing the word "GUILTY", Jim waited for all the reports to come in before going forward with the prosecution of the case. Kathleen was the exact opposite. Her thoughts were always busy trying to fit each bit of information into the puzzle. Often, to her frustration, when the information changed, Kathleen's solution to the puzzle crumbled before her eyes, and she had to start over, reforming her solution.

Jim continued working on the evidence submission forms. He listed each exhibit, starting with the description: one sealed brown paper bag. Then, he described the contents in each bag and listed the type of analysis needed for each exhibit. This was one of the most time-consuming parts of evidence collection, but it had to be done correctly. The crime lab used the paperwork, first to inventory the evidence, then to organize all the tests that were requested. As thousands of pieces of evidence crossed the counter of the crime laboratory, the evidence log was the mechanism to ensure all the tests were done and performed in the proper order. Once all the evidence was inventoried at the evidence counter of the crime lab, the details were entered into their computer system. This allowed the laboratory staff to track the progress of the evidence through the sections of the laboratory.

The paperwork also had another important purpose. It told the forensic scientists what types of tests the police wanted done on the evidence. A single tube of blood might need a DNA work up, or toxicology tests, or a paternity test, or all three. A firearm with a bloody fingerprint would travel to many sections. First to the firearms section to ensure there were no chambered rounds or bullets in the weapon. Once the firearm was cleared, it would travel to the latent print section for photographs of the bloody prints; then, to the DNA section, where they would remove a sample of the blood for testing before they returned it to the latent print section. The firearm would be thoroughly tested for any latent prints before the journey back to the firearms section, where test shots would be made for a bullet comparison. Jim knew the more detailed he was in outlining the testing and description, the more smoothly the evidence would move through the crime laboratory.

"Kathleen, as I finish each page, could you review my descriptions to make certain they are correct? Check my requests for analysis, too. If you can think of other tests that might need to be done, add it in," Jim said as he slid the first sheet across the desk to Kathleen.

Kathleen had been Jim's partner for about six months. It seemed like a very short time but was the longest six months of her life. She wanted to take in every bit of knowledge her partner had, absorbing it into her own mind. But Jim was not always in a giving mood. Kathleen would never complain about Jim. As partners go, she had drawn well. He was patient, kind, and had a cuttingly sarcastic sense of humor she enjoyed. She guessed he probably worked out at a gym, but he had never mentioned it. He had a thin but muscular frame, however age was beginning to show in his walk. Kathleen noticed every now and then a stiffness as Jim rose from his chair, a limp that came and went after sitting too long in their police car.

Jim had completed almost twenty years on the force and would be eligible for retirement at the end of the year. Everyone was certain that, even when he became eligible, he would never retire. Kathleen was not so certain. She did not have the history with him that the others in the force did, so she could evaluate him without the past sneaking in to color the truth. When Kathleen looked at Jim, she saw someone a little tired, a little stiff, a little beaten by life, someone who might want a break from dead bodies and politicians. Most of all, she thought, Jim might want to break away from his memories.

For nine years prior to Kathleen's time, Jim Jarred's partner had been Pete Stone. Jim had never spoken of Pete to Kathleen, and, Kathleen knew enough not to ask, but she had heard an ear full from everyone else in the department. Jim and Pete had both started at the police academy the same year. Jim was right out of college and Pete was right out of the Marines. They were an unlikely pair but since their Academy days, they had been close. Pete was the best man at Jim's wedding. For ten years, their careers paralleled each other. They rose up through the ranks separately but together, working their way up to the rank of detective. In hopes of working together, they both requested the same assignment to the Crime Scene Bureau and asked to be partners.

Normally, newly-assigned officers were paired up with experienced detectives, but Jim and Pete were allowed to be partners on a trial basis. The trial soon became permanent when the captain saw how well they worked together. Both were instinctive in their ability to understand the crime and read the signs and clues people left behind. The bond between Jim and Pete seemed to be a secret weapon. Each would play off the other's thoughts. Each knew the other's move before it was made. Everyone on the force knew them and liked them, but there was always a hint of underlying jealousy when all the major cases and all the high profile cases started being passed their way. No matter how unsolvable the case appeared, they would solve it. They were at the height of their career and they knew it.

Kathleen thought about how different her progression had been. After undergraduate work, she spent years earning a master's degree in Criminal Justice. During that time, she had been fascinated with forensic investigations. She had followed all the major forensic cases, reading about how they were solved. During her graduate work, she had studied the arsenal of tactics available to an investigator. She studied each individual case, mastering the steps to solve investigations correctly and incorrectly. Her thesis focused on a comparison of successful and unsuccessful investigation patterns. After she received her master's degree, she entered a doctoral program. She was close to obtaining her Ph.D. in Forensic Investigation when on a whim she had taken the police entrance exam.

Captain Freeman had been familiar with several of Kathleen's articles published in law enforcement journals and was impressed with her work. Captain Freeman was a man who believed one should never stop learning. He was constantly reading articles, meeting with other agencies, discussing new advances. He liked the way Kathleen did not focus only on the wildly successful investigations. She dissected the disasters and made correlations between the two. When Kathleen's name came across his desk as the first person ever to make a perfect score on the police exam, he called her to confirm she was the same woman who authored those publications.

His phone call grew from just confirming who she was to a profound discussion of the department. Captain Freeman was very impressed with Kathleen's knowledge of police investigation and by the end of the phone call he had convinced Kathleen that if she were willing to come on board, he would hire her through a special hiring process where she could become a lead crime scene investigator in just a couple years. The offer so excited Kathleen that she accepted it and hung up without asking a single question, or finding out where she would work or the captain's phone number. There was a sign of relief when he called her back with more information.

Her next six-months were spent at the cadet training academy going through standard police training class. It was grueling. She had long passed her thirtieth birthday, yet she still had to do pushups and take some tackles. She had to learn the proper arrest procedures, laws and policies. At one point during her police training, she felt every muscle and every brain cell hurt.

After graduation, a whirlwind tour through each of departments. A three month rotation on "patrol", which she hated; then "narcotics" which introduced her to some very dirty people living in some very dirty places. "Gambling" was next and finally the internal affairs units where no one really wanted to work except those who worked there. They loved it.

As unlikely as it seemed, after being with the Washington, DC Police

Department only a little over a year and a half, she was given the rank of detective and assigned as Jim Jarred's partner.

When Kathleen finally arrived at the position she had been promised by Captain Freeman, she guessed there might be a lot of resentment from the officers who had worked their way up to detective. Since she hadn't climbed her way up the ranks, she was prepared to ride out the wave of disgruntled officers who felt they deserved the position, but the wave never came. There were times when Kathleen felt her inexperience drew eyes of scrutiny upon her, but never resentment. Probably because they all thought Jim needed a partner like Kathleen.

Kathleen looked at her desk and knew she had made it to where she wanted to be. Although looking at the evidence inventory receipts made it a little difficult to acknowledge at that moment to acknowledge how much she wanted this job, paperwork was part of the package.

Kathleen glanced at Jim. He had just about finished the second inventory receipt for the evidence. Kathleen studied the first one. With a sigh, she began to check through what Jim had written.

Exhibit 1 - One sealed manila envelope containing unknown hair samples from the victim's clothing

Analysis request -hair characteristic evaluation, DNA if applicable.

Exhibit 2 - One sealed manila envelope containing a hair standard pulled from the victim's head.

Analysis request - comparison to Exhibit 1

Exhibit 3 - One sealed brown paper bag containing victim's blouse

Analysis request - check blouse for hairs/fibers/other foreign substances and human body fluids - DNA on any body fluids detected

Kathleen read through item by item, trying to remember where and when each exhibit was collected, trying to remember why they had thought that item was significant.

"On exhibit 6, the fingernail scrapings, we wanted DNA on that, didn't we?" Kathleen asked.

"Didn't I write that?" Jim asked as he pulled a third sheet from his pile of blank forms.

"It says, 'Check for human tissues,'" Kathleen replied.

"I am certain they would do DNA if they found anything, but it is probably better to write it down." Jim said as he looked over the twenty-second bag for description on the Evidence Inventory sheet.

Jim was meticulous in everything he did and even though his side of the desk was covered in a sea of brown paper bags and manila envelopes, it still seemed neat and organized.

Everyone had told Kathleen how different Jim was before she had met him. She had heard all about his boisterous laughter, and how his hint of a smile usually indicated an impending joke. Kathleen had never seen that side of him. In fact, the first time Kathleen met Jim was the day that both his partner, Pete, and Jim's wife, Jennifer, were buried. Kathleen had attended the funerals. She had not known either of them, but she wanted to attend.

Looking back, Kathleen felt that was probably a bad decision. Stepping into Jim's life during the middle of such tragedy did not help their relationship. Hundreds of their friends attended the services. Pete's funeral was in the morning with full police honors. Jennifer's was in the afternoon. Everyone attended both funerals, offering their support. The church was so crowded only half the people could sit. Kathleen recalled how she had watched Jim's response as people came by to tell him what a wonderful woman Jennifer had been. It took Kathleen most of the day to muster the courage to introduce herself to Jim. She wanted him to know that she was also there to support him. Kathleen had often asked herself, whatever had possessed her to introduce herself as his newly assigned partner? Why had she stepped into his life so thoughtlessly? She should have stayed in the background, absorbing the moment; but she hadn't. She had always regretted how they had met.

Pete and Jennifer were driving together late at night. The crime lab reported both had a high blood alcohol. Pete was driving when he lost control of Jennifer's car after a light frost had dusted the road. When interviewed, Jim had said there was an evening flower show Jennifer wanted to attend. It was the last day of the show and Jim couldn't go so Pete said he would take her. It was obvious from the blood alcohol level that they must have spent the evening drinking. Investigators noted that no alcoholic beverages had been served at the flower show. No one ever found out what bar they had gone to. Caught dead, together after a night on the town led half the people in the department to believe they were having an affair. The other half, usually the ones who knew them better, knew Pete and Jim were like brothers and an affair was impossible. The case was closed as a drunk driving accident but the questions always lingered.

Kathleen had heard all the stories and all the speculations. For the first three months of her assignment to Crime Scenes, half of her conversations ended with a person asking in a low whisper, "Has Jim ever said anything about it to you?" or, "Do you think anything was going on between Pete and Jen?" Out of Jim's hearing everyone talked about it. The only one who didn't, of course, was Jim, who had never spoken one word about the incident. Kathleen had learned that even the slightest reference to it would turn Jim's jaw to stone and his blue eyes to a steel gray, and she would quickly change the course of the conversation.

Kathleen turned to the evidence in front of her and reviewed it for a third time. She placed the evidence bags into several boxes so they would be easier to carry to the car for the drive to the crime lab.

Jim said, "Before we go, let me call the ME's office to see if there is anything else we need to pick up."

As Jim reached for the phone, Kathleen carried the lightest of the boxes down to the car. By the time Kathleen was back for the second box, Jim was off the phone.

"We have to stop over at the Medical Examiner's office before we go to the crime lab," Jim said as they each picked up one of the remaining boxes to bring to the car.

"You're kidding me," Kathleen said, surprised. "There was evidence we missed?"

"Oh, yeah." Jim nodded. "There was some evidence we missed, alright."

Kathleen once again went over the crime scene in her mind, reviewing each piece of evidence they collected, knowing they could not have missed anything.

"Victoria Young was pregnant."

Kathleen's eyes widened. "Interesting."

CHAPTER TWO

WHEN JIM AND Kathleen arrived at the Medical Examiner's office, Dr. Hayes, the Chief Medical Examiner, had everything prepared. He had taken photographs of the fetus. He had also drawn a fetal blood sample and a small amount of tissue.

"Well, of course you knew it was a bullet wound to the right temple that killed her." Dr. Hayes started talking the minute they were close enough to hear. "Not much stomach contents. She probably hadn't eaten dinner. It will all be in the report when I finish. I should have it done in a day or two. Here are the samples," he said, handing Jim a 10-milliliter test tube with a red rubber stopper and a specimen cup.

Jim looked at the samples and estimated the tube contained ten drops of blood. He knew this was not nearly the amount they usually brought to the crime laboratory. There was more tissue present, which appeared as an unidentifiable glob of red, meaty material.

"There is not enough blood in a fetal blood sample for a toxicology screen," continued Dr. Hayes. "The tissue is for the tox screen. A general screen for drugs would be good. Quantitations are probably not necessary. I don't know how much data there is on fetal drug concentrations. Some drugs won't even pass through the placenta. If there were drugs involved, we should be able to detect them in the mother's blood.

"Although," Dr. Hayes said thinking for a moment, "you know, fetal liver function is not consistent with adult liver function, so we might have a wider window of detection of any drugs. An interesting notion, don't you think? Well, anyway," he said, waving his hand and shaking his head as if to brush away the distraction. Dr. Hayes had a way of discussing his work that assumed everyone in the room knew exactly what he was talking about.

After a long pause Dr. Hayes continued. "It's your decision what tests to have done. There is plenty of blood for a DNA test. You might try running it through their DNA database to see if we can match a father. They will probably have to manipulate that data a bit. You know," he nodded at Kathleen, "they will have to remove the mother's DNA. If they eliminate the mother's DNA profile, the profile that is left is from the father. Of course; it would only be half a true profile, but, there's a chance you might get a hit."

Dr. Hayes was all business. There were seldom the formalities of a handshake or a "How's it going?" When he talked, it was about a case. Sometimes his conversations contained so much information that it was easy to miss a key point which he had slipped between two other thoughts. Kathleen had been burned by this in the past. She had missed the words "probably female" during his elaborate description of the possible suspect in a robbery/homicide case; her first case as a detective. When she put together a summary of possible suspects for the lead investigators, she listed seven men. Everyone had a great laugh at her expense, and the next morning, someone placed a copy of Grey's Anatomy on her desk.

If someone had told Kathleen to picture in her mind what a chief medical examiner would look like, she would have pictured Dr. Hayes. Beneath his white lab coat was a white dress shirt and tie. He looked like he could have retired years ago with his silver hair and gray beard, but he had no intention of retiring any time soon. A little bit of a paunch made the lab coat taut around his waist. He wore his eyeglasses slightly down on his nose and peered over them from time to time. Although he looked like he was someone's grandfather, he was not. He had never married.

"Hold on, Dr. Hayes," Kathleen said, raising her hands and gesturing him to slow the flow of information down to a safe speed. Dr. Hayes abruptly stopped talking, surprised at the interruption to his stream of thought.

"Doc," Jim stepped in to the conversation, "I don't know if we mentioned that this woman worked for a U.S. Rep."

"Oh, my," said Dr. Hayes. "Well, I knew she was not poor. Her nails, her teeth, her body were all in excellent condition. That is usually a sign of a person with some degree of affluence. I guess you might not want to run the DNA through the database. Who knows what you might find. Let's hope you don't find anything too significant in a DNA check," he said with a slight laugh at the thought. "Politics always makes things a little more complicated," Dr. Hayes said, smiling over the possibility of a little scandal added to the case.

"We live in Washington, DC," Jim said, patting Dr. Hayes on the shoulder. "We just get the evidence and it tells us the answers. Politics is just what goes on around us. We'll run the blood through the DNA convicted felon database, but I'm fairly confident we probably won't find anything." Jim collected the evidence into a box. "Like you said, she was a pretty up-scale girl."

"Ah, yes." Dr. Hayes nodded. "The Combined DNA Indexing System the crime lab just brought on line. How exciting."

"I don't know about CODIS. It's more of a headache for them, I heard." Jim chuckled. "They got some federally funded program to qualify the lab, now they have to have inspections, follow all these extra rules but it lets them search the FBI database."

Kathleen stared at her partner for a moment, before asking, "Where do you pick up that kind of stuff? I've been with you the whole time the CODIS system has been online and I never heard that."

"I pay attention," Jim said.

"Well, keep me posted on what you find," said Dr. Hayes as he opened the glass door for Jim and Kathleen to exit, carrying the two new exhibits he had collected.

From the Medical Examiner's office, Jim and Kathleen drove directly to the crime lab, housed in a relatively new building. It was modern, red brick with thin strips of windows about a foot wide. Wire crisscrossed the windows for security reasons, the panes tinted so sunlight would not affect the temperature of the lab or the instruments inside. Entrants could open the front door and walk in, but could not pass through the next set of doors without someone on the other side of the security door pressing the security lock release.

Jim stared at the video camera. "Hello," he said, almost yelling. He pressed the door buzzer. "Just dropping the evidence off on a case," Jim waved at the camera. A clicking sound indicated the lock had been released. Kathleen pulled the door open.

A man behind the counter said, "What do ya have?" The man was Jack Johnson, a relatively new figure in the crime lab. He was hired about two years ago as an evidence technician. Prior to that, the crime laboratory had never utilized an evidence technician concept. In the past, the officer would speak directly to the forensic scientist, and the forensic scientist would review the case with the officer.

"It's a homicide case," Jim said, pulling the bags out of the box.

"Yeah, homicide," Kathleen echoed. "We're the leads. Lead detectives on this one. Our case, big case, murder on the Mall."

Jack stood behind the counter, looking unimpressed.

"We have already gotten a call on this case. It's hard to give people answers when you don't even have the evidence yet."

Jack grabbed the first bag, looking at the exhibit number.

"Let me get a case number on all these bags. How many exhibits do you have?"

"I think it was twenty-five," Jim said, looking over the receipts.

"Twenty-seven," Kathleen quickly corrected him. "Fetus blood and tissue."

"I stand corrected, twenty-seven."

Jack walked over to the computer and quickly typed the numbers as the printer started printing out twenty-seven labels with the case number and exhibit numbers.

As Jim watched Jack meticulously check each exhibit on the inventory receipt, match it to the exhibit and then assign it an exhibit number, Jim thought back to his introduction to the new evidence technician concept. Pete was adamantly opposed to the idea. He complained about not being able to discuss the case in the same way with an evidence technician as with a forensic scientist. Pete felt Jack wouldn't listen to him and was certain that some of their evidence had been mislabeled or mishandled. Pete had had several heated discussions with Jack Johnson about evidence Pete thought had been worked incorrectly. Eventually, when Jim and Pete brought evidence to the crime lab, Pete would wait in the car.

Jim could never quite figure out if it was the idea of an evidence technician that Pete didn't like or if it was Jack Johnson. It probably all went back to the first day Jack and Pete were introduced. Pete had mistaken Jack for a man who had served with him in the Marines, a George Prendergass. It was pretty clear Pete detested Prendergass.

"Thank heavens you're not Prendergass," Pete had said, only half-sincerely. "Boy, you sure look like him, though. Well, at least what I think he would look like after twenty years. Be happy you never met him," Pete said, keeping a sharp eye on Johnson's expressions.

Pete kept on, "What a psycho. You know, the kind of guy you would never want to have a gun because you fear they will frag everyone in the company. Every time I saw him, all I wanted to do was get away. Lord, that man was born to go to prison." Pete paused, waiting for some kind of reaction from Jack, but Jack just continued to log in the evidence.

"Prendergass beat up half a dozen people. If Prendergass heard you say anything he didn't like, he was on you like a pit bull. He put one man in a coma for six days. Do ya know why?"

"Knock it off with the Prendergass stuff," Jim had cut in.

Jack appeared uninterested in the story, mumbling something about never having been in the Marines.

Jim remembered Pete being so insistent after they left the lab.

"There is no way you could look that much like a guy and not be that guy," Pete argued.

"A twenty-year-old memory?" Jim would argue back.

"A damn good memory," Pete would end.

Jim studied Jack. He looked like he could have been in the Marines. He stood about 6 foot 2 with a 280-pound frame with barely an ounce of fat. His hair was trimmed close on the sides with a short cut on top that he brushed slightly to one side. Jack definitely worked out at a gym, somewhere but Jim was not certain where. Unlike the old days with the forensic scientists, Jack never chatted or talked about himself. He did his job and, from what Jim observed, he did it well.

Jim and Kathleen discussed with Jack how the body was positioned, which would help the forensic scientist know where to look for certain evidence. They discussed what trace evidence Jim and Kathleen were hoping to find and how the exhibits were collected. Then they left, knowing Jack would inform the forensic scientists.

As Kathleen and Jim walked back to the car, Jim said in a low voice, "Pete never liked Jack."

"What?" Kathleen said, thinking that came out of nowhere.

"Pete never liked Jack," Jim repeated.

Kathleen waited for Jim to elaborate, but instead he said, "The public is going to want answers on this case quickly. They will want answers because it's not a murder they can explain away by a drunken boyfriend or an angry bar fight. A young, bright star in an up and coming job, working with highly respected professionals. That's the kind of murder that scares them.

As they drove off, Jim mentally listed the people they would have to interview but Kathleen quickly tired of silently concentrating on the case.

"So, do you have a guess on why this woman was murdered?"

"I don't know," Jim replied.

"I know you don't like to guess but a rich girl, working for a congressman, had to be murdered for a reason, don't you think?" Kathleen rolled down her window to get a breath of the fresh spring air.

"I can turn on the vent," Jim said.

"That's it? You are just going to turn on the vent? I want to discuss the case," Kathleen said in a disgusted tone, rolling the window back up.

"We need to wait and see what the evidence tells us," Jim responded. "Don't decide how the case is going to be solved before you have any information."

"Are those your words of wisdom for the day?" Kathleen said, not hiding the sarcasm in her voice.

"What is with you today?" Jim snapped back.

"I am trying to learn the fine art of crime scene investigation, and all

I ever get from you are four word sentences and a lot of crappy assign-ments," Kathleen replied irritably and loudly.

"Crappy assignments? Like what?" Jim said, painfully aware he had only said four words.

"You don't think that burglary was a crappy assignment?"

"That was a learning experience. I thought it was a good opportunity for you to learn about latent fingerprints."

"You had me check for latent fingerprints on pages of a phone book," Kathleen nearly shouted.

Jim paused as he thought over the assignment.

"Fingerprints on porous paper are permanent. They remain on the paper no matter how old the paper is," Kathleen said slowly as if she were explaining it to a child.

"I know that," Jim said defensively. "It was an open phone book at a burglary scene. Checking the book for prints was good detective work. The burglar could have looked at the phone book. He could have touched the page."

"It was opened to the restaurant where the victims went to dinner. They told us they had looked up the phone number in the motel room," Kathleen continued annoyed that she needed to explain how ludicrous this assignment had been. "The phone book was six years old and from a MOTEL. I found 188 prints on those two pages. It took me three weeks to process that book."

"Entering the prints helped you become familiar with the Integrated Automated Fingerprint Identification System. It was good practice," Jim said.

"I already knew I-AFIS," Kathleen quipped back. "I even know the mathematical algorithms they use for that system."

"So, do I," Jim said with a chuckle.

"Don't laugh," Kathleen said indignantly. "I spent three weeks tracing enlargements of 188 finger prints. It's not funny. Isn't the crime lab supposed to enter the prints into I-AFIS? "

"Well, generally they do."

Jim knew he was not going to win this argument. He looked at Kathleen sitting in the passenger seat of the car. Frustrated with the conversation, she had chosen to go back to her notes, flipping through the pages in her note pad. Her long hair hung past her shoulders. Without thought, she hooked it behind her ear to keep it from interfering with her work. Her bangs danced around her forehead from the breeze of the vent. She sat with her legs crossed as she tried to write notes on her lap. She was curled up in an agile, flexible way that reminded Jim of a child. In the six months he had worked with her, he had never tried to get to know Kathleen.

Long before Kathleen had been hired, the department had developed a plan to separate Jim and Pete. Each would take a younger partner and teach them how to be a forensic investigator before they retired. Jim knew Kathleen would be assigned to him long before they had met. He followed her progress through the academy, through her rotational assignments.

As he watched her now, he thought of the distance he tried so hard to maintain. Jim knew Kathleen was exceptionally smart, but there was an awkwardness in how she handled the cases. Perhaps it was inexperience. Six months was not long. But, it was six months of her presence reminding him of everything he didn't want to think about.

Kathleen felt Jim's stare as she looked up from her notes. Her brown eyes caught his. Her distinctive thick eyebrows and a hint of a Roman nose wrinkled together in a questioning expression. Jim turned forward, focusing on the road.

"OK. You made your point," Jim said breaking the silence. "Maybe I haven't been treating you like a partner. Maybe I have been treating you more like a student." Jim paused, thinking about what to say. "I don't want to be buddies with you. I don't want to be your best friend. But, I'll try to be a better partner to you. You at least deserve that." Jim gave her a quick smile. "Would you like to get a late lunch before we go back to the office?"

"Sure." Kathleen was surprised at Jim's statement, but she didn't want to comment further, deciding to check around for the fast food sign that must have prompted Jim's question. She saw no signs. There were no hamburger signs, no fish signs, no taco signs. They weren't even in an area that had a restaurant. In fact, Kathleen had not been paying attention to where they were driving. The neighborhood was completely unfamiliar. Jim pulled over next to a small shop with an enormous plate glass window and an old style of brickwork that could have been done a century ago. A sign hung from the building just above the doorway, hand painted, and swinging ever so slightly in the gentle spring breeze. In beautiful lettering that had been weathered by the years, it read, "Stone Soup Café."

As Kathleen walked passed the window, she could see her reflection in the hazy rippled glass. She studied her reflection in front of a hazy rippled world. Kathleen's dark eyebrows were pronounced as they were reflected by an outwardly curved ribbon of the glass. The rest of her face sunk back into the shadow. Brightly painted houses behind her reflected a mismatched rainbow as the backdrop. Somehow, she thought, life seemed a little prettier when viewed out of focus in the reflection of a hundred year old glass. Kathleen noticed for the first time, it was a beautiful day.

As they walked into the café, they stepped back in time. The twenty-foot ceilings were covered with intricately stamped tin squares. The café was long and narrow, with booths on one side and tables on the other. The plaster walls were painted a peach color, the same color as the ceiling. White ceiling fans hung down ten feet from the ceiling, but they sat fixed, not turning on the cool spring day. Wainscoting covered the lower walls of the room. The wood had once been light in color, but time had turned it dark.

In the back of the room was an elderly woman putting drink glasses away behind on old fashioned soda fountain. The wooden counter was almost as tall as she was. Behind the counter on the wall was a massive mirror, allowing her actions to be easily seen.

For the time of day and the neighborhood, the café was surprisingly full. A couple dined by the front window, a mother with her children in a booth, several couples occupied the tables lining the wall, and an elderly man in the back table loudly slurping soup. It could have been the cover of an old *Saturday Evening Post*.

As Jim walked toward the back, the woman behind the counter exclaimed, "Jimmy! Oh, my Jimmy!" She ran from behind the counter with her arms stretched out, ready to hug Jim the minute he was close enough to touch.

"Hello, Mama," he said.

Confused by his greeting, Kathleen said, "I thought your Mom was in Arizona."

"She *is* in Arizona," Jim said.

"Oh, don't be silly," the elderly woman said, waving one arm as if Kathleen had said the most ridiculous thing in the world. "Everyone calls me Mama. Don't they, Jimmy?"

"Well, everyone who wants to stay on your good side," Jim bent over slightly to kiss the elderly woman on the cheek. Mama hugged him for a moment and then drew his head back so she could see his face clearly.

"Oh Jimmy, it has been so long. You look good, very good. How are the boys?" she said, slowly releasing her hold on Jim.

"Thanks. The boys are growing. They are doing well. I am very proud of them. I'll bring them by some time," Jim said, almost apologetically.

"I would love that. They are good boys," Mama said pulling a tissue from the sleeve of her white, ruffled blouse. "I would love that." She patted first her eyes then her nose with the tissue.

"Mama, we're here for lunch," Jim announced, changing the subject in such a loud manner his words echoed off the high tin ceilings. "We'll both have your special. Can we eat out back?"

Mama threw him a sharp look. "Jimmy," she said in a voice that seemed like she was about to cry. "That place out back is yours. It will always be yours. Don't you ever forget that, O.K.?"

Jim bent over and kissed Mama on the cheek, and said softly, "Thank you, Mama. I won't forget."

Pleased with Jim's response, Mama smiled. "I'll have two specials for you right away. Now you go out to the back and enjoy. I will bring you some tea, too." As Mama ran off into the kitchen, she nodded her head happily and waved her hand toward the back.

"You'll like this. It is a very special place," Jim assured Kathleen.

Kathleen and Jim walked down a narrow hallway to the back door of the café. As Jim pushed open the wooden screen door, it was like unveiling a painting. Crossing the threshold, Kathleen stepped into an old English garden. Several wrought iron tables with glass tops sat in the small courtyard which had walls on all sides but, because it was on a hill, it opened onto the city below. Bright azaleas in full bloom covered one courtyard wall. Orange, purple, and pink flowers covered the bushes. One could barely see their deep emerald green leaves though the petals of the flowers. In front of the azaleas were lilies, just past their prime, bowing slightly from age. On the other side peonies just started to show their pink fluffy petals and irises jutted through the outer leaves of the peonies, with crimson and blue flowers, firmly announcing their presence. The tables were painted a beautiful sage color, which made them melt into their surroundings.

The garden's placement on a plateau of a hill allowed a wondrous view of the city. In the distance, Kathleen could see the monuments of Washington, DC. The Washington Monument and the Capitol building towered above the skyline. Farther in the background was a misty view of the Potomac River. The courtyard was an oasis in the middle of a tired old neighborhood. It was as if someone had cut out a piece of Monet's garden and placed it on the top of a hill behind an old cafe.

"What kind of place is this?" Kathleen said, taking in the scene. "It's beautiful. It's perfect," she said with a sigh. Leaning toward Jim, she whispered, "How do you know that woman?"

Jim's stare gave no acknowledgement that he had heard anything Kathleen had said. He walked slowly down the length of the yard, running his hand along the crest of flowers.

Mama breezed through the doorway with placemats and silverware. "Excuse me, Ms., uh Mrs.," Kathleen stumbled through the terms, not quite sure of how to address her.

"I forgot how pretty these spring flowers are," Jim said as Mama nodded in agreement.

Mama looked at Kathleen as she set the table. "It's Mama," she said, correcting Kathleen. "Everyone calls me Mama."

"Oh yes, uh, Mama," Kathleen said, feeling a little uncomfortable calling a woman she did not even know by such a familiar term. "Mama, my name is Kathleen Jackson. I am Jim's partner. I mean, we work together in the crime scene investigations unit. He's my partner at work, you know, not my partner outside of work."

Kathleen felt foolish rambling on. She didn't know why she kept talking. Maybe it was the look on Mama's face that made Kathleen think she needed to explain things further. Kathleen was the only one talking and she feared that if she stopped there would be a sudden awkward silence. Finally, Kathleen ran out of words.

"Oh, sorry," Jim said as he walked back to the table. "Mama, this is Kathleen Jackson. She's a detective, like me."

After a moment or two, Mama patted her arm and said, "I hope you are a good partner for Jimmy."

Mama went inside and within a minute she was back, carrying two plates. Each plate had a beautiful china bowl of soup. Cut in quarters and arranged around the bowl was a sandwich.

"Here you go," Mama said, setting the plates on the placemats. Jim and Kathleen eased into big wrought iron chairs. Kathleen felt so comfortable she relaxed for the first time all day.

"Two orders of Stone soup and sandwiches," Mama announced. "Don't you worry, dear. There are no stones in my soup. It's like the story. You remember that story about the stone soup. It's like that. It just means the soup has a little bit of everything, only it has both meanings." Mama spoke with such pride that Kathleen knew she had made the soup herself.

As Mama went back into the kitchen, Kathleen tasted the soup. Perhaps it was because she had only had coffee for breakfast and was hungry, but the soup truly seemed to be the most delicious soup ever made.

Jim picked up his spoon and swirled it around in the bowl for a moment, thinking about the last time he had eaten this soup. It had been a lifetime ago. He looked around at the garden and suddenly didn't feel hungry.

"This is delicious. This is really delicious!" Kathleen continued finishing the last drops of her soup. She set down her spoon and with the back of her hand hit Jim on his shoulder. The sting of the slap on his shoulder pulled him back from his thoughts.

"What?" Jim responded, somewhat surprised to have been hit.

"How many lunches have I spent with you eating cold hamburgers in our car?" Kathleen said loudly."We could have been having lunches here!" she said, smiling. "Or is your idea of a good meal something you can super-size?"

Jim took a spoonful of soup and sipped it slowly.

"You have a Mama who is not your mom, you have a delicious lunch place, DELICIOUS, where you don't eat lunch," Kathleen started to tease Jim, but the look on his face she knew too well and knew it was time to move on to a different topic.

"Why don't you talk about your kids with me?" Kathleen said in a more serious voice.

"You don't have kids. I thought you wouldn't be interested," Jim replied as he took the first bite of his sandwich.

Kathleen looked over at Jim as he ate his sandwich. She thought about all the people who would go on and on about their kids, how smart their kids were, or talented, or athletic. It was true; Kathleen did not have a lot of patience in this area. But Jim was different. He was her partner.

"The older boy is Robert, right? What is your youngest son's name?" Kathleen asked, wondering if the question would get his standard silent stare which was the usual response when Jim did not want to talk about something.

"David," Jim replied without a hint of hesitation. "My sons' names are David and Robert." He added, "Robert is seventeen. David is fifteen."

Jim ate the rest of his meal in silence while Kathleen enjoyed the view. There was something about the garden which seemed to put everyone at peace, she thought.

They left the café only after a long discussion with Mama, who insisted their money was no good in her café. Jim eventually slipped a twenty-dollar bill into her apron before they left.

When they got back to their office, there were messages. Representative Thatcher's office set up an appointment for them at 4 p.m. Captain Freeman had called to get an update on the case, and Jack Johnson had left a message that the lab would be batching any DNA they found in the case together so no DNA analysis would be done until all the evidence was screened for possible stains. This meant that the DNA evidence would not be worked for several days.

Before their meeting with the congressman, Jim and Kathleen reviewed the information they had on Philip Thatcher, the U.S. Representative from Alabama. There were seven representatives from Alabama, Thatcher being the most senior. He had been in office for twenty-two years, and was on several committees, the most recent being the Homeland Security Committee. No scandals appeared in his background, and no issues stood out in his history. Philip Thatcher seemed to be a pretty straightforward guy.

Kathleen and Jim arrived at the congressman's office at 3:30, time enough to look around and mark the comings and going of a few people in the office.

They waited about fifteen minutes before being shown into Congressman Thatcher's office. It was a big, beautiful office that showcased the grandeur of the South. On the wall behind the congressman's oak desk was a huge white satin flag with a scarlet X across it. It made such an impression on Kathleen and Jim that both their heads were drawn upward to look at the state flag of Alabama rather than the man standing beneath it.

"Ah, the crimson cross of St. Andrew on a field of white. It is a beautiful flag. Don't you think?" The congressman's drawl was so slow and thick there was no mistaking he was from the deep South. "It's one of Alabama's best kept secrets. Although there are a few more," he said with a thin smile and a wink of his eye toward Kathleen. Looking at Jim, he continued, "Or perhaps, this flag is more your fancy," Congressman Thatcher said as he pointed to a much smaller flag on the adjacent wall. "The eagle, globe and anchor. It is certainly one that brings a glowing pride to my heart," he said, gazing affectionately toward the United States Marine Corp emblem.

"Sorry, sir, I was never in the Marines," Jim said as he stepped forward to introduce himself with a handshake. "My name is Jim Jarred and this is my partner, Kathleen Jackson. We are with the Washington, DC Police Department."

"Oh, yes, I will do any thing I can do to help in the investigation of the tragic shooting of Miss Victoria," the congressman interjected. "I assume that is why you are here. Is it not? One of my aides informed me about the tragedy this morning."

The congressman led them to a round conference table where they all settled into plush leather-seated chairs. Representative Thatcher then answered the questions Jim and Kathleen had about Victoria

Young. Thatcher knew a significant amount of information about the woman.

Victoria Young had been born and raised in Alabama. Her family was middle class. They worked hard for a living and expected success from their children. Victoria was above average in school, eventually receiving a scholarship to college. She attended George Washington University at the Foggy Bottom Campus, graduated magna cum laude in political science and had been working in the congressman's office for a little over fifteen months as an aide. Victoria's work had been fairly routine: researching bills and summarizing information for the congressman. She was a hard worker. Generally, she stayed late in the office with work but never complained about it nor even seemed to mind the hours.

"She was a striking young woman, very beautiful. The world was hers. What a loss." Thatcher stopped speaking for a moment to contemplate what he had said. He had an obvious affection for the woman and showed genuine sadness over her death.

"Did you know she was pregnant?" Jim asked his eyes fixed on Representative Thatcher.

Sitting upright in his chair, the congressman brought his elbows forward to rest on the table. He held his hands together in a fist to hide the nervous shaking of his hand. It was a fact that did not escape Jim's attention. After a deep breath that expanded the Congressman's chest greatly, he finally replied in a loud and firm southern voice, "No, sir, I did not know that."

Almost as if he was deflating as he exhaled, the congressman leaned back in his chair and continued, "Not having known Ms. Young is your misfortune. She had such a presence about her and so charming. Her death is a tragedy. Now, doubly so with the death of her child, too. Her life senselessly snuffed out by the bullet of a crack-head gang member."

"Sir," Kathleen interrupted, "we don't know who killed her, yet. We are still investigating that. Do you know something we don't?"

"Not at all. Not at all," Thatcher said, waving his hands as if trying to retract the statement. "Just a guess." He rose abruptly, as if to signal the end of the interview.

Jim stood. "The lab results won't be in for several days. When we know something more, we would like to come back for further discussion. While we're here, would it be possible for us to interview the rest of your staff?"

The congressman seemed eager to oblige their request as he ushered them out of his office and turned them over to his white-haired secretary, who guided them through the various work cubicles.

Kathleen and Jim painstakingly interviewed the rest of the office staff. Each seemed to confirm Thatcher's opinion. They all respected Victoria. Victoria worked hard. She had an uncanny ability to command a room when she entered it. It was obvious she was someone they all had admired.

"Well, that was not very useful," Kathleen said as they walked to their car. "We could have gotten that information over the phone."

Jim looked over at Kathleen until she noticed.

"What?" she said, realizing she had missed something.

"What did you notice when we interviewed the congressman?" Jim said slyly.

Kathleen hated this game but she was also too competitive to pass it up. "Well, let me see. The congressman was a Marine."

"Too obvious to get any credit."

"He has a wife who died, a daughter in her late thirties," Kathleen continued.

"That was in the report we read!" Jim laughed. "You can do better than that."

"I saw their picture on his desk. I forgot about the report," Kathleen said, trying to defend herself. "From his liquor cabinet, it looks like he has expensive tastes. He needs to have his carpet cleaned. He has a television hidden in the armoire. Do you think he watches Oprah?" she asked rhetorically. "He cared about Victoria, but I don't think it was anything romantic. Oh, and he over plays his southern charm. Did you pick up something I missed?"

"I guess you don't play poker."

"I play poker," Kathleen snapped, annoyed with his condescending tone.

"Oh, I mean, I guess you don't play poker well," Jim said, correcting himself.

Kathleen stopped walking and turned into Jim's path. She hated when he did this to her. He had picked up a key piece of information from a look, or a smile, or a picture. Now, she was going to have to guess what it was she had missed.

"What are you talking about?"

"Thatcher knew Victoria Young was pregnant," Jim explained.

"OK, I guess I missed that part of the conversation. You know, the part where he said he knew she was pregnant. I was only there for the part where he said he DID NOT KNOW she was pregnant. Where exactly did you get that idea?"

"Did you watch him *at all* when we were asking questions?" Jim was toying with her now. "When I asked the congressman if he knew she was pregnant," Jim continued, "did you notice the way he sat up in his chair?" Jim tried to act out what he was describing. "He sat up in his chair. He put his arms on the table, brought his shoulders forward and puffed out his chest. When people bluff in poker that is exactly what they do. They want to appear stronger, more intimidating than they really are. He wanted to let us know he was absolutely firm in his answer. It's what people do when they lie. They want to make you think they are in a stronger position than they really are. Thatcher is lying about not knowing Victoria Young was pregnant. I know he is. The question is why does he feel he needs to hide that information?"

"I don't know. A puffed up chest seems like pretty thin evidence," Kathleen said. "Every time someone takes a deep breath, it doesn't always mean something."

"Sometimes thin is all you have," Jim said. "Sometimes it's not a big piece of evidence that sends you in the right direction. It's a glance or a look or sitting forward in their chair."

Kathleen knew this was what Jim did well. He took in information that no one else noticed and used it. When Jim talked to people, he didn't just listen to what they said. He read their faces and their tones… and sometimes their breathing.

As they turned the corner of the building, Kathleen pondered their conversation. After a few minutes, she ventured, "But he has no reason to lie. What would it matter if he knew she was pregnant or not? There's no reason for him to lie." Kathleen wanted to convince herself that what

Jim said could not be true.

"Oh, there is always a reason," Jim said confidently as he opened the car door. "We just don't know the reason… Yet."

CHAPTER **THREE**

THE LANDLORD LET Jim and Kathleen into Victoria Young's apartment. As the door opened, the curtains billowed into the room. Instinctively, Jim reacted to the unexpected movement and reached for his Beretta Cougar from the holster strapped to his belt. Just as quickly, he realized there was no threat and relaxed his posture. The landlord, slower in his reactions, gasped, his eyes darting around looking for the imaginary intruder. Fearful that danger might be lurking in the apartment of a murdered woman, the landlord gestured quickly for Jim and Kathleen to enter, then exited as he explained he would be in apartment 6 if needed.

The room reflected the same elegance and refinement that Victoria Young had portrayed in her death. Hunter green walls were accented by golden oak floors and large impressive woodwork. A huge bay window wrapped around the far wall. Long, off-white curtains breathed in and out, as the breeze from the open window brought them to life. There was a starkness to the room, highlighted by only a few pieces of furniture. However, the furniture that was present was striking. It was neither cheap looking nor ostentatious. Clean refined lines of wood and cloth covered the sofa and chair. A bookcase was filled with books, not books for show but books that were read. Some of the books had slightly torn covers, some had well-worn spines, all had a sense that they belonged there.

Scattered among the books on the shelves were silver-framed pictures of family — captured moments in time Victoria Young wanted to remember. A tarnished frame held a picture of her family hugging her as she donned the black robes of graduation. Shiny silver frames showed a vacation near a river, a family reunion, with a dozen smiling faces and a large picture of a woman who looked remarkably like Victoria standing next to her, beaming with the pride of a mother.

Jim walked out of the bedroom. "Well, it's a pretty clean place, pretty nice too," Jim said, hardened to the lives of the people he investigated. "We'll have someone go through her papers, check her bills, phone calls, see if there's anything there. Nothing here seems like obvious evidence. Do you want to look through anything else in her apartment?" Not waiting for an answer, Jim continued walking across the room. "I'll check the kitchen."

Kathleen imagined how all those people in the pictures would look today. Their hearts emptied by the death of the woman they loved. The apartment seemed undisturbed, as if Victoria was expected back any moment and life would continue on. Feeling uncomfortable, Kathleen yelled to Jim who had just opened the refrigerator, "I'm ready to go."

"Go? I would have thought you would have wanted to go over this apartment with a microscope." Jim patted Kathleen on the shoulder. "That woman didn't eat much. At least not much I would eat. I wonder if she was a vegetarian." Kathleen did not feel like responding.

The next few days passed slowly as they waited for the reports from the officers, the sections in the crime lab, and the Medical Examiner's office. The newspapers and television all covered the homicide as headline news. Various groups and organizations demanded a crack down on gangs, a clean up of drug dealers, and more police on the streets. The mayor assured the community that the crime would be solved, and the public would be safe.

Jim and Kathleen managed to close three unrelated cases while they waited. They called Ms. Young's parents who assured them through tearful gasps that no one would have a motive to kill their daughter. Victoria Young's father spoke with a deep southern accent, answering questions in a somber monotone voice. The mother's voice was different. Her words rolled off her tongue like a song, her inflections were subtle and rhythmic. Kathleen was caught up in the melody of her words as she tried to place the dialect but by the time she had decided it was from neither North nor South America, she heard Jim thank them for their time and promise to keep them informed. The call yielded no new information, only that awful feeling which always comes when talking to the parents of a murder victim.

On the fourth day, they started receiving the some of the reports. From the crime lab, they found out that the single blonde hair Captain Freeman had collected was definitely made from synthetic material. It was a cheap variety of spun polyester. Most of the evidence collected from under her fingernails proved to be dirt, probably acquired when she fell to the ground, clenching her hands in the last moments of life. As they read through each of the reports, none of them revealed any information that would help the investigation, until they got to the toxicology report. Jim read aloud the findings of 0.129 grams per deciliter of ethanol and 1557 micrograms per liter of cocaine in her blood.

Kathleen reached over and turned the page to the next report, which was from the firearms section. The bullet that had killed Victoria Young could be linked to half a dozen shootings in the area in the last three months. The gun was a 9-millimeter Glock, linked to a man named Syrus Sandman. Sandman's fingerprints were at five of the six crimes involving the Glock. Syrus Sandman was a twice-convicted felon who was released from prison last year. The gun was submitted two days after the submission of the Victoria Young evidence.

"Now that *is* a coincidence!" Kathleen said, pausing for a moment before she continued. "The 9 mm Glock was recovered at a crime scene in a justifiable shooting case in which an officer, who was attempting to arrest Sandman, shot and killed Sandman after he drew the 9 mm Glock."

"You have got to be kidding me," Kathleen said to herself. Shaking her head, she looked up at Jim who was standing over her shoulder reading the reports with her. "So the guy who killed Victoria Young was killed two days ago. Is that what this report is saying?" It was almost a rhetorical question. "Wow, talk about justice."

Kathleen flipped over the firearms report and began reading the next report aloud. "DNA - clothing - no suitable stains found for DNA analysis. Fetal blood findings DNA profile matched to the mother - Victoria Young. DNA match to the father - Syrus Sandman. Syrus Sandman!" Kathleen repeated the name again in disbelief. "Can you believe this?"

"Well, this case is coming together pretty quickly." Jim walked over to his desk. "So what do we have? A woman on the fast track who likes to have a drink and use a little cocaine now and then. She meets up with a not-so-nice guy to get her drugs. They have an affair. She gets pregnant. He doesn't want the baby. He shoots her. Two days later the police shoot him. He probably thought he was being arrested for the murder of Victoria Young. Maybe that's why he drew his gun." Jim looked at the pile of reports. As he flipped through the pages one more time, he added, "This hardly qualifies as a puzzle."

Kathleen stared at the floor, thinking for a minute. "There is something about this that just does not feel right. It is almost too clean cut. Everything is wrapped up with a few lab reports? Does that happen very often?"

"Sometimes, you just get lucky." Jim shrugged his shoulders.

"Every person we talked to tells us Victoria Young was a hard working, determined individual. Now, the evidence tells us something completely different. Should we have to discount everything we heard? There is something about this that just does not feel right."

"People hide things. Not everyone is going to tell you their deep dark secrets," Jim said. "She never told them that she used cocaine or was pregnant by Sandman. She kept it to herself."

Kathleen interrupted, "Do you think she told Representative Thatcher?"

"It doesn't make sense that she would tell Thatcher. I'd think she wouldn't want him to know. A U.S. Representative could help someone like Young in a lot of ways. She would not want her reputation to be blemished in the slightest in front of Thatcher." Jim rubbed the top of his head with his hand, trying to think through the evidence. "I do think Thatcher knew she was pregnant. But why would he lie about it? If the evidence is true, he has no reason to lie."

"Maybe he was trying to protect her reputation or maybe to protect his reputation. I have heard some politicians do lie from time to time," Kathleen said with a smile, trying to make a joke that might bring a smile to Jim's face as well.

Jim laughed as he leaned back in his chair. "Actually, politicians generally take great care not to lie. They may not always be helpful. They might hold back some information, but lying outright can be dangerous to a political career."

Jim sat rocking in his chair looking up toward the ceiling. "Why would he lie?" he said quietly asking himself. "Why would he lie?"

"Well there is one other possibility," Kathleen said. "He might be telling the truth."

Jim laughed as he grabbed his jacket from the back of his chair. "That would make me wrong and that just does not happen. Thatcher is lying," Jim said confidently. "Now, come on, let's go over to the Medical Examiner's office. We can get a copy of the death certificate for the file. Bring your coat, it's raining."

Just before they made a successful escape out the door, the phone rang. Jim picked it up. "Hello, Captain Freeman."

"Oh, no," Kathleen mouthed to Jim. This was not going to be an easy call, Kathleen thought. To the captain, this case had become personal. It was going to be hard telling him the woman who had charmed him so completely, even in her death, was a cocaine-user killed by a gang member with whom she had been involved and by whom had become pregnant.

"Yes, sir," Jim said in a very military tone. "No, sir." There was a slight pause, then, "Yes, sir, we are still waiting on some reports. Nothing yet, sir. I will keep you posted."

Kathleen looked at Jim in disbelief as he hung up the phone. "You are actually lying to a captain? Are you crazy?"

"Well, it's not really lying. We don't have all the reports. We're missing some paperwork from the Medical Examiner's office. Besides, Captain

Freeman seemed really concerned about Young's death. We should tell him in person what we found, not over the phone."

"Chicken," Kathleen mocked.

"True," Jim confessed. "It's not a conversation which I'm looking forward to. I want to plan how to tell him. He's not going to take it well. When we have everything together, maybe we can add something positive."

"Positive? Good luck!"

When Kathleen stepped outside, she took a moment to inhale the damp spring air. The rain had stopped, replaced by a gentle, misty drizzle. The sun was just peeking though the passing clouds, and everything glistened with a wet, dripping shine.

"There is something wonderful that happens after a rain, don't you think?" Kathleen said as she got into their car.

"Yeah, it means I don't have to water the grass tonight," Jim said in a flip response.

"You have grass?"

Jim rolled his eyes as he pulled into traffic, knowing Kathleen was mocking him.

Kathleen said, "I just pictured you more as a condo kind of guy. It is nice you are finally opening up. Maybe next week you can work yourself up to telling me whether or not you have a dog."

It was cutting sarcasm but Jim knew he deserved it. It wasn't that Jim did not like Kathleen. He liked her a lot. She was funny, nice looking, smart. She tried so hard to do everything well and her struggles often brought a smile to his face. The only thing he had against Kathleen was that his whole life changed the day she walked into it.

As Jim and Kathleen opened the glass front doors to the Medical Examiner's office, they noticed a citrus, menthol smell.

"Oh, no!" said Kathleen. "This is not a good day to visit."

"Come on," Jim said, grabbing her arm so she wouldn't turn back to the car. "You have to get used to the smell someday. We might as well begin today."

As they walked farther in, they began to detect the smell of the decomposed body. The truth was no one ever got used to the smell. When the Medical Examiner's office received a radio call estimating the time of death in days instead of hours, the office staff started putting up air fresheners. They were not the type of air fresheners sold at Wal-Mart for a $1.99. These came from a medical supply store and were specifically designed to mask the odor of death.

Kathleen hated the air freshener even more than the smell of a decomposed body. It was like a beacon, warning all who smelled it that worse was yet to come.

The hallway they walked down was wide with glass windows on both sides looking into the autopsy rooms. The entrance to the examination rooms was at the end of the hallway. This prevented unwanted visitors from entering the rooms, yet allowed easy viewing of autopsies without risking contamination of evidence.

About halfway down the thirty-foot hall, Jim stopped. The smell of decaying flesh permeated the air. Kathleen felt like she was covered with a blanket on a hot, sweaty summer day. The smell clung to her and dripped off her body.

Jim said, "It might be best if we went back to the front office and had Dr. Hayes paged."

"Whatever you think," Kathleen said, trying to be nonchalant, but a slight gagging noise came from the back of her throat, she tried to conceal it with a cough.

"I have got to play poker with you," Jim laughed as they turned toward the sunlight and fresh air at the front of the building.

Minutes later, Dr. Hayes entered the front conference room. "Sorry about the smell. We had a drowning. They didn't recover the body for three weeks. Do you have any news on the Young case?"

Jim started with the toxicology report. He explained how the fetal tissue report had come back negative for drugs and alcohol, but that Young had a high alcohol and cocaine level. Dr. Hayes listened carefully.

"Can you explain this inconsistency?"

"Yes, I suppose." Dr. Hayes rubbed his beard slowly. "If the woman was not a drug abuser, a scenario like this might be possible. It would be very unusual, but hypothetically possible."

"Why did you say the woman could not be a drug abuser?" Kathleen asked.

"Well," the doctor continued, "drugs stay in your body a long time. Much longer than you would think. When cocaine enters your system, you feel the effects for a few hours and then you think the cocaine is gone. But it is not gone. Your body has broken it down into a metabolite. Cocaine has a metabolite called benzoylecgonine. The lab can detect benzoylecgonine for many, many days after the cocaine is gone from someone's system. The fetus is a part of the mother's body. If the mother used cocaine routinely, cocaine and benzoylecgonine would be in both the mother and the fetus. Since there were no drugs in the fetus, Ms. Young must have taken the cocaine very shortly before she was killed. To get such a high level in her blood without affecting the fetus, I would say she probably smoked some crack cocaine. Smoking would allow the drug to move into her system very quickly but not have time to go across the placenta into the fetus. She would have to have been killed within a few minutes of her smoking the drug."

"What about the alcohol?" Jim asked.

"Oh, well that is a little easier to explain," Dr. Hayes said, resting one leg on the edge of the conference room table. "I gave you a tissue sample not a blood sample. Ethanol evaporates very easily unless it is in a liquid such as blood. I collected the tissue sample in a specimen cup. If the evidence was not worked for a day or two, that tissue could have easily dried out. The laboratory should have stored it in a refrigerator or, even better, a freezer to preserve the evidence. If they didn't store it that way, the sample would dry out. A dry sample would show no ethanol. Of course, you could still detect the drugs. Drugs don't evaporate. Seldom do we care if a fetus has ethanol in its system. It's not illegal to drink when you're pregnant. It should be, I think, but it isn't."

Jim looked over at Kathleen and nodded his head with satisfaction that things were coming together. Every unexplained inconsistency was being tied together in a clean, tight case.

"Well, Doc, I always feel better after talking to you," Jim said. He rose and offered a handshake to Dr. Hayes. "Oh, one final thing you might be interested in – the father of Young's baby was Syrus Sandman."

"I know the man, Syrus Sandman. I did an autopsy on him two days ago. He is not the father," Dr. Hayes said in a matter of fact manner.

"Doc, we got the DNA results. The DNA says Syrus Sandman is the father." Jim tried to sound apologetic for pointing out Dr. Hayes' error.

"Well then, I guess your DNA tests are wrong," Dr. Hayes replied simply.

"He had the gun that killed her. He sold drugs. The fetus had his DNA. I think we are pretty solid in saying the baby was Victoria Young's and Syrus Sandman's."

"You can have all the tests and reports in the world," Dr. Hayes protested, "but, I can tell you, that man did not father THAT child."

"Wait a minute," Kathleen interrupted. "Dr. Hayes, you are saying there was some kind of evidence you found during the autopsy that leads you to believe that Syrus Sandman could not father a child?"

"No…" Dr. Hayes hesitated. "I am saying I examined the fetus of Victoria Young. Syrus Sandman did not father her child. I can tell by just looking at the fetus."

"Doc, it was just a fetus. That is a pretty small and under-developed individual to be looking for any family resemblances. Don't you think?" Kathleen tried to make it sound more like a question than an argument.

"That fetus was old enough to have developed characteristic features AND the features of Ms. Young were very distinct. Her long legs, very thin body, the high cheekbones on her face, her ebony skin. She has the look of someone from the Masai tribe in Africa. Masai have very distinct features. They are unmistakable. Masai are known for their great endurance and speed. Much of that comes from the genetic factors that make them distinct. Ms. Young carried her mother's genes. Ms. Young clearly carries the features of the Masai people."

"Wow, that's incredible." Kathleen said, carefully studying the photographs Dr. Hayes had provided. She noticed Young's high cheekbones, her nose very narrow and flaring out slightly at her nostrils. Young had broad shoulders for a woman, long legs and a slender well-formed body. Young was unmistakably a beautiful woman.

"Are you telling me that you can tell this woman is descendant from Masai just by looking at her?" Kathleen asked, wondering how he had become so knowledgeable in Masai features.

"Well," Dr. Hayes said, looking a little embarrassed. "I think maybe I could have guessed a Masai link, but I actually got a call from her mother. Her mother is from Kenya. She called the other day to get some information about her daughter. Ms. Young's mother told me she was Masai." Dr. Hayes paused for a moment, having had a little bit of thunder stolen from his performance. "But, my point is, her features are also very similar to Mr. Sandman's. Here is a picture of Syrus Sandman," Dr. Hayes said as he found the picture on his desk.

Syrus Sandman's features were remarkably similar to those of Victoria Young. He was tall and slender in the face with dark ebony skin. There were markings of a difficult life that ended harshly. Dr. Hayes looked down at the picture, tapping Syrus face with his finger. "What I am saying," Dr. Hayes said in an increasingly firmer voice, "is that baby had too many Caucasian features to be fathered by Mr. Sandman. That baby was half white!"

"Half white! How could you tell that?" Kathleen was pretty certain that he had not done any validation studies on that hypothesis and a bit surprised that he could be so firm when all the scientific evidence said he was wrong.

"For thirty-five years, I have been doing autopsies. Do you know murder is the number one killer of pregnant women?" Dr. Hayes sighed. "Over time, you begin to notice things. You notice the women who are killed for no reason. You observe the babies dead in their womb. You notice subtle things that are impossible to describe. There are things you just learn to see."

Kathleen looked at him uncomfortably. "Do you have any journal articles describing these differences? Maybe you could find some research papers?" Kathleen asked as she scrunched up her shoulders and softened her voice to make her request seem less offensive to the doctor. "Maybe even just some notes on various cases that would support your opinion? It's just that to act on an opinion like it is fact is hard when there isn't any data to support your opinion."

The doctor shook his head slowly. "All I have is what I know. And, this I know." Then he nodded to both Kathleen and Jim to let them know he was not going to change his mind.

"Well, we can have the lab recheck the results," Jim said, trying to come to a compromise.

As Kathleen and Jim walked to the car, both their heads stared at the ground intently, trying to put the facts together in some way that made sense.

"With the backlog the crime lab has, the last thing they are going to want to do is recheck a DNA sample," Kathleen began.

"Especially when the results exactly fit the case," Jim added.

As they got in the car, Kathleen asked, "What do you think should we do?"

Jim started the car. After a moment, he said with a deep breath, "I think we should go home, get some sleep and think about this tomorrow."

CHAPTER FOUR

THE NEXT MORNING Kathleen went to work early, early enough to re-read the DNA report a dozen times. When Jim walked in, he didn't look like he had gotten any more sleep than Kathleen had.

Jim sat at this desk. Kathleen watched patiently, waiting for him come up with an idea. Waiting for him to say the first words. For several minutes, he sat staring off at a distant spot on the floor, rubbing his chin with his thumb and index finger. Neither of them wanted to call the crime lab and suggest that their work needed to be checked, but both also knew Dr. Hayes did not make statements based on guesses.

Suddenly Jim's voice erupted loudly, "What's the phone number to the crime lab?"

The words were so abrupt they startled Kathleen. She glanced at the reports she was holding and turned the pages so they were facing Jim. He picked up his phone and dialed the number listed.

"Hello," he said, "is Teri Sedgwick there?"

"May I say who is calling?" came a voice from the other end of the line.

"Detective Jarred," Jim said as he stood, placing his hand on his belt.

Kathleen watched as Jim straightened his shirt and brushed the creases out of his black pants. It was almost as if Jim were making himself presentable, getting ready for a formal greeting.

"You know she can't see you. You're on the phone," Kathleen whispered. She was surprised he was acting so foolish toward some unknown woman.

Jim waved his hand dismissively and turned so he was not directly facing Kathleen.

"Hello, this is Teri," came a voice on the phone.

Teri Sedgwick was one of the smartest people Jim had ever known. She had started in the crime lab about the same time he had started with the Crime Scene Bureau. Her area of expertise was DNA, but she worked in many other areas of the lab. She had spent some time working on a validation study identifying amino acids in latent prints through an enzyme method, which she had demonstrated to all the detectives several years earlier. Jim had known Teri a long time, and he knew if anyone could help, she could.

"Hello?" the voice said again.

"Oh, hello, Teri. This is Jim Jarred."

"Oh, Jim it's wonderful to hear from you. We hardly ever talk any more. What can I do for you?"

"Teri, did you work the Young case?" Jim asked.

"No, that was Aaron's case. Do you want to talk to him?"

"No," Jim said quickly. "I was just wondering if you could look over the case for me."

"I can, but Aaron would be better able to answer any questions you have," she said with a slightly questioning tone. It was not common for an analyst to draw conclusions from another analyst's work. Cases were worked from start to finish by a single analyst to ensure they could describe exactly how the analysis was performed in a court of law.

"Well, I just…it's more…" Jim stumbled through what he wanted to say. He did not want to reveal such a tenuous suspicion of bad lab work to Teri. "I am asking you more as a friend than a forensic scientist. There are some little things that just aren't adding up in this case. I would like you to look it over, just to make certain everything is kosher."

"OK, give me a minute to get the file." After a few minutes, Teri spoke again. "OK, I have the file. What would you like to know?"

"Can you find the DNA analysis on the fetus? Is there any way the results could have been misread?"

"No, the results are good. The data shows two sets of peaks, one from Young, which Aaron eliminated through computer enhancements. The second set was from Sandman. The peaks are good-sized, no obvious stutters. This was an easy call," she said.

Jim paused to choose his words carefully. "OK, second question, is there any chance that Aaron contaminated one case with the other?"

"No, federal regulations require that only one case be open at a time. That is part of the DNA auditory board standards. Aaron has to list the dates and times each case was open to show that no two cases are open at any one time. There is no way he was not following that protocol. Everyone here knows not following protocol could cost us our accreditation and our CODIS lab."

"OK, one last question," Jim hesitated for a minute. "Is there any possibility that the DNA profile of Syrus Sandman is incorrect?"

"Well, that is always a possibility," Teri said. "But, not in this case. The original hit to our local database was confirmed in CODIS. Since Sandman was a convicted felon, Aaron had run the blood standard submitted by the Medical Examiner's office through our CODIS system. The blood collected at the autopsy of Syrus Sandman matched this case. I have both the CODIS profile and the blood standard profile here. They are a dead on match."

"Oh, well, Teri. You have been a lot of help," Jim lied.

"I'm pretty certain I have not been a LOT of help, but it is nice talking to you. I miss those conversations over the evidence counter. Don't be such a stranger," Teri replied in the cheerful, friendly voice Jim remembered.

"Oh, one other thing before you go," Jim said. "Syrus Sandman's blood was submitted for what type of work?"

Jim heard some clicking of computer keys. Then, Teri came back with "two ten-milliliter tubes of blood submitted for toxicology -- drugs and alcohol testing in addition to the DNA database check." It was information she was obviously reading from a computer screen.

"Thanks. Talk to you soon," Jim said as he hung up the phone.

Jim and Kathleen discussed the case for the better part of an hour. Finally, Kathleen summarized the circular conversation. "Either the lab is wrong or the doctor is wrong. It's that simple. Both seem absolutely positive of their results. How do you crack a case when neither side will budge?"

Jim looked at the file on his desk which was becoming thicker and thicker. He thought about the available options. His eyes narrowed as he thought. "We crack this case," he said as he turned his gaze to the outside window, "by hitting it at its weakest link."

"I wasn't aware there was a weakest link," Kathleen pointed out.

"Oh, yeah and his name is Thatcher," Jim said as he reached for his jacket. "Let's see what he has to add about who might be the father of that baby."

When they arrived at Congressman Thatcher's office, they were surprised to see the staff seemed to be expecting them. The front receptionist directed them to the inner lounge, assuring them the congressman would be able to receive them in a moment.

As they waited, Jim leaned over and whispered to Kathleen, "Remember, read the man not the words."

Just then, the two large wooden doors leading into Congressman Thatcher's office opened and his private secretary appeared. "The Congressman will see you now. Right this way."

Following her, they found Congressman Thatcher standing in front of his desk, his hands grasping the lapels of his coat. It was such a bizarre look that Kathleen almost laughed aloud when she saw it. The congressman's overweight body was twisted so his shoulders were squarely facing them as they walked in the door, but his legs were slightly twisted to the side with one leg extended more than the other. It was like a painting of a seventeenth century nobleman standing pompously in the center of Kathleen's view.

"Ah, the keepers of peace; the protectors of society. It is so nice to see you again," the congressman said in a round full voice. "Do you have any news for me?"

"Well, it appears drugs may have been involved," Jim said as they walked further into the room.

"Drugs, drugs. How tragic," the congressman continued in his theatrical presentation, his southern drawl as thick and as slow as ever. Slowly, he paced in front of his desk. "I am sad to say it is not an unheard of story. A young girl seduced by the trappings of a big city. The bright lights of the city blinding her from the evils that can steal your soul before you even know you have even been seduced. It is a tragedy. A tragedy I wished I had known about. I wish I could have reached down and pulled this poor child out of the murky waters in which she was slowly drowning. However, she preferred to keep me ignorant of her misfortunes, and because of that, I fear it may have cost her her life. Do you have any suspects who may have committed this heinous crime?"

"Not yet," replied Jim quickly.

"Not yet?" Thatcher stepped back a little surprised. "Well," he continued in his rolling, rounded words, "if you need anything at all, just ask. I will have the forces of the entire federal government at your service, if necessary, to bring a speedy close to this tragedy."

"Oh, thank you very much for your assistance, but I think we'll be fine working with our own staff," Jim said with a hint of condescension which escaped Thatcher's notice. Jim reached over to shake the congressman's hand good-bye.

"We will be sure to keep you posted on any new information we find," Jim said as he started for the door. Kathleen still faced the congressman. This trip had been pointless, she thought. They had not gotten any new information from this man. The only thing she could determine from this meeting was that the congressman was a little odd and loved a bit of drama, to say the least.

As Kathleen changed her gaze from the congressman to Jim, she was surprised to find him staring directly into her eyes and then a wink.

Jim swung around on his heels with his index finger pointing in the air. "Oh, there was one last thing I forgot to mention about Ms. Young's pregnancy. We don't know who the father is, but we do know he was a white man. Not much to go on, just a little fact. I thought you might be interested."

Kathleen watched as Thatcher took a step backward, his hands searching for the edge of the desk to brace himself. Once his hands found the safety of the desk, they firmly clenched the edges, and his arms straightened for support. The congressman's head wobbled ever so slightly, almost as if he were about to faint. In a soft, silky southern drawl, he said, "How extraordinary," and then walked to his desk to sit.

The congressman's words shriveled from an elegant, polished speech to a desperate search for something else to say. Kathleen mentally catalogued the barely noticeable tremor in his hands as he shuffled some papers before managing to say, "Good day, detectives."

Neither Kathleen nor Jim said anything until they cleared the building and quickly walked a half a block toward their car. Each had an unconscious fear someone might overhear what they were about to discuss.

"OK," Kathleen said, a little out of breath. "That man was lying. The congressman not only knew Victoria Young was pregnant; he knew the father was white. Thatcher knows who the father is. That means Hayes is right. Do you think that means he is the father?"

"Who, Hayes? I don't think Dr. Hayes is the father," Jim answered back, having a little fun with Kathleen's excitement.

"Not Hayes! Thatcher!" Kathleen responded, faking a disgusted look at her partner. "That means the lab results *are* wrong. Wow. We have to ask the lab to retest the sample. They should be able to tell us if they made a mistake."

"No!" said Jim emphatically. "This was not a mistake. The lab did not accidentally mix up the samples. This had to be deliberate. No one accidentally switches the DNA of a fetus to a convicted felon. There is something really wrong going on here. Teri said the DNA files were perfect. She said there were no mistakes in the lab work and that means someone at the lab is covering up something. We need to figure out what's going on before we start pulling more people into this investigation."

Kathleen stopped. "Unless you know how to get into the lab and retest a DNA sample, we need someone's help," she said trying to point out the contradictory nature of Jim's statements.

Kathleen resumed walking. "What about Teri Sedgwick?" she asked. "How well do you know her? Her area of expertise is DNA. She could do the retest. Do you know her well enough to ask for her help? Do you trust her?"

"I know her through work. I consider her a friend, but I really don't know her that well," Jim said, pausing to look up and down the street, checking to be sure there was no one there, who might overhear their conversation. "But, I trust her."

When they got back to the office, Jim called Teri to see if she would be interested in meeting them after work to go over the entire case file.

"You know, these major case reviews are usually between the police and the analysts who actually worked the case," Teri said in an insistent tone. "I have not done any work on this case!"

"I know, that's fine," Jim assured her. "It's better that way. You will just have to trust me," he said. "Bring the file so we can go over it. Where do you want to meet?"

There was a sudden stop in the conversation as each realized they had stumbled into awkward territory.

Teri finally broke the silence apologetically, "I know we used to go to Stone's place, but maybe we could think of somewhere else."

Jim breathed deeply but didn't say anything. Finally, after what seemed like an hour, he responded flatly, "That's fine. Let's meet at Stone's at 6:30."

Jim turned to Kathleen. "We are going to meet at the Stone Soup Café for dinner. Teri will bring the case file."

Kathleen's face immediately lit up. "I love that place! This is wonderful. I am starving. What kind of dinners do they have there? Any specials?"

"Calm down, Kathleen. It's just a restaurant. You haven't won a Hawaiian vacation. It's just someplace to meet where we won't be seen."

It still made Kathleen happy to think of dining under the stars in a lovely courtyard with wonderful food talking about a case with coworkers. It was the small things like that that made Kathleen smile. With her job as a detective, she appreciated those moments more than she ever had in the past, at least she imagined she would appreciate those moments.

Kathleen and Jim parked about a block away from the café. Looking at the street signs, Kathleen realized that they had come in a different way than the first time they had eaten here. This place would be very hard to find without Jim, she thought. It was in the middle of a blue-collar neighborhood. Houses that were probably built in the 1950s lined the street, and because it was on a hill, Kathleen could see more houses dot the hilly streets for several blocks. As they turned the corner to the café, Jim saw Teri walking from the other direction, carrying a briefcase and her purse.

They waited at the front door of the café as Teri approached. Teri's looks were unmistakable. She had long straight black hair with red highlights. Kathleen thought she must have had some American Indian ancestry because her face was slightly rounded and her skin always had a hint of bronze, even after months of winter. However, by far the most unforgettable thing about Teri Sedgwick was her piercing blue eyes. It was particularly unusual for someone of her coloring to have blue eyes. Everyone stared at her eyes the first time they met her and Kathleen was no exception.

"Teri," Jim said, gesturing toward Kathleen, "this is my partner, Kathleen Jackson. Kathleen, this is Teri Sedgwick."

Kathleen stepped forward to shake Teri's hand, holding it hand an extra moment, staring at Teri, which made the introduction slightly awkward.

Teri tilted her head and gave Kathleen a big smile, as if to let her know it was OK because this was how every introduction went. Then she turned to Jim. "Shall we go in?"

Jim held the door as Teri entered first, then Kathleen, and finally Jim. Mama was clearing a table when she turned to see them.

"Hello, Mrs. Stone," Teri said bending slightly to meet Mama at eye level.

"Teri, Oh Teri. It is so good to see you once more. What is this Mrs. Stone? You call me Mama or I will be hurt." She put down her dishes to give Teri a kiss.

"Ah, Mrs. Stone," Kathleen sighed softly. She made her statement more to the room than any one person. "I get it, now. It's Mrs. Stone. Stone Soup Café. It's like a pun. I didn't know her last name was Stone.

It's very cute. I get it now." Kathleen's voice faded off as she laughed to herself.

Teri threw a questioning look toward Jim, but he had no time to respond before Mama saw him and ran to give him a hug.

"I don't see you for so many months, and now I see you last week and this week. It is a wonderful thing, a gift from God," Mama bubbled over as she kissed each of Jim's cheeks.

"Mama, we need to do a major case review. Could we use the room in the back?"

"Oh, yes, yes, certainly. I will make coffee. Just like I used to. Go to the back, I will bring things for you to eat," Mama spoke with such excitement in her voice that Kathleen thought maybe Mama was going join them for the review.

As Kathleen stepped into the conference room, she could not believe her eyes. It was the most elegant conference room she had ever seen. In the center of the room stood a large oval oak table with eight leather chairs surrounding it. The floor had Victorian-style area rug on a beautiful wood floor. Mahogany panels covered the lower portion of the walls, with exquisite wallpaper above the chair rail. On one wall was a fireplace with ornate ironwork around its sides and a thick oak mantel, upon which stood a lone antique clock. On both ends of the room, the walls contained a white board and a pull down projection screen and in the corner were both an overhead projector and a computerized projector. On the back wall was a marble buffet counter. Its back splash was covered in beautiful Italian tile, and an immense silver coffee urn and chafing dish waited there.

After taking in the room for what seemed like minutes, Kathleen said in utter disbelief, "Who puts a conference room like this in the back of a café? Who in their right mind would build a conference room like this? Who would come here to have a meeting?"

"We would," Teri said as she threw her briefcase on the table.

Jim turned back to the doorway, indicating he was going to assist Mama in the kitchen with the coffee. As he left the room, Kathleen flopped down in one of the big leather chairs.

"I feel like I am the odd man out in a very complicated game," Kathleen said taking a deep breath. "Why would you come here to meet? It seems like a strange place to come."

"How many major cases have you worked on?" Teri asked, trying to make conversation.

"Well, actually, this is my first high profile case," Kathleen admitted.

"Some high profile cases *are* major cases," Teri said with a sincerity that put Kathleen at ease. "But, major cases are not just high profile cases. Major cases are cases with a lot going on. For example, if a senator got arrested for driving under the influence of alcohol, I can assure you it would be a high profile case, but it would be a simple case. The officer makes an arrest, has a blood sample drawn, the blood sample is sent to the crime lab, and the crime lab sends back a report with their findings. It's simple.

Teri went on, "Major cases are the complicated ones where there are a lot of people involved in the investigation or there is a lot of evidence being collected and submitted to the crime laboratory. In this case, we have dozens of pieces of evidence, seven laboratory sections involved, twenty officers doing background checks, searching for witnesses or canvassing the crime scene. With a case like this, it is easy to forget to submit a bullet for testing or miss some witness's story. Sometimes there is evidence that is contradictory. When that happens, a new theory of how the crime unfolded must be developed. Eventually, all the evidence will point to one theory. That will be the correct theory.

"A major case review is a way to make certain all the facts of a case are supported by all the evidence. Normally we, or at least we used to, have all the analysts involved. They would talk about their findings with the officers. The officers would ask questions. It really helps in an investigation. We haven't really done one since we started using our evidence tech in the lab. I am not certain why we stopped. I always thought they were a good idea but for some reason, Jim didn't want everyone here for this review."

Teri paused then asked Kathleen, "How many years have you been with the force?"

"Uh, well, two years, actually," Kathleen said, knowing that her limited time on the DC police department was not very impressive to someone routinely working with detectives.

"Two years?" There was no mistake in Teri's surprise at the answer.

"No one is assigned to the Crime Scene Bureau after two years."

"Well… I was." Kathleen hesitated, wondering how much of the story she should tell Teri. "I was hired as a planned replacement for Jim and his partner, when they retired. My background is academic, but my field of study is Forensic Investigation. I think the department thought it would be a good fit. I'm not always certain it is," she laughed. "I went through the Academy for their initial training and spent a year rotating through the different departments. You know, learning the ropes; then, transferred to the Crime Scene Bureau as Jim's partner. It was incredibly bad timing. I got my assignment the day his partner and his wife died. My report date was the day of their funeral."

She paused briefly, but then continued, "Because I was always rotating to a different assignment, I never really got any major cases assigned to me. The point of the rotations was more to learn how things were done."

"Jim and Pete always got *all* the big assignments," Teri said with a smile, remembering when she worked with them.

"So you knew Pete?"

"Oh, yeah. Jim and Pete, they were the GO TO men," Teri explained. "They were incredible. You would not believe some of the cases they solved. They never missed a detail. They could read people better than a lie detector. You got a good assignment when you got Jim. He knows how to do the job better than anyone." It was obvious Teri had a deep admiration for Jim.

Teri continued, "Did you know Pete and Jim invented the major case review concept nine years ago? That's why they put this room together. It was some place where they could come. Sometimes, we would be here all night working through a case. Mama would make us sand-wiches. It was great."

"Jim put this room together?"

"Well, Jim didn't really. Pete did. Actually Pete's mom did. You know Mrs. Stone," Teri replied. "The first year they were assigned to the Crime Scene Bureau, they put in so much overtime reviewing cases she thought this was the only way she could make certain Pete got a good meal. You know how Italian mothers are."

"Pete Stone?" Kathleen said in amazement. "Mrs. Stone is the mother of Jim's partner, Pete Stone? I never made the connection."

"I didn't think so," Teri smiled.

"Pete and Jim were the best, best detectives, best of friends. Together they were unbeatable. Then that car crash. What a nightmare," Teri, said not knowing how much Kathleen knew about Jim's past.

"He never discusses it." Kathleen desperately wanted to know what Jim was like before his wife and partner had died, and Teri nodded, acknowledging Kathleen's silent request for her to continue.

"It was a terrible accident. Pete had been driving way too fast. The accident re-constructionist estimated his speed at over 90 miles per hour. The driver's side wheel went off the road, hitting soft dirt. He was driving Jennifer's SUV. The center of gravity on the SUV was so high. Once the car hit the dirt, it was all over. The SUV began to tumble and rolled for a hundred yards. Even though they both had on their seatbelts, they didn't have a chance."

Teri stopped for a moment, thinking about how terrible the accident must have been. Then she continued. "The first responding officer thought it might have been a two car accident. You know, someone might have hit them. He thought he noticed a different color paint on the rear passenger side of the SUV. The lab got the evidence on the case. No one could believe the results when the analysis was complete. The headspace gas chromatograph measured high level of alcohol in their blood. Pete and Jenny had to be both really drunk, three times the legal limit, I think. When the trace analysis on the car showed no other car involved, it was obvious it was a single car accident with an intoxicated driver."

Kathleen shook her head. "It just seems so….so off that Jim's wife and his partner…were together."

"I know," Teri said. "Jim told me Pete and Jenny met here to go to some flower show. It's still hard to believe. With that high of a blood alcohol level, you have to wonder. They certainly didn't go to any flower show. They had to be drinking together all night long. It wasn't just a glass at the bar before they went somewhere else. They each had ten or twelve drinks in them. It just didn't make any sense. I will say, Pete did enjoy a beer from time to time, and he was quite the lady's man; but Jenny, not with Jenny. Nothing about the story sounded like Jenny. Then after their deaths, it was terrible. You know," Teri said in more of a whisper, "the rumors that go on in the department. Only half of them are ever true. I didn't believe any of them, but I had no explanation for the evidence."

Hearing footsteps in the hallway, Teri stopped talking and began opening her briefcase.

Jim walked through the door with a tray of coffee, cups, milk and sugar.

"OK," Jim started. "Are we ready?" he reached for the file he brought. "Let's see, Teri, you have the lab file, correct?"

"Right here," she said holding up a three-inch bundle of paperwork.

"Then here, Kathleen, you can go through all the other reports," he said as he slapped a two-inch stack of papers in front of her.

"Let's go." Jim walked to the white board and grabbed a marker.

"OK. Was the body moved after death?"

Kathleen looked down at her papers and began flipping through them. "My examination at the scene has it as No." Kathleen flipped through a few more papers. "And, it looks like the Medical Examiner agrees with me. He says no. So, I guess everyone agrees -- No."

"So the woman was found at the scene of the crime where she was killed," Jim said flatly. "Were there any witnesses?"

Kathleen thumbed through more pages. "No witnesses. Well…uh… one witness, who saw someone taking a picture. Wait, let me read this more carefully." Kathleen paused to read the whole report before she continued. "A witness was outside with her dog and thought she saw a flash of light in the general direction of the crime scene at the correct time but believed it to be a flashbulb from a camera. Interesting. Who would walk a dog at one o'clock in the morning?"

"Let's assume the witness saw something," Jim said. "It could be the flash of a camera or…"

Teri jumped in, "Or the flash of a gun being fired."

"There was no mention of any noise," Kathleen protested.

"Yes, so it would be a gun with a silencer or maybe the witness can't hear very well," Jim suggested.

"The witness can't hear a gun but can see the muzzle flash?" Kathleen said with a chuckle. "That is one deaf witness."

"Regardless, we are going to need to talk to that person," Jim said as he wrote a column on the white board of things left to do in the case.

"Cause of death?" Jim fired.

"Rifle shot to the right temple," Kathleen responded.

"Recovered bullet?"

"Nine millimeter."

"Identified murder weapon?" Jim asked.

"Nine millimeter Glock," Teri looked up from her pages confused. "A Glock isn't a rifle, it's a handgun."

"The ME's report says rifle shot to the head," Kathleen clarified.

"Teri, any chance the lab made a bad ID?"

Teri flipped through the case file to the firearms paperwork. She pulled out the digital photographs that the firearms examiner had taken as documentation.

"No," Teri said shaking her head. "The bullet looks good. It's not a fragment. It is a good, clean bullet. This should have been an easy match," she said as she held up two large pictures of nine-millimeter bullets.

Jim added to the white board --Check with ME on rifle identification, then made another column on the board labeled "DISCREPANCIES". Under it, he wrote RIFLE/GLOCK.

"Well, as long as we are listing discrepancies, I'll add the tox report," Jim said as he wrote MOTHER/FETUS TOX.

Teri looked puzzled as she flipped through her pages to the toxicology report. "Oh," she said. "So, the mother had cocaine and ethanol but the fetus results were negative for drugs and alcohol. That does seem to be a discrepancy."

"Well, Dr. Hayes explained how a discrepancy like that could occur," Kathleen interrupted. "It sounded like it might be a one in a million chance, but it could happen. The drug discrepancy could have been from an acute dose which did not get into the baby's system yet, and the alcohol could have evaporated from the tissue."

"Hayes said the alcohol would have evaporated if the tissue had dried out," Jim corrected. "Teri, is the tissue listed as dried?"

Teri scanned the lab notes made by the toxicologist. "No. The tissue sample is listed as having normal color and consistency."

"Wouldn't the toxicologist have noted if the sample had dried out?" Jim asked.

"Yes, anything out of the ordinary would have been noted in the case notes," Teri replied. "If there is one thing we're taught in our training, it is to note everything. He would not have missed noting the changes in the condition of the sample."

"So the tox results are a discrepancy," Jim said as he underlined them on the white board.

"Now, the DNA results," Jim continued. "Dr. Hayes says the fetus could not have been fathered by Syrus Sandman." Jim wrote PATERNAL DNA TEST on the white board.

"What test did he do to determine that finding?" Teri asked, perplexed.

"Don't even go there," Kathleen broke in.

"We went over this on the phone," Teri said, knowing the direction the conversation was going.

"Hayes says the baby has Caucasian features," Jim explained.

"Those results are solid. There is no discrepancy in the DNA results. The DNA analysis shows two donors to the fetus' DNA, Victoria Young and Syrus Sandman. Dr. Hayes is guessing," Teri argued. "There is no scientific data that shows you can tell the racial make up of a fetus. You have to rely on the scientific testing."

"Then, we need those samples retested," Jim said firmly. "We need to make certain the DNA results are correct."

"The lab director is not going to authorize retesting of samples based on a hunch. Especially a bad hunch, like you thought the fetus didn't look like its father. Do you know how many DNA cases we have on our backlog?" Teri said just as firmly. "Even if it was approved, it wouldn't be high priority. There's no evidence there were any problems with the analysis of the samples. Going through chain of command, the re-analysis would take weeks to get approved if it even did."

"That is why we don't want to go through the chain of command," Jim said staring at Teri with a look she knew very well. It was a look Jim got when he wanted something done, but didn't necessarily want to follow the rules. In these situations, the answer "No" seldom stopped him. "I want the samples re-tested," Jim said bluntly.

Teri fixed a stare back at Jim, slowly realizing what he was asking.

"I can't retest the samples. Do you know what you are asking?" Teri argued. "I'm not authorized to do any testing in this case. This is Aaron's case."

Teri argued on, hopelessly. "It takes a couple days to do a DNA test. It's not like I can just skip a lunch or test it on my break! It takes an hour just to bleach down the work area. Then, you have to extract the DNA from the sample. Once the DNA strands are extracted, they have to be amplified. There is a lot of prep work that has to be done before it goes on the instrument. Once it gets to the capillary electrophoresis which produces the DNA allele profiles, you need to have calibrators, and blanks run, then your samples run. DNA analysis is not done in fifteen minutes. That is time that I absolutely don't have and that's not even mentioning the cost of reagents or the time it will take to make the interpretation of the results. If I did an unauthorized test like that, I could lose my job!"

Jim continued to look at Teri. He realized what he was asking her to do was a lot, but there was no other way to find the answers in the case. Jim walked over to where she was sitting and bent down to look her in the eyes.

"We need to know the truth in this case," Jim explained in a soft voice. "I don't want you to lose your job, but there is something very wrong in this case. I don't know who we can trust. The only thing I know is that I trust you. I know you can do this."

Teri stared at the case file she had smuggled out of the lab. She knew she had already made one policy violation by removing the materials without signing it out. Now she was being asked to violate more policies. No one moved or spoke, letting the ticking from the clock on the mantel fill the room, as they each thought through their dilemmas. Finally, after what seemed like hours, Teri gave in. "OK, I will help."

CHAPTER FIVE

JIM, KATHLEEN, AND Teri worked all night, combing the case files. Reviewing every witness's statement, every case file note, they looked through each piece of paper in every file. By the next morning, it showed on their faces. When Teri got to the lab, everyone could tell she had had a rough night. For most of the day, she made reagents, cleaned up some old case files, and did some housekeeping in the lab, knowing she did not have the concentration to open a new case. Teri's thoughts were focused on how to test the Young fetus sample.

Kathleen and Jim's day started off badly, too. When they got to the office in the morning, Captain Freeman was there to greet them.

"What the HELL do you think you are doing?" Captain Freeman bellowed as they walked through the doorway. "You knew days ago the results of the Young case," he said waving over his head the thin, practically empty working file of Victoria Young. "The last thing I need is two detectives who think they can lie to me. Where the hell is the main file for this case? This file is empty."

"Calm down, Captain," Jim said. "We had some reports in, but the case is not closed. We still are waiting for some information. We were working on the case last night, and I have the file right here."

"What kind of information? Information like Young was involved with a gang-banger? That she was involved in drugs? Her mother has called me twice asking for information on the death of her daughter. What am I suppose to tell her? Or, do you want her to find this all out in the newspaper?" Most detectives knew not to keep the captain out of the loop during their investigations; most had felt the fury of his wrath but usually only once, never to make that mistake again.

"Captain, we are not done with this investigation," Jim repeated. "Nothing is going out to the papers until we finish. I am telling you as a detective who served under your command for 5 years that this investigation is not complete. You have to trust me on this. When we know the truth, you will be the first person we call. I promise."

"OK, OK," Captain Freeman said, taking a deep breath. "I want to know the results the minute you have concluded this case. Do I make myself clear?"

"We will," Kathleen whispered as she watched the captain march out the door.

After Freenan had gone, Jim turned to Kathleen and said, "We need that DNA sample tested. Teri has got to come through for us on this."

It was a few hours before they got a call from Teri.

"Can you reanalyze the sample for us?" Jim asked Teri, hoping she had come up with a plan.

Teri answered with much hesitation, "I think I can do it. But I can't do it during the day. It's impossible to conceal testing from the other analysts. I'll have to do the analysis at night. Once everyone has gone, I'll analyze the case. It's going to have to be late, though. There are a lot of people on flextime, and I don't think I can have private access to the lab until after 8 pm. Depending on how much I can get done, it might take me three or four days to analyze the case. Is that all right?"

"All right? That's wonderful. Can you start tonight?" Jim said, pleased that Teri would take this risk for him.

Teri thought about how tired she was. She knew it would be a long night. She wanted to say "No," but in the end, she answered, "Yes."

Teri spent her first night bleaching down the analytical area. It was what they called clean technique protocol. She removed the sample from the vault, checking the label on the side, reconfirming the case number. She took out an evidence inventory log and began to list the description of the tube of blood. She carefully wrote, 'One 10 mL grey-stoppered tube of whole blood approximately 2 mL of blood.' Years of experience had taught her to document everything. Inventorying and describing the evidence was standard operating procedure. Teri did it automatically.

She then brought the sample over to the biological hood, put on her gloves, lab coat and mask. She turned on the hood, which sounded like a muffled motorcycle starting. The bio hood looked like a large cabinet beginning waist high and had a glass sash window that slid up and down. Teri slid the glass window down past her face, and looking through the glass at her gloved hands, she opened the tube of blood. Using a pipette, she removed a small amount of the blood sample and placed it into a little plastic vial with a snap-on cap. Adding a buffer and an enzyme to the vial, she mixed the solution rigorously with a vortex.

Teri fell into the rhythm of the lab work she was so comfortable in doing. Time slipped by until she was ready to store the samples until her next nights work. She wrapped the samples up so no one could what they were and carefully secured them in her personal lock box. "If this doesn't work, I'll fix it tomorrow," she thought. It was 3 am and she was exhausted.

The next night Teri extracted the DNA and began the process of creating the short tandem repeats, known as STRs, of selected DNA strands. By 6 am, she was almost finished when she heard the first people of the day coming into the lab. Obviously on a flextime and started their day early. Exhausted and slightly panicked, she sat down in her chair at her desk and struggled to think of what to do.

Teri knew Scott from the questioned documents sections was the first to arrive and his office was in the back of the lab. Once he went to his office, she would have time to leave the lab for a few hours sleep. She heard Scott's footsteps walking down the hall. When there was silence, she waited a few moments longer, then got up and left for the stairway leading to the exit. She made it to the front door before she saw John Kragg getting out of his car and heading for the lab. Just as

John got to the front door, Teri opened it.

"Teri, what are you doing here so early in the morning? I thought you started at eight," John Kragg said, surprised.

"Oh, I couldn't sleep," Teri lied, wishing she were in bed. "I thought I would get to work early and see if I couldn't get out that Donner case." Teri paused for a moment hoping she seemed believable. Then continued, "I was just going back to check my car. I thought I might have left my car door unlocked. I just wanted to make sure. You know how it is when you come in early. Sometimes you forget the basics," she said with a weak chuckle.

"Oh, sure, I understand. These early mornings are not for everyone. I'm a little early myself."

Teri walked to her car and pretended she was checking her locks. With a casual wave of her hand, she pretended to laugh at herself. As she walked back to the laboratory, she knew she was too tired to analyze any cases. When the laboratory director came in at 8:00, she went to his office, and explained that she had come in early to finish the Calhoun case, but she really wasn't feeling very well and thought she might have to go home for the day.

"Check with the courts and make certain we are not close to a court date on that case. If there's no problem, go on home," the lab director said before adding more sympathetically, "you look terrible."

Teri signed out, using a sick day, and went home for a well-earned sleep.

That night, Teri was again ready to go into work. Knowing there was a chance some people might be working overtime, she waited until 10:30 to head back to the lab. When she got to the lab, the streets were dark and to her relief, the lab was empty. She thought about the morning encounter. Just to be safe, she parked her car at the back entrance, behind the building. This would give her some way out of the lab without being seen if there was a repeat of the earlier encounter.

That night, Teri continued with the reanalysis of the samples without giving thought to time. It was about 2 am when she thought she heard the front door of the lab slam shut. Teri immediately turned off the lights to her office.

"There is no reason someone would come to the lab this late," Teri said to herself, beginning to worry.

Could one of the evidence alarms be going off? She knew that all refrigerators and freezers were monitored. The alarm company would call the lab director.

"What if the lab director does a walk-through of the lab? How am I going to explain myself?" Teri tried to sink into the darkness. Then in a moment of clarity, she realized that the electronic alarms were also audio alarms. If one of the alarms had been set off, she would have heard it.

Pressing her ear against the office door, Teri could hear no alarms. She slowly opened the door slightly and listened again. There were no alarms. She peeked her head further out the doorway to see the stairwell and the darkened hallways on the first floor.

"No one is here," she tried to convince herself. "Anyone else in the lab would be here for a legitimate reason and not go sneaking around with the lights off."

Teri was disgusted with herself for being talked into such secretive behavior. She thought about her job. If she were discovered it would be a minimum of a reprimand and probably a suspension. As she was about to flip her office lights back on, she heard someone trip over a metal garbage can in the hallway below.

Teri looked out the doorway. All the lights downstairs were still off. She distinctly heard a man's voice say, "Damn it!"

The voice was muffled and unidentifiable, but it was clear someone was walking around the darkened crime laboratory.

Teri closed her door quietly, hoping whoever was in the lab would not come up the stairs. However, within seconds, she could hear footsteps echoing in the stairwell. She leaned against the door trying to breathe slowly as the adrenaline rushed into her system. Her heart started beating faster.

Teri looked around for some place to hide. There were no closets to vanish into. There were no big cabinets to curl up inside. Teri looked at the kneehole in her desk. Quickly without further thought, she squeezed her 5 foot 10 inch frame beneath her desk. With her knees pulled to her chest, she pressed against the back of the desk, hidden by both the desk and the office wall.

The footsteps were coming toward her office! Teri thought about how ridiculous it was that *she* was under her desk in the lab. Slowly she peeked around the corner of her desk, straining to hear, her heart stopped as the unknown intruder paused in front of her door then turned toward the file room. Teri breathed a sigh of relief. As she sat on the floor of her darkened office, feeling foolish and afraid, Teri remained frozen.

After several minutes, the person started to come toward the DNA section. The footsteps grew louder and louder, and the door opened slowly, Teri's heart thumped with hard, constricted contractions. She was certain whoever was in the room could hear her heart, too. She covered her chest with her arms, hoping to muffle the sound. She could see the shoes of the person walking around the office. It was a man. She did not recognize the little bit she could see of him. The pounding of her heart now seemed to be deafening.

Teri pulled herself back farther into the kneehole of her desk. The movement made the metal sides of her desk creak. The man stopped and turned toward the direction of the noise. The footsteps grew closer. Teri opened her mouth and tried to control her breathing with deep, rhythmic breaths. The man stopped at Teri's desk and turned on a flashlight. Teri could see the flashlight searching the room for the source of the noise. She tried not to breathe at all now, and with every controlled breath, her body felt like it was being deprived of oxygen. Teri could see the legs of the man standing directly in front of her desk. She wondered if the moist, warm breath she slowly exhaled could be felt on the legs of the intruder. Teri dare not turn the direction of her head. Except for the slow expansion and contraction of her lungs, she did not move at all. After what seemed like an eternity, the man turned toward Aaron's desk, and with his flashlight, flipped through the paperwork on his desk.

Teri felt suspended in space as the man looked through Aaron's papers, making noises of displeasure. After one last disgusted grunt, the man slowly turned and walked out of the office. Teri listened as he left the DNA section and headed toward the firearms section.

Grasping her cell phone from her coat pocket, Teri dialed the number for Jim Jarred. She was relieved when he answered the phone after only one ring.

"Jim," she whispered, still under her desk. "I am in the lab and there is someone else here. They are looking through files!"

It was about three in the morning and Jim was half-asleep. "Do you know who it is?" Jim yawned.

"It is an intruder!"

"Maybe it's someone finishing up a case," Jim said, hoping to calm her down.

"This isn't TV." Teri couldn't help but roll her eyes. "People in the lab don't work twenty-four hours a day solving cases. We go home at night. At least, anyone with any brains in their heads would go home at the end of the day!"

"If it is really an intruder," Jim said trying to make sense of the situation, "maybe you should call the police."

"I am calling the police, Jim! You are the police! I am calling you. I don't know who this person is. I need your help. What should I do?"

"OK," Jim said. "I'll think of something. Just sit tight. Wait until you feel safe then get out of there. I'll send someone."

Jim sat on the edge of the bed and rubbed his eyes. After a moment, he reached for the phone.

"Washington, DC Police dispatch, how may I direct your call?"

"Carolyn, is that you?" Jim yawned.

"Jim Jarred, is that you? What are ya callin' me for at this time of night?"

"Hey, Carolyn, could you do me a favor and patch me into Lincoln Bravo two-nine-seven. He's working tonight, isn't he?"

"He sure is and I can surely do that. Did you just wake up in the middle of the night and have a hankering to talk to Butch?"

"Something like that," Jim waited for the patch-in to the police car radio of an old friend who liked to work nights.

"This is Two Niner Seven, over."

"Butch, this is Jim Jarred. How ya doing?"

"Well, I'm doing fine, but what the heck are you talking to me for?" Butch said

"I was wondering if you could do me a favor."

"Anything," Butch replied.

"Could you go past the crime lab with lights and siren?"

"Sure thing. Is there a problem?"

"No, no problems. There have just been some kids showing up at the crime lab. You know, throwing rocks, jiggling doors. I just thought you might drive past and give them something to think about. I told the lab director I would try to help out with the problem. I forgot to put in the request when I was at work," Jim lied. "I must be feeling guilty for not taking care of it. It woke me up out of a sound sleep thinking about it."

"Sure thing," Butch replied. "The night's been kind of slow. It might give me some entertainment. If I see any kids, I'll make certain to give them a good scare."

"Thanks, Butch. I owe you one."

Teri could hear the siren coming from quite a distance away.

"Oh, no," she thought, "Jim really DID call the police." She pictured her whole career coming to an end. The police arresting her for unlawful lab work. She didn't know if there was even a charge of unlawful lab work, but she was certain they would come up with some kind of charge. The loud whine of the siren closed in on the lab. Teri wondered what she might do if she were no longer allowed to be a forensic scientist. Through her mind ran a gamut of jobs, all of which Teri thought she would hate.

Suddenly, Teri was brought back to the present. She heard footsteps lightly running down the hall, then pausing at the front desk. She could tell by the intruder's actions that he was also panicking and it gave her satisfaction to have the tables turned as she heard the police car enter the parking lot.

Teri realized the sirens had stopped. She could see faint reflections of the police lights flashing against the inner windows of the lab. She heard the rattle of the front door as someone checked to see if it was locked. Then, there was silence again and the dull passing of minutes. Teri peeked out from under her desk. She could no longer see the flashing lights or hear a sound. The police had driven off. She felt she was once again at the mercy of the unknown intruder. She listened carefully. To her relief, she could hear the intruder walk quickly down the steps, unlatch the locked front door, and leave the building.

Just to be safe, Teri stayed at her desk for another hour. She rested her head on the paperwork covering her desk and drifted in and out of sleep. By five o'clock, Teri felt comfortable enough to get up and go home.

While Teri was juggling her daytime job as forensic scientist and nighttime life as undercover DNA analyst, Kathleen and Jim tried to find the answers to the questions they had identified. They started at the Medical Examiner's office. Dr. Hayes was waiting when Jim and Kathleen arrived.

"Dr. Hayes," Jim said, surprised that the doctor was standing at the front door, "I didn't mean you had to greet us. I just wanted you to set aside a few minutes so we could talk."

"I know, I know," Dr. Hayes said, waving his hand as if to dismiss such a silly idea. "I was just so interested in what the reanalysis of the DNA was."

"Oh, uh, yes." Jim said, trying to think of what to say. "Yes, the DNA report. We haven't actually requested that sample be re-tested yet. We will." Jim did not want to reveal the fact that Teri was breaking all laboratory rules and analyzing the sample during the wee hours of the morning. "We are going to request a reanalysis. It's just that a reanalysis takes some time. You know," Jim shrugged, "extra paper work. We have to make a formal request, that sort of thing. We just haven't had time to do the paperwork."

Kathleen wanted to add something to the conversation, but wasn't certain what to add. She had not felt a need to lie since she was a child, and then, she had done it so badly that everyone knew she was lying. Now, the lies were becoming so complicated that she felt not saying anything was her best option.

Jim continued. "We wanted to talk to you about the bullet wound you reported in the Young case. You had in your notes that you thought it was rifle wound."

"Oh, yes," Dr. Hayes said, nodding. "It looked like a rifle wound. It was a distance shot. You know, no stippling, no gunpowder around the wound. It was definitely not shot from close range."

"But you said in your report 'Rifle wound to the right temple,'" Jim stressed.

"Well, yes." Dr. Hayes shrugged. "I mean, I leave the actual identification of what type of bullet to the experts at the lab. The wound definitely had the characteristics of a rifle shot. The bullet was some what fragmented, but it looked like a bullet from a rifle. I am not a gun expert, but it definitely looked like a rifle shot."

"Fragmented?" Kathleen said, finally contributing to the conversation.

"Did you take a picture of the bullet?" Jim asked.

"No," Dr. Hayes said, somewhat offended that they were questioning his procedures. "I put the bullet in an evidence bag. I sealed the bag. I marked across the seal with my initials and the date. I wrote on the bag what the contents of the bag were, and I sent it to the crime lab. That is how we've always done it. We don't have time to take photographs of everything. We did take photographs of the body, if you're interested in those."

"Sure, that would be great," Jim said as he looked at Kathleen.

Kathleen did not look happy. She could not think of anything worse than looking through numerous photographs of dead bodies. In a halfhearted attempt to conceal her feelings, she mumbled, "Yes, that would be great."

Kathleen and Jim spent the rest of the day going through the photos taken of Victoria Young's body, comparing them to those of known rifle victims. From their notes and drawings, they had been able to determine that the bullet entered at a slightly upward angle. That didn't seem so unusual. Young was close to six feet tall. Most people holding a firearm would have been pointing it slightly upward. Other than the partially fragmented bullet indicated in the notes, their efforts yielded no new information.

The next day, Kathleen and Jim headed back to the crime scene. Once there, they got to work with the basics. They spent most of the morning making measurements, putting up markers, and searching for any additional evidence. When they thought they had the position of the crime sufficiently marked, they went to find the witness listed in the police report. If they could bring her to the crime scene, the markings would better assist them in knowing where she was with respect to the crime and the other structures.

"The witness's name is Mable Cohen. She lives in apartment 801." Kathleen read the information in the police report as they walked toward the apartment building. "She has a dog. She is 77 years old. Lives alone."

As they entered the apartment building, Kathleen noticed that the building was old. The walls echoed with their footsteps as they walked across the marble floor that probably once had been stunning, but over time, dirt and grime had collected, adding a dull yellow tone to the color. What once had been white walls was now a dingy shade of gray. When they stepped inside the car, the old Otis elevator lunged once or twice before delivering them to the eighth floor."

"Here it is, 801" Kathleen knocked softly on the door.

A wiry woman with silver hair opened the door. Kathleen and Jim introduced themselves, and the woman invited them in. Mrs. Cohen's apartment was not tattered and old like the entrance lobby. Mrs. Cohen's apartment was flawless in its presentation. Everything was in its place. Everything was polished to a shine. The windows were freshly washed so the light streamed in to brighten an already colorful room. Elegant wood cabinets displayed an extensive collection of china and crystal. Jim and Kathleen sat on an old Victorian sofa, which was maroon with lime, orange and pink finely-sewn flowers as colorful accents. Ornately carved wood carefully framed the back of the sofa and wrapped around to make the arms.

"Mrs. Cohen," Jim started. "We are here to talk to you about the flash of light you saw the other night. We have the police report where you told the officer what you saw."

"Flash of *fire*," Mrs. Cohen said, immediately correcting him.

"Excuse me?" Jim said.

"I never said it was a flash of light. I said it was a flash of fire," repeated Mrs. Cohen, punctuating her point with her index finger.

"Did you tell the officer who questioned you that you saw a 'flash of fire'?" Kathleen asked.

"Of course I did," Mrs. Cohen said, offended that her accuracy of the account was in question. "I told him I had seen a flash of fire. But that young boy didn't seem to understand. He looked at me like I didn't know what I was talking about. That's when I told him it was like a flashbulb on a camera. You know, so he would understand what I was talking about. But it wasn't a flash of a camera bulb. It was a flash of fire."

"What exactly is the difference between a flashbulb on a camera and a flash of fire?" Kathleen asked.

"A flash from a camera lights up the whole area. That's what it's supposed to do. It's a big flash. That was not what I saw. What I saw was like a little shooting fire in mid-air, surrounded in complete blackness. It's hard to explain. It would be like pointing one of those butane lighters they use to start a fire. It was like someone was pointing that, and flicking it on for a second, only much faster and much more intense."

Kathleen and Jim glanced at each other with eyebrows raised, realizing what Mrs. Cohen had revealed. In perfect layman's terms, she described the muzzle flash of a firearm, which happens after a bullet has been fired from a gun.

"Where exactly were you when you saw this flash?" Jim continued with his questions.

"Let me see," Mrs. Cohen said, drawing her gaze up toward the ceiling as if to think the answer over. "I had been walking toward Tidal Basin. I guess I was drawn in by that beautiful aroma of those cherry blossoms."

"At one o'clock in the morning?" Kathleen said, hardly believing any woman would be walking alone around the Mall at one o'clock in the morning, let alone a 77-year-old woman who looked to weigh 100 pounds with her clothes on.

"Well, I wasn't walking over to see the blossoms alone. Duke, my dog, was with me. He needed to go for a walk. I think something he had eaten had upset his stomach, and he wanted to go out. Duke is very insistent when he needs to go outside. I always find it is most wise to heed the request of your pet when they are not feeling well. Don't you?"

"Well, ma'am, I don't have a dog," Kathleen said quickly. Then, looking at her partner she added, "The jury is still out on whether Jim is a dog owner or not."

Jim ignored the slight bit of sarcasm. He was nonchalantly, looking around the room for a dog. He did not see any signs of a dog in the apartment.

Mrs. Cohen immediately noticed his suspicions and added, "He's in the bedroom sleeping. I closed the door when I heard you knocking."

"Do you think it is prudent to walk your dog at one o'clock in the morning, Mrs. Cohen?" Kathleen asked, genuinely concerned for her safety. "You know it can be somewhat dangerous outside at that hour."

"I have never had any trouble, dear," Mrs. Cohen said, reaching over to pat Kathleen on the arm. "At my age, with anything I do there is some risk involved. Although, I will say when I saw that flash, I did think that it was time to come home." Mrs. Cohen sighed as she rose from her chair and said, "Could I offer either of you a cup of tea?"

"No, thank you, ma'am," Jim answered looking toward the bedroom. "What is your dog's name?"

"His name is Duke. Would you like to meet him? I know he is as curious to meet you as you are to meet him. With your scents left all over my apartment, he will be certain to notice. It will drive him crazy trying to figure out what strange visitor I've had. He is very protective."

"Sure. I would love to meet Duke," Kathleen stood. As Mrs. Cohen opened her bedroom door, Kathleen crouched a little to greet the dog she was certain would be scampering in towards her. Kathleen had always been good with animals, especially dogs.

As Mrs. Cohen opened the door, out sauntered a huge German Shepherd. It immediately moved between Mrs. Cohen and her two guests. Duke didn't growl or make any type of sound. He cocked his head slightly and sized up Kathleen and Jim from head to toe. Jim stepped forward, gesturing to Mrs. Cohen. As he did so, Duke stepped forward toward Jim. Duke did not relinquish his position in front of Mrs. Cohen nor did he take his eyes off Jim. Jim stepped back.

"Mrs. Cohen," Jim said still looking directly at Duke, "would you mind coming outside with us to show us where you saw this flash?"

Leaving Duke behind, the trio went down to the street to walk the block and a half to where Mrs. Cohen stood the night of Victoria Young's murder. Jim evaluated the scene. To their left they could see the color of the cherry blossoms coming into view, but the trees were definitely not in full view. Neither Kathleen nor Jim could see the markers they placed at the scene of the crime earlier that morning. Mrs. Cohen pointed straight ahead toward where she saw her flash of fire.

"You mean you saw the flash on this side of the bridge, not over there where the cherry blossoms are?" Jim asked, trying to understand exactly where she thought the shooting had taken place.

"Oh, yes," Mrs. Cohen replied firmly. "It was on this side, not across the water. It was there," Mrs. Cohen said, pointing at the beginning of the bridge that linked the street to the path toward the cherry trees.

The bridge Mrs. Cohen pointed to crossed over to the Jefferson Monument. From this side of the bridge, it was a very far distance to the scene of the crime. This information was not what Kathleen and Jim had been expecting.

Kathleen and Jim walked Mrs. Cohen back to her apartment, thanked her for her time, and said someone would be calling her in a few weeks to review her statement. They then walked back to the bridge and began looking over the area, but there was nothing of consequence they could find. They looked over toward the markers, which were far in the distance. As they stood where Mrs. Cohen had stood, they saw the flags they had marked but they were hundreds of yards away.

"What do you know about Glocks?" Jim asked.

"Do you want the short or the long version?" Kathleen said with a smile. "Austrian designed, it was made popular by the Austrian Army. It didn't enter the US market until 1985."

"I don't need a history lesson," Jim said. "Give me something an investigator can use."

"Sure," Kathleen said confidently. "What do you want to know? That it is often issued by law enforcement agencies or that the Glock 17, oldest and most common, uses standard nine-millimeter ammunition. It has three safety features, a drop safety, a firing pin safety and a trigger safety, which is good because it has a lighter trigger pull than other pistols. A Glock's average trigger pull weight is between five and six pounds, which is why a number of law enforcement officers are missing a toe or two. A Glock weighs a little less than 2 pounds with a full magazine. When fired using standard ammunition, a bullet will leave the chamber at a speed of approximately 1200 feet per second." Kathleen looked at Jim who was squinting toward the crime scene, apparently not paying attention to Kathleen's dissertation. "Do you want me to continue or maybe you would like to tell me what YOU know about Glocks?"

"I know that's one hell of a shot for a Glock," Jim said as he dusted some dirt off his hands. "Let's go back and clean up the crime scene."

The next morning, Kathleen and Jim arrived at the office to the sound of a ringing phone. Jim picked up the phone, listened for a second and then mouthed to Kathleen, "It's Teri."

"So how did our plan work last night?" Jim asked.

"*Our plan!*" Teri said, feigning contempt for Jim's casual response. "*My plan* was to have someone in a police uniform come and save me from an intruder. But all I got was some police sirens and severe leg cramps from hiding under my desk. All night! Where were you? You never even checked up on me! That was your plan?"

"I love it when a plan comes together," Jim said with a smile. Then, in a more caring tone said, "I had them run past the lab a couple more times with lights off. I knew if there were any major problems, they would notice. I'm glad you're safe."

"Yes, I am safe and done with my analysis," Teri said proudly. "I just need to interpret the results. That is probably going to take most of the morning. I called in and said I have a doctor's appointment so I would be a few hours late to work. I need a little quality sleep before I tackle the computer printouts of the DNA tests. That should take me two or three hours. When would you like to meet, this afternoon? I could probably have it done by 2 p.m."

"OK, we'll come by the lab around 2 o'clock. Could you reserve a conference room? We can go over your findings there. Please do not tell anyone about this, yet. If anyone asks, say it's a consultation on another case. Oh, and Teri, you're wonderful," Jim said. He hung up the phone and turned to Kathleen with a wide smile. "I love that woman."

It seemed like 2 o'clock would never come for Kathleen. Her concentration on some needed paperwork drifted and waned. It seemed like an endless sea of useless paperwork. Handwritten notes had to be transcribed into typed documentation. Times and dates of who was contacted, what they said had to be compared to the original notes. Pages were numbered so they were certain no information in the case file was missing. Page numbers had to be checked to ensure they were numbered correctly. It seemed beyond mindless to Kathleen, yet she knew if she made one mistake, wrote a number down wrong, transcribed a time incorrectly, it might cost them the case when it went to trial. A smart lawyer never missed a paperwork error, nor failed to exploit it to its fullest potential.

This constant redundancy of work never seemed to bother Jim. It seemed almost a peaceful time for him, a time when his thoughts focused on the ordinary and the simple. The straightforwardness of the work seemed to give his thoughts time to rest.

Frustrated because she had lost count of the pages of the witness reports for a third time, Kathleen groaned aloud. She looked at the clock feeling it had to be 1:45, but she groaned again when she saw it was only 12:30.

Jim decided to put an end to her suffering. He tapped her on the shoulder and said, "Let's catch some lunch and then go over to the lab."

To Kathleen's displeasure, Jim drove to a hamburger place near their office. Kathleen could hardly choke down the burger she ordered. She hoped they would have gone to the Stone Soup Café, but knowing it was such a link to Jim's past, she felt it was in poor taste for her to ask. It was hard for her to imagine how difficult it must have been for Jim to go back to the place owned by his partner's mother.

The silence of their meal made Kathleen uncomfortable; she tried to think of a line of conversation that avoided the subjects of good food or old partners. "What do you think Teri found out?" Kathleen asked. The anticipation in her voice was noticeable.

"I never wonder about the facts," Jim said dryly. "I always wait for the evidence to tell me what it has to say."

That was the extent of the meal's conversation. Kathleen tried to think of another comment, but the only thing that came to mind was the weather. They finished their lunch without Kathleen mentioning the weather.

As they drove to the crime lab, Kathleen could not help but consider other solutions to the mystery of the murdered woman. "What would the results unfold?" she wondered. "Could the tubes have been switched? Maybe Syrus was the father. That would make things easy.

Maybe there was a hit in CODIS to another felon," Kathleen thought to herself as she passed the time imaging one scenario after another, each more ridiculous and implausible than the last. By the time they arrived at the crime lab, Victoria Young had become an international spy.

Jack, the evidence technician, met them at the door to buzz the alarmed door open and let them into the evidence receiving area.

"Hi, Jim, Kathleen," he said nodding toward them. "What can I do for you? It doesn't look like you are carrying much evidence."

"No," Jim said scratching the back of his head, "not, today. We're here on a case consultation with Teri."

"Oh," Jack said, "do you want me to sit in? If you have a case name or number, I can pull the file."

"Oh no, that's OK. It's one of those old cases that never seem to go away. I thought I would bring Kathleen up to speed just in case she has to carry on with it after I retire," Jim improvised. "Teri knows all about it. She's probably already pulled the case file. Could you page her for us?"

A page sounded through the speakers in the ceiling, and Teri showed up a few minutes later. Her long dark hair did not quite shimmer as usual. Her eyes, although still striking, looked tired but pleased to see Jim and Kathleen. Kathleen wished she exuded the confidence she saw in Teri. Teri's tall, lanky body seemed to breeze down the hallway, the bottom of her lab coat flowing out behind her like a runway model. Although that trait was still present, Kathleen and Jim could now also see fatigue and anticipation.

"Hey," Jack said, nodding toward Teri, "you sure you don't want me to sit in on this consultation? Maybe there is some way I could help."

"We got this one covered," Jim slapped Jack on the shoulder and started walking toward Teri.

Teri brought them to the conference room and quickly closed the door. She was carrying a file folder and a videocassette tape.

"The intruder last night," Teri said waving the tape in the air, pleased with herself. "I once worked as backup for security. The lab is videotaped twenty-four hours a day. Twice a day they have to change the tape. When the person in charge of changing the tape was sick or on vacation, I would change the tape. Now it's Jack's job, of course, but I never turned in my key. I just got this out of the security room. It's a tape of last night. We'll see who was walking around the lab last night besides me."

As Teri put the tape into the VCR connected to the video conferencing system, Kathleen asked, "If you knew you were being video taped, why weren't you worried about losing your job?"

"These tapes are never watched," Teri laughed. "Well, I mean they are watched if there is a problem or they have to backtrack to trace down something, but no one ever reviews what happened the night before. There are hundreds of them. They just put them on a shelf until they might be needed."

"Why tapes?" Kathleen said as she scrunched up her nose. "I think I've got a better system at my house or at least a more updated system. Get a read-write DVD. It would make things some much easier, and smaller."

"That's one of the problems with crime labs," Teri sighed. "We use a lot of new technologies but we also have to be careful. Digital evidence can be altered much easier that a tape. That's why we use tapes. It actually would take a lot more effort to alter a tape than a disc. We're pretty secure, here."

They all sat down to watch the tape, intently anticipating another breakthrough in the case. On the television screen, there were four square pictures. The upper left square was a picture of the entranceway, the upper right picture was the main hallway to the back of the lab through evidence receiving, the lower left picture was the main hallway in the laboratory, and the lower right picture was the back door and the back portion of the lab.

"Who puts the tape in at night?" Kathleen asked.

"The last person leaving, when they lock up the building, puts the night tape in. The tapes can run for up to 15 hours so there is some overlap. Most of the time we don't use the full tape."

They watched as they saw the last person leaving the laboratory the night before. It looked like Jack Johnson. He got in his car and drove away. Teri fast-forwarded. The only thing moving on the screen was the time marker in the bottom right corner. The numbered time line flew past, but nothing else changed. Then in the upper left square they saw the sunrise, a car pulled into the parking lot, and John Kragg got out of his car. He walked into the building and down the hall to his office. A half-hour later, other people began coming in to start their workday.

"Maybe the tape was going so fast, we missed it?" Kathleen said with a question in her voice. "What time did you get here last night?"

"Around eleven," Teri said as she rewound the tape. She slowed the tape at 10:50 and then pressed PLAY. They watched all four squares but nothing happened. 11:00, 11:05, 11:15 came and went and there was nothing.

"Are you sure it was eleven? Maybe it was midnight," Jim suggested.

"No," said Teri firmly. "It was eleven. I was listening to the radio and the hourly news came on. The last thing I heard before I turned my car off was that it was eleven o'clock." She seemed totally perplexed. "This is not possible," she said, straining her eyes at the screen. "I have to be on this tape. I was here last night."

"Well, let's think about this later," Jim said, a little frustrated. "I am more interested in the data."

"Easy for you to say," Teri snapped back. "I am more interested in whether or not I might have been killed last night. But I *know* you will be interested in what I found out about the DNA sample." Teri slid her file across the table toward Jim, definitely pleased with what she had found.

"What did you find?" Kathleen could not suppress her curiosity.

"Well, I found the DNA of Victoria Young and the DNA of Syrus Sandman," she said with some satisfaction.

"So, it is exactly like the first test," Kathleen said with a shrug.

"NO! It's not. I found both the DNA of Victoria Young and Syrus Sandman in the blood sample of the fetus," Teri slowly said, looking at Kathleen and Jim as if she had just said the most astonishing thing.

"OK, we understand that. But, that does not seem to be any different than the original results. I am not certain we got your point. Could you give it to us in non-DNA terms?" Jim said, leaning forward in his chair.

"Babies get half their DNA from their mother and half their DNA from their father. They don't get their mother's entire DNA and their father's entire DNA; they get one DNA gene from each parent. Each single gene comes together to make a separate unique DNA signature," Teri explained. "Do you follow me?"

"Of course," Kathleen said. "I think that is pretty basic genetics. Half our genes are from our mothers and half from our fathers."

"What I found was ALL the mother's DNA and ALL the father's DNA," Teri said with excitement. "It's more like two blood samples, one from Victoria and one from Syrus, were mixed together. There is too much DNA in this sample to have come from one person. There are too many genes in this sample."

Jim leaned back in his chair, trying to absorb this information. "Could Aaron have missed this?"

"NO!" Teri responded quickly. "This was not what Aaron's results showed. Aaron's results showed half the DNA from Victoria and half from Syrus."

"Could Aaron have manipulated the data in some way?" asked Kathleen.

"Yes, he could." Teri responded, obviously displeased with the implication that Aaron had done something wrong. "But, he could not manipulate the results in the original data." Teri paused as she thought of how to explain her findings. "Let me try to explain. Data obtained from DNA tests is analyzed and the results are represented as a graph, which has a base line and peaks. Each peak represents a short section of the DNA. The height of the peaks represents the amount of DNA found in the sample. Where the peak falls on the graph corresponds to the number of base pairs in the strand. Each person will show two peaks at a specific DNA loci or section of the DNA strand that has been identified. We normally run 13 loci. So, any one individual will show no more than two peaks on each of the thirteen graphs. Sometimes there can be less than 2 peaks, but I won't even go there," Teri explained, hoping they were following what she was saying.

Teri continued, "The sample that I ran last night had four peaks at each locus. This is not unusual when a suspect and victim's DNA are mixed together in a sample. If that happens, we want to eliminate the peaks from the victim's DNA. To do that, we run a standard of the victim's blood. We remove the victim's DNA from the graph and what is left has to be from the suspect." Teri paused to give Jim and Kathleen time to digest what she had said.

"How do you remove these peaks? Is it easy?" Kathleen was wide-eyed with the possible implications.

"We have a computer program where we can click on a peak and remove it. It is very easy for us to remove the peaks from a victim. It allows us to focus on the important peaks of a suspect. But we do not change the original data of the analysis. We can't change the original data. We can only work with the data in a separate program. That way, if there are any mistakes, we can ALWAYS go back to the original data," Teri said emphatically. "I looked at the original data that Aaron ran. Aaron's analysis only showed 26 peaks. Thirteen DNA segments or half were from Victoria's DNA profile, and 13 DNA segments or half were from Syrus' DNA profile. That is exactly what you would expect in the child of two parents. Aaron's original data does not match what I found. I found all 26 DNA segments for Victoria and all 26 DNA segments of Syrus. My graphs show TOO MANY DNA segments to be from a single source blood sample!"

With a heavy sigh, Jim put his hands on his head and leaned back in his chair. "Is there any way Aaron could alter the original data?" His neck was starting to get stiff. He rubbed it for a moment before he leaned forward to listen to Teri's answer.

Teri was on the edge of her chair now, giving the question some thought. "Aaron would have to reprogram the safety precautions when the original data was being collected. Prior to the test being run, Aaron would need the DNA Technical Administrator's password. If he had that, he could disarm the safety features in the program. But the Technical Administrator is at the FBI. The FBI is who set up the program. Aaron knowing an FBI password is virtually impossible."

"Could he guess the password?" Kathleen asked, searching for a possible solution.

"Aaron's not a computer hacker. He is a Forensic DNA analyst." Teri said, trying to defend Aaron but feeling that she was not doing a good job.

"OK," Jim said, trying to simplify the information being presented, "let's go over what we know." He started listing the facts. "Your analysis shows there is something wrong with this blood sample. Aaron's results do not match your results. Aaron could have screwed up his work in some way, but we cannot conceive of how Aaron could have changed the results. He would have needed access to a password kept at the FBI. We know your results are accurate. That is the one truth we do know. You said it looked like the blood samples of Victoria Young and Syrus Sandman were mixed together and placed in the exhibit marked as the fetus blood sample. Is there anyway we can confirm that this is not fetal DNA?"

"No," Teri replied. "DNA from a fetus would look the same as DNA from an adult. But…" she said, thinking, "the DNA is the same, but the hemoglobin is not. We could test the blood to see if it contained fetal hemoglobin or adult hemoglobin. That would tell us which type of sample it was."

"What do you mean by hemoglobin?" Jim asked as he rubbed his forehead. An hour of intensive training in forensics was not helping his growing headache.

"Hemoglobin is the molecule that carries oxygen to the tissues in the body by way of the blood," Kathleen interjected, recalling her physiology courses in college. "It's what makes blood red. The blood is bright red when oxygen is present and a purplish red when it needs oxygen. Adult hemoglobin is designed to exchange oxygen and carbon dioxide in the lungs where there is lots of air. Fetuses exchange oxygen in the placenta, which means its hemoglobin needs to have a greater affinity for oxygen to be effective."

"Exactly," Teri said, impressed that a detective would know such information. "Because the fetus gets its oxygen from its mother, the actual structure of the hemoglobin is different. The lab can run tests to determine if something has adult or fetal hemoglobin."

"Can you do those tests?" Jim asked hopefully.

"No," Teri said flatly. "That test would be done in our toxicology department. They have a blood gas instrument. It works on the basis of a light wave being passed through hemoglobin. I know that test checks for fetal hemoglobin."

"I don't want any more people in on this. I don't want to involve the toxicology section," Jim said firmly.

"I don't know how to run it," Teri said.

"Is there any chance you could learn?" Kathleen asked.

"It's not like a coffee pot. It takes months to learn to use equipment properly. It is not just pressing a few buttons. You have to understand and interpret the results," Teri said then added, "maybe I could try and get someone to run the sample for me without telling them exactly what it was."

"Perfect. We need those results by the end of the day. DO NOT tell Aaron anything. He may be on the take or have some motive for what he has done." Jim rose and made his way to the door, abruptly ending their discussion.

"Hey," Teri said, trying once again to defend Aaron. "We don't know who has done what. All we know that is some data has been changed. Aaron is a good guy. Let's not write him off completely. And, what about this tape?" Teri added, trying to retrieve the tape from the VCR, "there has to be something wrong with it."

Kathleen shrugged her shoulders, "Just add it to the list".

Jim opened the conference room door and looked up and down the hallway, to see if anyone was close enough to hear their conversation. The only person in the hallway was Jack Johnson, drinking from a water fountain at the end of the corridor.

"Stone's tonight?" Jim asked quietly. Teri nodded in agreement. Kathleen smiled approvingly.

CHAPTER SIX

WHEN KATHLEEN AND Jim arrived at the Stone Soup Café, Teri was already there. As they walked into the room, Teri was leaning back in the big leather chair with her eyes closed.

"Hi, Teri," Jim said sympathetically, noticing the tired look in Teri's eyes as she turned to look at him.

"We can't make this a late night, Jim. I have got to get some sleep," Teri said, sitting up and rubbing her eyes. "I do have some interesting news, though. The blood sample was not fetal blood. It contained adult hemoglobin."

Teri pulled out the laboratory case file of Victoria Young. "Knowing what we know now, I re-reviewed the original DNA analysis very carefully. The original results matched mine and were altered."

"How can you tell?" said Kathleen with great interest.

Teri pulled out a piece of paper from her briefcase and held it up. There were lines across the 11-inch length of the paper and small narrow peaks, which jutted up from the line.

"This is an enlarged electropherogram of a DNA profile," Teri explained. "The peaks represent the DNA pattern. The baseline is what the detector sees when no peaks are being detected. If you notice the baseline," she pointed to the line across the page, "it's bumpy. When you enlarge the baseline, it looks like a line someone might draw if he were in a car on a gravel road. When you have very sensitive detectors like this, it is normal. It's called baseline noise. It can be caused by a lot of things like fluctuation in the electrical current, vibrations to the instrument, any minor changes in the environment. But, when you eliminate a peak using a computer program, the computer does not mimic the baseline noise. It draws a straight baseline, as smooth as glass."

Teri pulled out another piece of paper. "The peaks are so narrow it's very hard to see, but, I enlarged this one."

Kathleen and Jim studied the second piece of paper. They could see a jumpy, unsteady line for three quarters of the page, then for about two inches, a very smooth line, and then it returned to the unsteady line.

"I checked all of the peaks," Teri said. "One set of Victoria's DNA results were removed and one set of Syrus' DNA results were removed, making it look like a perfect DNA sample of a child they had together."

Jim rubbed his head looking up at the ceiling. "That's pretty sophisticated stuff. Who do you think could do something like that?"

For several minutes, each sat silently, letting the awful implications sink in. Someone had intentionally doctored the results in the Young case to make it appear that the father of her child was a convicted felon. Everyone knew the results from the laboratory would be trusted.

Jim finally broke the silence. "OK, we need to organize the information we have."

He started to list what they knew. "One. The woman was probably killed by a rifle shot, possibly with a silencer. But the lab matches the bullet to a Glock of a recently deceased gang member with felony convictions. Two," he said holding up two fingers, now pacing as he spoke. "The fetal blood sample was replaced with a mixture of blood of Victoria Young and Syrus Sandman. THEN, the DNA results were altered to make it look like Victoria and Syrus were having a baby. Three, fetal tox results are negative but the mother had both cocaine and alcohol in her system. I think those results are pretty suspect. Four, we have a U.S. Representative who is willing to lie to the police about his knowledge of Young's pregnancy."

"I think I have to go to the laboratory director," said Teri, concerned. "He has to know about this. He has to be told that there are problems in his lab."

"NO!" Jim said adamantly. "We have ONE, TWO, THREE sections involved. We don't know who else could be involved. It could even be the lab director. Hell, he could be orchestrating the whole thing. No one else in that laboratory is to be told anything more. Is that clear? Until we figure this out, until we know who is involved, we are the only ones who know this information," then Jim added quietly, looking directly at Teri, "there is one more thing we need."

Teri started to shake her head. "Do you have any idea how tired I am? Or, how scared I was?"

"I know. And, you did great," Jim said encouragingly. He stood behind her and began to rub the top of her shoulders as she closed her eyes and leaned her head back in the leather chair. "No," she said in a low voice. "I am not going back to the lab at night again."

"We need to get the DNA profile from the fetal tissue that was submitted," Jim whispered. "It's the only way we'll know who the real father is. It's the only way we'll know who might have killed Victoria Young."

"I can't," she pleaded. "It's too much. It's too hard. I can't work on no sleep. I wouldn't even trust my own results," she said, still shaking her head back and forth slowly.

Kathleen knew Jim was going to talk Teri into running the samples. How long it would take was another issue. She watched Teri and Jim together. Jim stood with his hands on Teri's shoulder, leaning over her. They seemed so comfortable together. Kathleen remembered Jim's words when she had asked him if he knew Teri well. 'I don't know her well. But, I trust her.' It appeared to Kathleen that Jim knew Teri extremely well. Kathleen wondered how Jim would describe his relationship with her if Teri had been someone he did not know well. Kathleen watched as Teri laughed at something Jim had just said to her.

Kathleen decided to get some coffee from the kitchen. As she walked down the hallway, she felt a pleasant night breeze brush across her face. It felt wonderful. She turned toward the back door to the courtyard where she and Jim had had lunch. It seemed like years ago. As she opened the screen door, she saw the Washington Monument and the Capitol glowing white as spotlights flooded their marble. She could smell the spring flowers in the crisp April air. Her thoughts melted away. She felt almost intoxicated standing there in the doorway. Then, she noticed a flicker of light from an orange citronella candle. Mama was sitting at one of the tables, her back to the door as she viewed the city from her garden.

"Sorry," Kathleen said as she saw her, "I didn't mean to interrupt you."

"No, no, dear." Mama waved her hand, encouraging Kathleen to join her. "You're not interrupting anything; just an old woman enjoying a beautiful night. Come enjoy with me."

"It is beautiful." Kathleen crossed the courtyard and sat in a chair at the small table.

"My son Peter bought me this place many years ago." Mama sighed. "He was such a good boy, a good son." She sat for a moment, remembering him before she continued.

"He was in the Marines, you know. When he graduated high school that was all he wanted to do. I didn't want him to go into the Marines. He was all I had. Oh, I missed him so while he was gone."

Kathleen watched the flickering light of the orange candle bathe the old woman's face in light. It made the wrinkles around her eyes cast deep, dark shadows on her face. Mama spoke with a slight Italian accent that seemed to match the rhythmic songs of the insects making their spring debut. The heavy night air muted the flowers' fragrance. Kathleen leaned back in her chair and listened to the lilt of Mama's voice.

"Do you know he saved every penny he earned while he was in the Marines? Well, maybe a penny or two went to buy a beautiful girl a drink from time to time, but he saved most of it," she said with a laugh as she patted Kathleen on the hand. "After four years in the Marines, he decided he wanted to be a police officer instead. Such a wonderful thing, I thought, a police officer. On Mother's Day, he brought me here for dinner. We were celebrating him entering the police academy. I remember the day like it was yesterday. He was so pleased, he could hardly contain himself. 'Mama' he said, 'I cannot be taking care of you forever. It is time you took care of yourself. It is time you got a job.' It was true," Mama said. "My husband died when Peter was fifteen. The social security we got after his death was barely enough to get us by. But of course, I couldn't work. I had no college, not even all of high school. I never worked. I kept house. So Peter worked. After school, on weekends, Peter worked so hard. He kept us going."

Mama pulled a tissue from the sleeve of her blouse. Wiping her nose, she turned to Kathleen, hoping she would understand. "But, what could I do with no training, no schooling? Well, Peter knew what I could do," Mama said firmly. "He had already bought me this place before we went to dinner. When they brought my dessert, it was a dessert plate with only one thing on it -- a key to the front door. Peter could not have been more pleased with himself. He grinned from ear to ear.

"He knew this was the place where I could do what I do best. I make certain everyone has a good meal in front of them; good food, good people, my family. This neighborhood is my family. I keep busy; work hard. It gives me a lot of joy doing this work and I have lived a comfortable life. My son, he gave me a very comfortable life."

Kathleen tried to picture Pete Stone, the man who had done so much for his mother, the man whose mother loved him unconditionally, the man who had killed his partner's wife. Kathleen tried to picture Pete in the story she was hearing, how he looked when he was talking to his mother, how he had told her that she owned the café, how he looked in his police uniform. "What did he look like?" she asked, astonished she had asked aloud.

"Oh, he was a handsome boy," Mama said, pleased Kathleen asked. "But, you have to realize, I see him through a mother's eyes so it's hard for me to see him other than the most handsome man. I do have a picture though."

Mama reached into her pocket and pulled out a small billfold. She took out a picture of a man standing next to her and handed it to Kathleen. Peter had been tall with a crew cut and a mischievous grin that told Kathleen he was a lot of fun. His hair was brown with definite hints of red. He was dressed sharply with pressed, pleated pants and an expensive dress shirt that was tucked in, broad shoulders and a narrow waist and hips, muscular but he was not bulging with muscles.

The faded picture showed a neatly trimmed mustache on a man whose arm was around his mother.

"He was very handsome," Kathleen said as she slid the photo back to Mama.

"There you are!" Jim said in a loud voice that shattered the moment. "Come on, we're ready to go. Thanks for the room, Mama. The boys and I will stop by next weekend to pay for it."

"Oh, I would love that," Mama said as she rose from her chair. "I would love to see those boys."

Kathleen walked with Mama to the doorway. Mama squeezed Kathleen's hand tightly. "Thank you for letting an old woman talk."

As they walked to the car, Kathleen asked, "So, is Teri going to analyze the tissue tonight?"

"Well, let's just say we came to a compromise," Jim said as he got in the car.

Teri and Jim had decided how best to accomplish the analysis of the fetal tissue the night before. Now the first and foremost task for Kathleen and Jim was to retrieve the evidence from the crime lab. That involved requesting the evidence's return to the main police vault. Early the next morning Kathleen and Jim drove to the crime lab to request custody of the evidence.

"Hey, Jack," Jim said as he walked up to the evidence-receiving counter of the crime lab.

"Well, hi, Jim. Are you here for another consultation?" Jack asked.

"No," Jim replied quickly. "We're here to pick up the evidence on the Young case."

"The Young case?" Jack said with some surprise. "That's a lot of evidence. Usually, you guys call ahead on big cases like that. No one notified me that you wanted the evidence back. It's going to take some time to put it all together," Jack said, slightly annoyed. "Why not take a late breakfast or early lunch and come back? I can get it all inventoried and packaged up for you."

"We'll wait," Jim said dryly. "They want it back in the main evidence vault. We might as well get it done now so I get them off my back." Jim tried to sound casual, not wanting to seem too insistent but not wanting to wait either.

"This is very unusual. You know, it causes a lot of disruption in my schedule. I have to put aside everything I'm working on to get this done. I don't appreciate it," Jack said, clearly angered with the request. Walking toward the vault, Jack took one more look at Jim, but Jim just shrugged his shoulders as if he was just following orders.

"That was a little strange," Jim said as Jack disappeared.

"What do you mean?" Kathleen asked, looking around for something strange.

"I never saw anyone get mad that we are picking up evidence."

It took the better part of the next hour to inventory and box up the evidence as Jack would bring out several pieces. Jim would cross them off his list, and then Jack would return to the vault to get more evidence. It was a tedious procedure

"OK," Jack said, "that should be it. Let me count." He started counting aloud ending with, "Twenty-five, twenty-six, twenty-seven. Yes, that looks like it." He spun the evidence inventory sheet around toward Jim to review once more and sign. "Yes, twenty-seven evidence bags were submitted, twenty-seven evidence bags returned," Jack continued. "Now if you would just sign that you have taken custody, I have work to do."

Before Jack could turn away, Jim stepped in. "I think we are missing one." He searched each label, re-checking. "I don't see exhibit 26, the fetal tissue sample."

"Well, it should be there," Jack said, still distinctly annoyed.

"Here's why," Jim said, looking through the inventory list supplied by the laboratory's computer. "Exhibit 25 was separated into two exhibits, 25 and 25a. I am still one exhibit short."

Jack turned to the computer and began typing. Using the mouse to scroll down the screen, he looked for the problem. "OK, I see why," Jack said after a moment. "Number twenty-six was placed in the freezer vault by someone. That's pretty strange. I'll get it."

After a few minutes, Jack came back with a specimen jar containing a small amount of dark tissue. "Here you go, Exhibit twenty-six. Now is there anything else I can do for you?"

"No, that's fine. Thanks for your help." Jim grabbed the heavier of the two boxes where they had placed the bags, and motioned for Kathleen to grab the other. They walked out to the car and placed the boxes in the trunk. All except the specimen jar, which Jim grabbed from the box. "This one is not leaving my sight," Jim said as he opened the car door.

"Where are we going with that?" Kathleen asked, unclear of the plan.

"Where else? We are going back to the office to secure the evidence," Jim said, looking over at Kathleen. Kathleen rolled her eyes, becoming accustomed to not being in on the plan.

They first stopped by central evidence receiving, which held the main police vault. They dropped off the evidence at the main vault, all except the fetal tissue sample, then they went up to their office.

"Call the lab. Ask for Teri," Jim instructed Kathleen.

"Why would I call the lab and ask for Teri? We were just there. We could have talked to her then," Kathleen said angrily. She was still in the dark. "And, why don't *you* want to call her? You seem to enjoy talking to her so much."

"What does that mean?" Jim said, surprised at Kathleen's tone. "I don't want to call her because everyone in the lab knows my voice. They don't know your voice as well." Jim flipped through the officers' names who initially assisted them during the sweep of the Young crime scene.

Kathleen dialed the phone. "Hello," she said, changing the timbre of her voice, hoping she had taken the cue from Jim correctly. "May I speak to Teri Sedgwick?"

"May I tell her who is calling?" It was definitely Jack Johnson who had answered the phone.

Kathleen mouthed to Jim as she held the phone to her chest, "Jack wants to know who it is."

"Court," Jim mouthed back.

"I am calling on behalf of an attorney in federal court," Kathleen responded politely.

"One moment," the voice said.

After a moment, Kathleen heard Teri say, "Hello?"

Kathleen relaxed her voice and her posture. "Hi, Teri, it's me, Kathleen."

"Oh, yes, certainly. I will be there as soon as I can," Teri said curtly, then hung up the phone.

"She hung up on me!" Kathleen turned to Jim, who was shaking his head.

"You did great!" Jim continued to flip through the names of the officers who had done the initial interviews at the crime scene. "I'm looking for the name of the officer who interviewed Cohen. He really botched up his interview. He left out key details that were significant to the case. It's nice to bring in rookies to canvas the area for witnesses, but when they screw up, they need to be held accountable. This guy should get a slap on the hand."

"He did get us the witness," Kathleen said, half-heartedly trying to defend the new officer. "Regardless of what he wrote, we would have had to interview her anyway. Even if he had written 'Witness saw something,' we would have followed up. I wouldn't be too hard on him. They come in without much knowledge of the case. They are asked to go up and down the city blocks asking if anyone had seen something. Mrs. Cohen may have been the hundredth person he talked to." Kathleen suspected that her interviews on previous assignments may not have been as thorough as Jim would have wanted.

"I wouldn't have learned anything if someone didn't tell me every time I screwed up, and believe me, someone *always* pointed out my screw ups. It's what has made me the man I am today. You might say I am one big screw up honed to rapier sharpness." Jim held his head in mock royal superiority.

Forty minutes later, Teri walked through their office door with a backpack and a briefcase.

"What are *you* doing here?" Kathleen said with surprise.

"Not keeping her in the loop, Jim? That's a bad habit you have," Teri said with a wink toward Kathleen and nod to Jim.

"Well, Kathleen has issues. The woman can't lie. Even if she is just thinking about a lie, her eyes get big, and her face turns funny," Jim said, grinning at Kathleen.

"My face does not look funny," Kathleen said defensively. "AND, I can lie. I'm obviously not as crafty as you. I have not spent years honing my lying skills like you. I opted out of taking Lying 101 in graduate school,

but I can lie if necessary. When I told you I liked your tie this morning -
- a lie," she said with some satisfaction.

Jim looked down at his tie. "Hey, this is one of my favorites," he said
defensively. Then, more seriously he added, "This was too important,
Kathleen. I thought it was just easier if I didn't say anything to you. Then
I knew you would act like your normal charming self," he said, trying to
make a few brownie points. "And that is exactly what you did. Hey, are
you short on clerical staff at the crime lab?" Jim said to Teri in an
attempt to change the subject.

"No, I think everyone is there today. Why?" Teri replied.

"Your evidence tech, Jack Johnson, answered the phone," Jim said.

"Oh, yeah. He does that all the time," Teri explained. "He answers the
phone, does filing, archives files. He even preps cases for us sometimes.
The city gets their money's worth out of him. He is nonstop all the time.
It's great for us. Whenever someone needs help with something, Jack is
right there to step in." Teri paused. "There is something about him
though. He kind of bothers me. I can't really put my finger on it. I guess
I shouldn't talk about him that way. He's been nothing but helpful to me."

Jim's gaze snapped from the specimen container and fixed on Teri.
With an intensity Kathleen had never heard before, Jim said, "Always
listen to your instincts. Sometimes, they can save your life."

Teri broke the silence that followed. "Shall we get to work?" she
asked.

Jim led them to a little conference room attached to their office area.
This small room had windows along one side, allowing them to look
out into the desk area. There was an old wooden table in the middle of
the room that Teri moved against the far wall. They rolled out the chairs
except for the one Teri was going to use. Teri put her briefcase and
backpack on the table.

From Teri's backpack, she pulled a lab coat, a surgical mask, surgical
hat and surgical gloves. She also pulled out forceps, a scapula, small
disposable deep-welled plastic trays, distilled water in a plastic squirt
bottle and a similar bottle of bleach along with a box of laboratory
paper wipes. "I packed this last evening before I left work. I hope I
remembered everything," Teri said as she put on the lab coat.

From her briefcase, Teri pulled a firm white plastic board. "Once I start bleaching down things, you cannot talk and do not come near me. Also, could you turn off the ceiling fan?" she said as she snapped on her rubber gloves.

"Why can't we talk?" Kathleen said, fascinated with the whole performance.

"When a person speaks, even the moisture from his breath has enough DNA to contaminate a sample," Teri explained as she organized the items on the board.

"In layman's terms, she doesn't want us spitting on the evidence," Jim said, grinning at Kathleen.

"I liked her explanation better," Kathleen smiled back. "It was more eloquent."

"That's why we pay her the big bucks." Jim laughed.

Teri gestured for them to step back. She looked like a doctor just entering surgery. The only parts of her body that could be seen were her feet, a portion of her long dark hair and her piercing blue eyes. The rest of her body was covered in a powder blue lab coat, a mask, and latex.

First, she bleached the table on which she was working, then the plastic board. She bleached each tool that she had brought using the lab wipes. As she bleached them, she moved them from one side of the board to the other, to ensure that nothing was missed. Kathleen was surprised how long the whole process took. Twenty minutes, thirty minutes, forty minutes went by.

Finally, Teri reached for the tissue sample. She removed it from its specimen cup and placed it on the white plastic board. She examined it carefully, making certain it was one solid piece of tissue. Pulling out a center section that seemed to be in the best condition, she cut off a small portion with the scapula. She chopped the sample thoroughly. Distilled water made a bloody paste of the sample. She then opened a small package of sterile swabs. The swabs had a long wooden shaft with cotton at one end. Carefully, she dampened two cotton swabs with distilled water and rolled each of them in the slurry she had made. The tips of the swabs became a dark, rusty red.

When she was done, she reached for several of the sterile test tubes she had brought. Popping the top off the red rubber stopper of one test tube, she slid the swab to the bottom of the tube and resealed it with the stopper. She did the same with the second swab, placing it in a second red-stoppered tube.

Two hours came and went. Occasionally, Kathleen would look over at Jim. If Kathleen had known how long this was going to take, she would have pulled in another chair. She could not believe how tedious the lab work was. She watched as Teri's focus never wavered. Teri was meticulous in every detail of her work.

After both tubes were sealed and she had checked the seal on the specimen container, Teri finally asked, "What case name do you want on this?"

Jim and Kathleen hesitated for a moment, looking at each other, waiting for the other to be the first to talk.

Teri pulled off mask and hat and shook her hair free. "It's OK, guys. Everything is sealed up. We're finished."

"Let's go with Freeman," Jim said as he breathed a sigh of relief.

"Freeman?" Kathleen was surprised. "You mean as in Captain Freeman?"

"What's his first name?" Teri asked.

"Yes," Jim said to Kathleen. Then he turned to Teri and answered, "Morgan."

"Morgan?" Kathleen said even more surprised. "The Captain's name is Morgan Freeman? Morgan Freeman, like the actor?"

"Yes." Jim was once again surprised by some of the information Kathleen didn't know. "Did you think his first name was captain? Don't ever call him that, though," Jim warned.

"I guess I didn't think about it. I can certainly relate to the problem," Kathleen said as she watched Teri clean up the table. "So, you don't think I could call Captain Freeman by his first name?"

"I would guess he would be pretty furious if someone called him 'Captain Morgan' -- like the rum," Teri said jokingly. "He doesn't have a well-developed sense of humor like us."

Kathleen pictured the encounter in her mind, then, nodded in agreement. "I just have one last question," Kathleen said, raising her voice, "What are we doing?"

"We are submitting a case to the crime laboratory," Jim said proudly.

"We are submitting two swabs of suspected blood to the lab. It's blood that Captain Freeman found on a brick, which was thrown at him while he was walking to work. Captain Freeman is furious," Jim said, inventing the story as he went. "He wants to know if a felon threw the brick. If a felon did, he wants to use the evidence to bring the jerk in for questioning."

Holding up the tubes which Teri had handed to him, he continued, "It's a rush case. The brick throwing could easily elevate into far worse crimes against the captain. Tomorrow morning Teri is going to conveniently be within ear shot and offer to run the rush case for us."

Teri nodded in agreement.

"Teri is going to get a DNA profile of the person who threw the brick," Jim said with a smile.

"I see. It's a pretty good plan," Kathleen contemplated. "So, we are submitting a sample of the fetus tissue under the captain's name to get the actual DNA profile of the fetus."

"By George, I think she's got it," Jim said with a pitiful British accent.

"And the best part is," Teri added happily, "I can analyze the case during work hours. No more late nights hiding under my desk. No more life-flashing-before-my-eyes moments."

"It's a good plan," Kathleen nodded finally feeling like a one of the three musketeers.

"It's a compromise," added Jim as he grinned toward Teri then looked at his watch. "Hey, I gotta get out of here a little early. I didn't think this was going to take as long as it did. Dave has a ball game tonight. Anyone want to come?" he said casually as he sealed the evidence bag and locked it in his temporary storage drawer. "This doesn't have to be refrigerated, does it?" he said, looking at Teri.

"No, the sample should dry at room temperature and I'm sorry, you're going to have to count me out on the game," Teri said, feigning a frown. "I wish I could go but I have some friends coming over tonight."

"What the heck," Kathleen jumped in, pleased such an offer had been extended. "If you let me swing by my apartment to pick up some things, I'd love to go. I think it would be fun."

Sitting on the cold, outdoor bleachers brought back memories for

Kathleen. She looked up to see the same grey sky of her childhood; a sky that demanded ballpark lights to brighten the daylight hours of a dreary spring day. Kathleen could have cut out the picture and placed it in her memory book and no one would have uncovered the deception. She smiled as she watched the pack of high school boys prance on to the field with both the enthusiasm and awkwardness of teenagers. A boy almost six feet tall grabbed a bat and sized up the pitcher. Kathleen recognized the boyish grin and gnarly hair as he gave a few practice swings. For the last few months, she had stared across her desk at a much older version of that same face. The boy was much less wiry than his father with a broad chest and muscular legs with a roundish face of a fifteen year old.

"Hi, Dad." David waved.

"Hit one out of the park," Jim yelled back.

As David walked up to the batter's box, he stretched his shoulders and his back, trying to stare down the pitcher before raising his bat. The first pitch was low and away but David couldn't help but chase it, giving him his first strike. The second throw got the inner corner; the umpire yelled, "Strike two!"

Clapping his hands, Jim yelled encouragement. "Shake it off, Dave."

With the third pitch came a hard, distinctive crack, letting the crowd know he had made contact with the ball. David took off running as he watched the left fielder run further and further back. David's hopes lifted as the thought of a home run sent him looking back at the crowd with a big grin, but a moment before the ball passed over the fence, a glove plucked it from the sky.

"You were robbed!" Jim yelled, as he watched his son run off the field. Turning to Kathleen, he said, "I'm getting a soda. Do you want any thing?"

"Yeah, something diet."

As she watched Jim walk down the bleachers, she suddenly became aware of the woman sitting next to her, who was inching her way closer.

"It's nice to see Jim dating. He's a good catch," the elderly woman said softly, leaning in toward Kathleen. "After his wife died in that tragic car accident, I didn't think he would ever find anyone else."

The woman looked over to make certain Jim was not in hearing distance before she continued. "Of course, he never talked about the accident, but I could tell it was hard for him when his wife passed on," the woman whispered with a nod of assuredness.

"We're not on a date," Kathleen whispered back.

"Of course, you're on a date."

"I work with Jim. We're not on a date," Kathleen politely persisted, trying not to sound like she was correcting the woman.

"Honey, you're sitting here watching the two worst teams in the league fight it out for last place. The only reason a woman would come to one of these games would be on a date," the lady insisted.

"You're here," Kathleen pointed out.

"Well, of course," she said indignantly. "My grandson's playing."

Kathleen could see Jim starting back up the bleachers and decided not to further continue the pointless conversation. By the time Jim handed her a soda, Kathleen had managed to move several inches away from the woman and put the conversation to rest.

"Your date seems very nice," came a voice.

Jim leaned over to see who was talking on the other side of Kathleen, briefly noticing Kathleen cringe at the woman's statement.

"Ah, Meredith, nice to see you," he said before looking over at Kathleen, a bit confused. "You told her we were on a date?"

"Yes," the woman added, feeling on obligation to help Jim out. "She told me she was having a wonderful time on her date with you."

"Uuggh!" was all Kathleen could say before the grey sky opened and a drenching rain began to fall. Within seconds, the few people left in the stands fled to their cars and the players left the field, relieved to end the game.

Kathleen pulled her jacket over her head, looking at the sky to see if the clouds hinted at how long the downpour might continue. Her attention was drawn back down as she heard a hand-slap Jim on his back.

"Hi, Dad," said Rob. "Can I have twenty bucks?"

"Twenty bucks? For what?" Jim raised his hand to get some protection from the rain as he looked up at his son.

"The team's going out for burgers. You know, to celebrate," Rob grinned. "The game was called before they lost. It's kind of like they won."

"Twenty bucks for a burger?" Jim questioned as he looked through his wallet.

"I'll buy Dave a burger, too."

Jim relinquished two ten dollar bills and watched his son scramble down the bleachers.

"Let me take you home," Jim said, shaking off some of the water that had collected on his coat as the rain began to slow.

After several minutes of what Jim believed was a senseless argument about her taking the subway, he pushed Kathleen into his car and drove back into the city center.

"Why don't I make us some dinner?" Kathleen offered as he pulled up to her apartment building. "I could throw something light together."

"Too much of a bother, I'll just pick up something on the way home."

"Now who's being stubborn?" Kathleen said, contented with her jab. "I'm already going to cook dinner for myself. I'll just throw in another cup of whatever; It's not going to be anything special but it didn't sound like you had a better offer. You know, I'm actually a pretty fair cook."

Jim relented and followed Kathleen up to the top of the three-story walkup. Slightly out of breath, he stood at the doorway, taking in her apartment. Kathleen's living room had bookshelves that covered three walls. The bookshelves were put to good use, volumes of books were stacked floor to ceiling; stuffed into every crack and crevice. Where they could fit standing, they stood. Where they could fit sideways, they were slid in sideways. The room was no bigger than Jim's den but it didn't need to be big to hold Kathleen's belongings. There were only two pieces of furniture in the room, a well-worn brown leather sofa and a telephone table where Kathleen threw her keys. The starkness of the room made Jim wonder how anyone could spend much time in the apartment but the well-worn binders of the books led Jim to believe Kathleen did.

"This is your apartment?" Jim asked.

"No," Kathleen said sarcastically. "This is the show model where I bring people to impress them. My apartment is much smaller."

"It's nice," Jim lied.

"It's not nice," Kathleen said as she drew back a curtain that covered one side of the room exposing a small kitchen and kitchen table. "But, it's all I need right now. Make yourself comfortable. Is crab salad OK?"

"Yeah, I love crab," Jim said as he pulled one of the books from the cramped shelf. "You've got a lot of books."

"Yeah, it's a compulsion. There doesn't seem to be a book I can pass without buying," Kathleen admitted as she rattled through some pots and pans.

Jim walked over to the two photos sitting on the telephone table. One was of Kathleen grinning from ear to ear as she stood next to a bearded man who was holding a three-foot long blue fish.

"Who's the guy in the picture?" Jim asked.

"Oh, that's my ex-fiancé."

The statement brought a surprised look from Jim but Kathleen did not notice as she pulled out a cutting board and chopped some mint leaves.

"I didn't know you were engaged," Jim admitted, with a raised brow, still looking toward Kathleen. "What happened?"

"Ah, he wouldn't relocate," she answered nonchalantly, searching through her refrigerator for some lettuce.

"And the other picture?" Jim asked.

"Oh, that's of my Mom. That was taken the night before my nineteenth birthday. She had my birthday party that night so I could get an early start the next morning," Kathleen explained. "It was my first chance to leave Burke, South Dakota. That's where I grew up, and nothing was going to slow me down. Are you OK with toasted cheese on French bread?"

"Anything's fine, Kathleen," Jim assured her as he put the picture down.

"Yeah, I thought a friend had gotten me a job in New York City but when I got there, it had all fallen through," Kathleen explained. "I slept on her sofa for a few months, trying to find something but with the only a high school diploma and no experience, the only thing I could get was waiting tables. Do you like Dijon salad dressing? Try it," she added before getting an answer from Jim. "I make it from scratch. I think you'll love it."

"But now you're working on your Ph.D.," Jim said, honestly

impressed she was so close to her degree with such a rocky start.

"Yeah, my Mom died a few months after that picture was taken. I used the insurance money to go to college. University of Florida."

"Not South Dakota?"

"God, no! Well, actually, I started at the University of Florida but I didn't like the weather so much so I finished my degree in psychology at the University of Rhode Island in New Haven. But, you know, psychology, it's not so marketable. So I got a job as an assistant buyer at a clothing store, then I tried my hand at designing clothes, but I was terrible." Kathleen laughed.

"In New Haven?" Jim asked, pulling another book from the shelf.

"No, by that time I was in Boston."

Kathleen pulled out a bowl and added some Dijon mustard to some lemon juice and then slowly began to drizzle in olive oil. Jim walked over to look at what she was doing. It seemed a bit complicated, so he returned to his inspection of the hundreds of books.

"All your books are non-fiction," Jim observed. "Biographies, history, calculus, no novels, no mysteries?"

"What's the point of reading fiction?" Kathleen asked, surprised at his question.

With a shrug, Jim flopped down on the couch. "So you went to graduate school in Boston?"

"No, I found out about a program in Criminal Justice in Pittsburgh so I went there. Well, actually I went for a couple years but didn't get my degree. One day, I just had an urge to head down to Mardi Gras in New Orleans. I loved it and just couldn't bring myself to leave so I landed a job shucking oysters. That lasted over a year."

"Drawn in by the glamour," Jim joked.

"Something like that," Kathleen chuckled before announcing proudly, "Dinner is served."

Jim sat down at the small kitchen table. Each plate had a mound of crabmeat, a small green salad and a couple of slices of French bread covered with broiled, bubbling browned cheese.

"This looks great," Jim said, trying not to show his hesitation as he forked through the crab. "What's the green stuff in the crab?"

"I chopped up a little mint and added some lime zest. Do you want something to drink?" Kathleen asked, standing at the open refrigerator. "I have iced tea, and… Well, ah, it looks like I only have iced tea."

"Iced tea is good," Jim nodded before continuing with his questions. "So you finished up your degree in New Orleans?" Jim said, trying to taste the food while Kathleen was not looking. To his surprise, the bright citrus of the lime was balanced by the fresh mint and mingled into a taste that matched the fresh spring day.

"Hey, this is really good. Very refreshing."

"You sound so surprised. So I guess you thought I was lying when I said I was good cook?"

"Ah, so, ah," Jim said, struggling to change the subject. "So what did you do for a year in New Orleans, aside from shucking oysters?"

"Well, I got engaged to Joe, the man in the photo," she smiled. "He was an oyster fisherman. We had a lot of fun together. He was a great guy, but I felt a little guilty about not completing my degree so I went back to school. I finished my degree in Criminal Justice in Seattle," Kathleen said as she poured the tea.

"And, your fiancé didn't want to go to Seattle?" Jim pondered.

"That's my story and I'm sticking to it."

"Somehow, I think there's more to it, but I not certain I want to go there." Jim laughed. "So after you got your degree, you moved to DC?"

"Not exactly, at least not right away," Kathleen confessed. "I started a job in Mesa, Arizona but a few months after I started I found out about this new Ph.D. program in Forensic Investigation here in DC and I knew it was for me. Ten journal publications and almost a Ph.D. later, I got handed to you as a bright-eyed, bushy-tailed police detective."

"I guess that explains a few things," Jim said, crunching on the last piece of bread. "But, your family must think you're very successful."

Kathleen laughed at the thought. "They only count success in the number of years you've been married and the number of kids you have."

Jim brought his plate to the sink and turned back to look around the room. "You know, now that you're a detective, you should look into getting a bigger place. You aren't going to impress anybody with this one."

"Just throwing out compliments right and left, aren't you," Kathleen teased.

"I've got to get back home," Jim said as he reached for his jacket draped over the back of the sofa, still damp from the rain. "Thanks, for the date."

"Hey, I'm not your type," Kathleen shouted, as he opened the door.

"I know," he winked. "See you tomorrow."

The next morning, Jim and Kathleen met at the office. Kathleen couldn't help but grin when she saw Jim. He was her partner and for the first time she finally felt like he was her partner. Jim was unaware of Kathleen's sudden change in the assessment of their relationship as he focused on getting the new evidence to the crime lab, insisting they immediately drive there first thing. About a block before they arrived, Jim called Teri.

"We're about a block away," Jim alerted her.

"OK, I will head up to evidence counter."

As Jim entered the crime lab, he saw Jack standing at the evidence counter, taking evidence from another officer. Teri stood behind Jack with her back slightly turned, reading a case file.

"This might work out after all," Jim whispered to Kathleen. "Teri can assist Jack. She can sign in the case, helping Jack out while he's involved with evidence from another case."

As Jim and Kathleen moved to the counter, Jim motioned to get Teri's attention.

Jack took a side step over to stand in front of Jim. "What can I do for you?"

"I have a DNA case," Jim said.

Teri looked up from her case file. "Oh, I can sign it in if you're busy, Jack. You're always helping me out. I might as well pay back the favor," Teri said, stepping up to the evidence counter.

"That's OK," Jack said as he waved Teri back. "It's my job. I can handle it. What do you have?"

Jim gave Jack the whole story about the brick being thrown at Captain Freeman and stressed how much of a rush case this was because there were concerns for the his safety.

Teri stepped forward to the counter again. Picking up the tubes, she said, "This evidence was *very* nicely collected. I can do a quick wash of the swabs and put the samples on with the analysis I was about to start. Jack, if you could sign in the case within the next half an hour, I could probably have the result to them by late tomorrow."

"Will that do, Jim?" Jack asked.

"That will be perfect."

"We aim to please," They both signed the paperwork, turning over the custody of the swabs to the crime lab.

"I am just going to use the restroom before we leave," Jim said as he patted Kathleen on the shoulder. "I guess I shouldn't have drunk so much coffee."

Kathleen stood in front of the evidence counter as Jim turned the corner toward the men's restroom. She watched quietly as Jack logged the tubes into the lab's computerized evidence tracking system. Jack labeled each of the tubes, assigned them a case number, and placed a unique exhibit number on each tube. Then, Jack looked at Kathleen. "Will you be submitting the brick?" Jack asked.

"No," Kathleen answered firmly.

"You probably should. There are a number of things we could do with it. We can check it for prints. Fingerprints can show up on bricks, especially bloody prints. They show up very nicely. We can also identify the manufacturer of the brick. We may even be able to tell where the brick was sold,"

Kathleen stood there for a moment. She took a deep breath and looked down the hallway for Jim.

"Uh, well," Kathleen started slowly trying to drag out her response. "That's not…. You see, well, the brick was destroyed."

"The brick was destroyed?"

"Uh, yes. The brick was destroyed. There is no longer a brick," Kathleen stammered. With a slow swallow, she knew she would have to explain further.

"How was the brick destroyed?" Jack said with curiosity.

"Well," Kathleen braced her arms on the counter and started rocking ever so slightly back and forth on her heals. She paused for a moment to listen for Jim's footsteps coming down the hallway. She heard nothing. "Actually, I destroyed it. You see, we were going to bring the brick here, you know, to have all that stuff done to the brick. So, we were bringing it here," Kathleen repeated herself trying to stall for time to think of what could have happened to the brick.

"Then, Jim remembered the tubes with the swabs which he had forgotten on his desk. He put the evidence bag containing the brick down on the ground and went back to the office. I thought I would be nice and drive to the front door to pick him up. I didn't realize the bag containing the brick was right in front of the driver side tire," Kathleen said trying to suppress any facial expressions that might betray her lie.

"You drove over the brick?" Jack asked in disbelief.

"Well, uh, yes. Or, no. I just drove on top of the brick. Then, when the wheel was on top of the brick, I got out of the car to see what I had driven onto. When I got out, I saw the wheel there on top of the evidence bag. That's when it just, well, um, it just exploded. Completely destroyed," Kathleen said, relieved her story had finally come to an end.

Just as Kathleen finished, Jim walked around the corner. Both Jack and Kathleen looked toward Jim as if they each wanted to say something to him. Looking back and forth between Kathleen and Jack, Jim knew something was wrong.

"I told Jack how I destroyed the brick," Kathleen blurted out to Jim.

A thin smile grew on Jim's face as he imagined the story she must have told. He could imagine the awkward, nervous way she must have told it, probably rocking on her heels, taking deep gulps of air. Jim also knew unless Jack was an excellent study of character, he probably would have mistaken Kathleen's nervousness for embarrassment, understandable if a detective had destroyed a valuable of a piece of evidence on a potentially important case.

"Is that right?" Jim said biting his lip trying not smile. "Well, it's probably all over the department by now anyway. It's better Jack heard the truth from you, now, rather than through the grapevine in a couple weeks. You know how those stories grow. After a while, there's not an ounce of truth in them. Isn't that right, Teri?" Jim yelled over the counter at Teri who was still looking at her case file.

"Don't I know it," Teri smiled back. "Kathleen won't be living this one down for quite a long time."

"Let's go, my protégé," Jim said as he grabbed Kathleen by the arm. "Thanks for all your help, guys."

As they eased out into traffic, Jim could hardly control his curiosity. "So you destroyed the brick? I can't wait to hear how you did that. Don't keep me in suspense. How could one possibly destroy a brick? Of course, we all know a piece of evidence like a brick can so easily be destroyed so I'm certain whatever story you came up with was perfect."

Kathleen turned her head to the window defiantly. "You'll just have to hear about it through the grapevine, like everyone else," she answered.

CHAPTER **SEVEN**

THE NEXT DAY, Kathleen and Jim were in their office once again completing the endless paperwork that was a department staple. Jim summarized his list of people who had been interviewed and cross-referenced it to the list of officers who had done the initial interviews at the crime scene. Kathleen made a few notes on the dates and times they spoke with Dr. Hayes and Teri Sedgwick. Both were intently writing at their desk when their concentration was interrupted with the word, "Sir."

Kathleen and Jim looked up in union to see a young man in a perfectly cleaned and pressed patrol uniform; his patrol hat under one arm. As he stood at the side of their desks, Kathleen noticed that the patrol officer stood straight and strong as they had been taught at the Academy. His shoulders filled out his shirt perfectly, but he was too skinny to fill the rest of his uniform. His short black hair was trimmed just above his collar and around his ears.

"Antonio Sanchez, reporting as ordered, sir," he said in a way only a young rookie would.

Kathleen remembered all the "Yes, sirs" and "No, sirs" she had to recite at the police training academy. The cadence marches, the standing at attention, her hair tightly pinned up to keep it off her uniform collar. They were experiences Kathleen preferred to forget. The day of their graduation was the last day she had ever said "Sir, Yes, sir" or wore her hair in a tight bun.

Kathleen glanced over at Jim and wondered if he had ever looked so young or so green as Sanchez did right now.

Jim stood and leaned on the corner of his desk. "Officer Sanchez, thank you for coming so promptly. Do you know why I have asked you here?"

"Sir, No, sir," responded Officer Sanchez, still at attention.

"I wanted to ask you about your assignment at the Young crime scene. Do you recall exactly what it was?" Jim said as he casually walked around to the back of his chair.

"Well, sir, I was asked to conduct interviews to determine if there were any possible witnesses to the crime. I conducted 54 interviews, sir. I was assigned to check a three-block area which contained four apartment buildings and twelve business establishments. I asked individuals entering and leaving both the establishments and the apartment buildings if they had seen anything suspicious in the early morning when it was suspected the murder took place." Sanchez's response was articulate and exact.

It was policy at the Academy to constantly train recruits to practice how they presented information. Juries in court often watched the witness more than heard their words. Inarticulate officers, stumbling through their statements, often were perceived as not believable to a scrutinizing jury. Sanchez had learned his lessons well.

He continued, "If a witness gave an affirmative response, I indicated it in my notes. Those notes were transcribed into my report. With each individual, I left instructions if they remembered any additional information they were to call the department. I also noted each individual's apartment number, place of employment, and address if they did not have a local address. In the apartments in my assigned area, I made certain someone in each apartment was contacted."

"Did you obtain any significant information from any of the individuals you interviewed?" Jim said, stretching his shoulders as he braced his arms on the chair.

"No, sir, nothing that I recall," Sanchez replied, now wondering where this questioning was going.

"What is a muzzle flash, Officer Sanchez?"

"Sir?"

"A muzzle flash. You do know what a muzzle flash is, don't you?" Jim stared directly at the young man. The act was one that questioned Sanchez's knowledge as a good officer, which Sanchez did not like.

"Sir, yes, sir. A muzzle flash is the bright flash that results at the end of the muzzle of the firearm that has been fired. The flash results from propellant particles emerging from the barrel of the firearm behind the projectile being discharged. The propellant particulates ignite when mixed with oxygen in the air, sir," Sanchez repeated in a loud monotone voice as if he were reciting a manual he had memorized.

Jim nodded with satisfaction. "Now, describe a muzzle flash the way a 77 year old woman would, one who has never owned a firearm."

"Sir, I do not believe I would know how a 77 year old woman would describe a muzzle flash," Sanchez responded, obviously confused.

"Oh, I think you do," Jim said correcting him. "I think you know exactly how a 77 year old woman would describe a muzzle flash. Why don't you just stand there and see if it doesn't come to you."

Sanchez stood at the side of their desks staring off into the distance. It was painful for Kathleen to watch him thinking through the question. She could see his mind reviewing each interview he had done that day. Kathleen saw the moment of recognition as it came to him. His straight broad shoulders drooped, and his gaze fell to the floor. With a deep sigh, Sanchez raised his shoulders back.

"Sir," Sanchez said, pulling himself back to attention. "I believe a 77 year old woman might call a muzzle flash a flash of fire."

Jim walked over to Sanchez and patted him on the back. "Well done, Sanchez," he said warmly.

"Sir, will I be reprimanded for not bringing this witness to your attention?" Sanchez asked with noticeable concern on his young face.

"Will a reprimand teach you anything more?" Jim asked as he sat back in his chair.

"No, sir."

"Then, I really don't want to waste my time doing the paperwork for it," Jim said, glancing at the mounds of incomplete paperwork.

Sanchez remained at attention waiting for instructions. None came. Jim sat pretending to be absorbed in his paperwork. Finally, Sanchez said, "Thank you, sir," and walked out of the office.

"So now, I guess, I need to call you Grand Master -- Teacher to All," Kathleen said, rolling her eyes.

"I didn't want to go up the chain of command and make a big deal about him missing a key witness. But I also didn't want to let it slide. Sanchez is going to be a good cop. He is a good cop. Now, he's going to be a better cop. I'm not asking for a pat on the back," Jim said dryly.

Kathleen studied Jim as he explained his logic. His shoulders were broad like Sanchez's but Jim could fill out the entire uniform. Jim kicked up his feet on the desk and leaned back in his chair reading a piece of paper. The cuffs of his black cotton pants had picked up a cobweb from somewhere. Kathleen knew Jim would immediately swipe it away if he saw it, but it gave her some pleasure not to tell him about it. She let it hang from his cuff.

Why Jim would do this for a rookie he had never met and not do it for her? He never let her figure out the answers. He always just told her the solution. Kathleen thought about all the mistakes she had made in cases they had worked together. Jim was always there to take care of the situation. Someday, she thought, he won't be there and then everyone will know that having her on a case was about as helpful as carrying a set of encyclopedias in the trunk. She began to worry about her first big case if and when Jim retired. She feared that day. Kathleen was lost in her thoughts when she heard Jim's voice.

"Don't worry, you'll find your way," he said with a warmth and depth that surprised her.

"What, now you're a mind reader, too?" Kathleen said sarcastically, trying to cover up the gratitude she felt for his statement. Kathleen regretted the words the moment they passed her lips.

Before Kathleen could apologize for her quick sarcasm or explain how she felt, Teri walked through the door.

"Well, I have your answers," Teri said, holding up a manila folder.

"Was there a DNA hit?" Kathleen asked, excited at the prospect of

Teri's news.

"No. The DNA sample was not in CODIS. But we have the profile. It won't mean much until we have a suspect," Teri said.

Kathleen noticed Teri looked a million times better than the last time she saw her. Her hair was once again the shimmering brown with red highlights; her walk had regained the bounce and presence that Kathleen had come to admire.

"What do we do next?" Kathleen asked.

Teri reached for the crime laboratory case file. "I say we shake this case up and see what comes out," Teri said with a confidence that Kathleen envied.

"Captain Freeman?" Jim said, raising his eyebrows.

"That works for me," Teri replied. "I guess I better try to make going into the lab in the dead of night to analyze someone else's evidence sound as good as possible."

"It doesn't sound *so* bad," Kathleen said. "We can work on it in the car."

"Let's go. The faster we hand off this case to someone else, the better," Jim said as he rubbed his forehead trying to get rid of a slowly growing headache.

At District Headquarters, they learned that Captain Freeman was in a meeting with Catherine O'Connell. This was not good news. Catherine O'Connell was the Deputy Director for the department. As her name implied, her Irish red hair was a warning beacon for the fires that burned below. No one would dare call her hot-headed, at least not to her face; but everyone in the department had felt the heat of her fury at one time or another.

"Would you like me to tell them you are here?" asked the officer at the reception desk.

Kathleen looked at Jim. Jim looked at Teri. Teri looked at Kathleen. Then, in one unified voice, they all said, "NO."

The three sat on the benches in the front hallway waiting area. They knew they could probably find more comfortable chairs in the back offices, but they also knew there was a possible cost for those comfortable chairs. Typically, there were only two reasons why

Catherine O'Connell might be visiting the District HQ. The first reason, and by far the more pleasant of the two, was there was a rush project that needed to be done. A select few would be chosen to drop everything they were doing to work on it. This at first might not seem like a bad thing, however, those who knew the horrors of being sucked into the vortex of a rush project knew that it was something to be avoided.

The second reason was invariably that someone very high up, and in Washington, DC that very high up might be as high up as one could go, had called the Deputy Director to complain about a police officer. Having weighed those costs with the gravity of their case and the weariness of their bodies, they opted to sit outside on the wooden benches, waiting for the meeting's end.

The minutes ticked by. Forty-five minutes turned into an hour. Each was absorbed in their own world, reviewing their role in the case and how they were going to present it to the captain. No one felt the need to talk.

The ringing of the phone at the front desk interrupted the silence

"Hello," answered the desk officer.

Then Kathleen and Jim heard words they dreaded. "Detectives Jarred and Jackson? Yes, sir, I can track them down for you, Captain. In fact, I think I can do that fairly quickly, sir. They are sitting ten feet in front of me."

The officer hung up the phone and motioned to them. "Hey, Jarred, Jackson. Captain Freeman wants to see you in his office. ASAP."

"Great," Jim said with as much sarcasm as a one-word sentence could manage. Stiffly standing up from the bench, he added, "Teri, you might as well come back. You can sit outside Freeman's office. At least those chairs are padded."

The three walked to the entrance hallway where they waited for the front desk officer to release the security lock on the door. As they stepped through the doorway, they stepped into the main Office of Administration. Unlike Operations, which was comprised of sworn officers, civilians almost exclusively manned Administration. This was where all the dreaded paperwork was generated, requested or required. Fiscal, timekeeping, payroll, quartermaster and archived case files were all processed here. Also in the building were offices for the District Commanders who ran the various zones in the Police Department.

As they walked down the passageway of cubicles, they could hear typing on keyboards and the answering of phones. Several officers milled around the office area and none looked happy. Some officers were from Internal Affairs, which occupied the second floor. Some were officers working on special assignments. Some were officers called over by their District Commander for a variety of reasons, none of which were considered good.

They walked to the end of the corridor where Captain Freeman's office was. A row of large windows faced the main room, framing the captain and the deputy director who were involved in an intense conversation.

"I'll wait here," Teri said, quickly picking up on the expression on the captain's face.

"Chicken," Jim said, as he walked to the door of Captain Freeman's office.

"Here they are now," Captain Freeman said, motioning Kathleen and Jim into his office. "This is Detective Jim Jarred and Detective Kathleen Jackson."

"Yes, Deputy Director, I believe we have met several times before," Jim said, stepping forward to shake her hand.

"Yes, yes, I am sure we have," she said, shaking his hand without looking at him. O'Connell's gaze was toward Kathleen, which made Kathleen extremely uncomfortable.

"Deputy Director, I am Detective Jackson. It is nice to meet you." Kathleen reached to shake O'Connell's hand. Kathleen felt the Deputy Director's hard, firm grip, a handshake that unmistakably said the Deputy Director was all business.

"Yes, Detective Jackson. I don't believe we have met, but I certainly know about you. Captain Freeman fought very hard to get you hired. He felt you would be an asset. 'A shining star', I think he said. Normally, I like to see officers earn their badges, like I did," she said as one eyebrow rose to show her disapproval. "Especially for women; it's best they prove themselves in the field before they become detectives, don't you agree?"

Kathleen gave careful thought to what she should say before she answered. "I am proving myself in the field, I hope."

"That's not what Congressman Thatcher has led me to believe," Deputy Director O'Connell replied. "Congressman Thatcher believes you are harassing him. Congressman Thatcher has indicated that he has cooperated with you to the fullest degree of his capabilities and yet you keep coming back to his office with undignified and insulting innuendos. Is that true?"

"No, Ma'am," Jim said, stepping into the conversation. "We did question Representative Thatcher regarding the homicide of one of his aides, but we did not harass or insult the congressman."

"Is your questioning of the congressman completed?" O'Connell asked.

"Yes, at this time we have no further questions for Representative Thatcher," Jim answered.

"Then, you have no further reason to contact him or visit his office. If you do feel the need to contact the congressman, please clear it with me first, along with the questions which you intend on asking him."

"Yes Ma'am," Jim responded obediently.

Without further comment, Deputy Director O'Connell collected her things and left.

"I guess the DD got a call from Thatcher. We must have hit a nerve with him," Kathleen remarked thoughtfully.

"Deputy Director O'Connell eats Congressmen for breakfast. She has no need to follow the whims of an Alabama official," Jim said sarcastically. "Whoever rattled O'Connell's chain was higher up than Thatcher."

Captain Freeman ignored Jim's comment. "What are you two doing here, anyway?"

"Captain, however bad your day has been, it's about to get a lot worse." Jim waved his hand at the window, signaling Teri to come into the office.

Together they presented to Captain Freeman all the information they had collected. It took the better part of two hours. They were meticulous and convincing. After the captain had a thorough understanding of the issues, he put his head in his hands and rubbed his forehead.

Then, he walked over to his phone, hit the intercom button and said, "Jenkins, I want Laboratory Director Michael Marino on the phone, please."

"Yes, sir." A minute later, the captain's phone rang.

"O.K. Thanks, put him through," Captain Freeman waited patiently. "Hello, Mike, this is Morgan Freeman. Mike, we have a little problem over here at the District Headquarters. Would it be possible for you to stop by?" He waited for an answer then continued, "Great, tomorrow morning it is. See you first thing. Oh, and Mike, just to be on the safe side, it would probably be wise not to mention the meeting to anyone in your lab." The last statement was certain to raise the laboratory director's interest by several degrees, Kathleen thought.

"How do you know the laboratory director is not involved?" Kathleen said with some concern. "We're not talking about one rogue person with some bad results. This involves at least three sections that we know about. The DNA was definitely altered. The tox results we can't trust, and, firearms identified a rifle as a Glock. This is either a group conspiracy OR someone pretty high up in the system is pulling some strings."

"Mike Marino is not involved. Mike is straight as an arrow," Captain Freeman said firmly.

"Captain, she has a point," Jim said, trying to defend Kathleen's assessment. "It's not just one person trying to cover up a mistake. When you look at the results, you know the intent was to deceive and mislead us. The link to Syrus Sandman, that took a lot of work. Someone had to locate his blood and know he was dead so there would be no witness to deny the child. Someone also had to make test fire shots of Sandman's Glock. Then, they had to open up the evidence bags, remove the real evidence, and replace it with the Glock bullets. Who knows what the actual tox results were, but I'm pretty certain what ever they were, it was not what was reported. How many forensic scientists not only know the ins and outs of every section but also have access to all those areas?" Jim turned to Teri. "Teri, do you know if any of the DNA analysts are checked out in firearms?"

Teri cleared her throat loudly. "I think just me. I've done some special projects so I'm qualified to perform certain tests. One of them is doing test shots in firearms." Teri looked around the room. With all they had found, she knew someone in the laboratory was guilty of manipulating evidence, but she knew it could not be Mike Marino. She knew integrity meant everything to the man.

"I agree with the Captain," Teri said finally. "There is no possibility that Mike is involved in this. At least, there is no way he is knowingly involved."

The drive in to work the next morning was hard for Kathleen. She had not slept well all night. Her dreams were punctuated with appearances of Mike Marino doing various acts of destruction. She had one dream where Mike Marino had gotten into her computer to change her Doctoral thesis, making all her data useless. Mike Marino had also sabotaged her car, stolen her checkbook, and overdrawn her bank account.

As she lay awake, Kathleen's feelings toward Marino changed from a slight suspicion to growing contempt for the man. Kathleen imagined what it would be like as Marino entered Captain Freeman's office. She envisioned the four of them questioning the laboratory director, imagining his intimidating glare as question after question was thrown at him. Marino would break down as piece after piece of evidence of his corruption was laid out before him.

Would he break down sobbing, she wondered. Would he immediately ask for an attorney? Stories still circulated around the force regarding Captain Freeman's ability to interrogate a suspect. Would Captain Freeman unleash his powerful and commanding interrogation skills? As Kathleen pulled up to the District Headquarters, she knew that in a few minutes she would get the answers to her questions.

Kathleen, Teri, and Jim had all driven their own cars directly to the District Headquarters. By the time Kathleen had gotten there, a half hour before Mike Marino was to arrive, Teri and Jim were having coffee in the conference room.

"Do we have everything?" Jim asked as he looked through all the evidence he had brought.

"I think so," Teri said. "I also brought the tape of the lab the night the intruder showed up. I thought Mike might have some ideas on that."

"Or excuses," Kathleen added coldly.

As they settled into their conference room chairs, Captain Freeman entered the room, carrying the case file from the crime lab. He looked as tired as Kathleen felt. All sat in silence, staring at the oak conference table; each dreading what would happen in the next few minutes.

As Mike Marino turned the corner to the entrance of the conference room, Teri stood.

"Good morning, Mike," she said as he walked through the doorway.

"Good morning," Mike said as he eyed Teri with an eyebrow raised. The surprise on his face was apparent to all. "Is the Washington P.D. stealing my best DNA analyst away from me?" he said, looking over at Captain Freeman.

"No, Mike," Captain Freeman said, his demeanor revealing the seriousness of the situation. "Please sit down. We have something we need to talk to you about."

Mike Marino was tall with salt and pepper hair, more salt than pepper. He had worked in forensics for over thirty years and had been the laboratory director for almost fifteen years, one of the youngest ever appointed to that position. Mike had experience and knowledge, but he also had a certain sophistication about him. He was dressed in an expensive dark suit, with a crisp white shirt which always seemed to have an animal embroidered on the left breast. He wore a shimmering silk tie. His last name explained the olive tone to his skin and brown eyes. He moved to a chair as he studied the room and the people.

"Certainly," Mike said in such a charming way that surprised Kathleen. "But, first, I think introductions are in order. Jim, it's certainly a pleasure to see you again. And, of course I know Teri very well," he said. "But, this lovely lady, I don't believe I have had the pleasure of meeting you," he said, turning his hand toward Kathleen.

"Oh, please. The man thinks he is going to charm his way out of this," Kathleen thought as she stood up to shake his hand. "Kathleen Jackson, sir. It is nice to meet you. I am sorry it is under such unfortunate circumstances."

"Unfortunate circumstances?" Mike said, turning a questioning eye to Captain Freeman.

"Yes, well, Mike. That's what I asked you here to discuss. Some issues appear to have arisen from the lab work we received from your laboratory," Captain Freeman said politely.

"Issues in my laboratory?" Mike Marino's tone went from pleasant to serious. "Please, explain."

"You'd better take a look at this," Captain Freeman said as he threw down the laboratory case file. The case file slid across the conference table, spinning slightly as it reached Mike's end of the table.

From the inner pocket of his suit coat, Mike pulled out a pair of reading glasses. He slowly opened the case file and began to review it. As he studied each report, he would find and examine each associated piece of evidence. Everyone watched him, but he appeared unfazed by the probing eyes. He took his time reading and re-reading the case file, cross-referencing the notes with the evidence, absorbing every detail.

Kathleen leaned back in her chair and glanced around the silent room. "Was this the ferocious interrogation Captain Freeman was so famous for?" she wondered. "This approach was just giving the crime lab director time to think about his excuses. Time was what Marino needed to create some elaborate, embellished performance, and we sit here and hand it to him. They will get nothing from him," she thought in disgust.

After almost an hour, Mike Marino finally spoke "Is this everything?" he said, closing the case file.

"Well," Teri started. "There is one more thing." She reluctantly explained her involvement in the case. She told him how she had come in at night to test the samples so the police could confirm or deny their test results. She told him about the intruder who entered the laboratory in the early hours of the morning. She told him everything. They quietly waited for his response.

"Let me see the tape," Mike directed Teri.

Teri got up and placed the tape in the VCR. As she played the tape, she outlined the timeframe. "This was when I entered the laboratory," she started.

"Where is the date stamp on that tape?" Mike asked.

"The date stamp?" Teri questioned. "Well, you can see the time scrolling by. This is the time I entered the lab. As you can see, I'm not in the picture. There is no indication that I entered."

"I see the time scrolling by," said Mike Marino, focusing on the numbers imprinted in the bottom corner of the screen. "Those tapes should have a date stamp on them. We should be able to see both the time and the date. Was Scott at work on this date?"

"Yeah, I think so."

"The tape shows John Kragg as the first one coming in so we know whatever date this tape was made, either Scott was off or it was made before the changed his schedule. With out a date stamp, how do you know what date that tape was made?"

"By the label on the outside of the tape," replied Teri.

"Whose handwriting is on the label?" Mike questioned.

"It looks like Jack Johnson," replied Teri. "But, that is pretty typical. Jack does most of the morning tapes. He has access to the security room, and he is usually there before the other security staff."

"Which begs a question," said Mike directly to Teri. "How did you get access to these tapes? The only access is our security staff and a backup person."

"I used to be the back up person until Jack volunteered. I guess I never turned my key back in."

Mike stared at Teri. A wrinkle of concern creased his brow. "Really. Well, I guess that is a loophole we will have to fix."

Mike began to recap the problems he saw in the case file. "From what I reviewed, we have a fragmented bullet collected by the ME's office and submitted, but the analysis shows the bullet to be in pristine condition and from a Glock submitted to the laboratory two days later. Second, we have toxicology reports that do not agree. Third, we have a video tape which has been tampered with. Fourth, we have fetal blood that was submitted by the ME's office that has now turned out to be adult human blood which has doubled in volume."

Teri interrupted, "What do you mean 'Doubled in volume'?"

Mike peered over the top of his reading glasses at Teri. "The ME's office described the fetal blood as less than one milliliter. Both your notes and the notes taken by Aaron describe the blood as two milliliters," Mike paused, then looked at the case file again. "Fifth, we have a fetal tissue sample that has a DNA profile that does not match the blood profile. Lastly, the adult blood sample does match a DNA profile of blood that was submitted to our laboratory two days after these samples were submitted, apparently, mixed with the blood of the victim." Again, Mike peered over the top his reading glasses. "Have I missed anything?"

"I think that pretty much sums it up," Jim said.

"I think you have a clear picture of the evidence we have," said Captain Freeman. "It appears there are a few issues that need to be investigated."

"Agreed," Mike said acceptingly. "They are issues that would have been investigated were they brought to my attention."

"Yes, I know they would have been," Captain Freeman agreed. "But now that they HAVE been brought to my attention, we can work this one of two ways. You can go back to your laboratory and begin an internal investigation."

"What!" Kathleen blurted.

"As I was saying," the Captain said in a slightly louder voice, glaring at Kathleen. "We can have you investigate the discrepancies in the lab work, but we both know that if you find anything criminal in nature, you will have to turn it over to us. Once we are informed, we'll also have to conduct an investigation. There is a strong suggestion that something criminal is going on. Your internal investigation is only going to prolong the inevitable."

Mike leaned back in his chair, took a deep breath and thought for a moment before he said, "Agreed. How do you want to proceed?"

"We need to interrogate everyone who had access to the evidence," Jim said bluntly.

"Until we identify a criminal action as opposed to a series of mistakes or poor judgments, I prefer you consider these as interviews and not interrogations," Mike said with some insistence. "We still do not know exactly what is going on. The interviews will give us all a better idea. My staff consists of forensic scientists. I don't think lying is in their nature, so I trust they will tell you what they know, and this can be cleared up fairly quickly."

Mike stood. Still wearing his reading glasses that had slipped halfway down his nose, he looked at Teri as a teacher would sternly look at a student who had misbehaved. Slowly, he took off his reading glasses and put them back into his pocket as he turned to Captain Freeman. "I will send my staff over here to answer your questions. It will cause less of a stir among them if they don't see you questioning everyone. Who would you like to question first?"

"That evidence tech, Johnson. I never liked that evidence technician concept from the start. He might be screwing up all this evidence," the captain answered quickly.

Mike ignored the editorial comment by the captain. "Jack Johnson it is then. Do you want me to call the lab? He can probably be over here in half an hour or so."

"Just tell him when you get back to the lab. We'll expect him around 10:30," Jim said, knowing this must be a very difficult thing for a lab director to accept but not seeing on Mike's face. His lab was stepping into the very unfriendly spotlight of a police investigation. Jim respected him for the professional way in which he handled it.

"Thank you," Mike said, appreciative of the courtesy. "One last issue," Mike said as he turned to Teri. "Pending an investigation, you are on suspension."

"What?" Kathleen said loudly, quickly embarrassed that "What" seemed to be the only word she had contributed to the conversation all morning.

Teri, however, was not surprised.

Mike turned to Kathleen. "Forensic scientists base their whole career on very fundamental ideals. Two of them are being able to say 'Always' and 'Never'. In my laboratory, we *never* tamper with or test evidence in someone else's custody. We *never* falsify data. We *never* sneak around or hide what we are doing. We *always* report suspected problems the moment they are detected. We do this to protect our cases. We follow those rules so in court we can say the words *always* and *never*. Teri violated all of those rules. She knows it." The intensity of Mike's voice established no room for argument. His clenched jaw did not move as he took one last look at Teri.

Teri did not say a word as Mike Marino left the conference room. She gazed down at the table. When she did look up, only Kathleen noticed there was a faint glistening of her beautiful azure eyes as if she wanted to cry but she was too stubborn to give anyone that satisfaction.

"How about I take you out for some coffee?" Kathleen said to Teri softly. "It's going to be awhile before Jack gets here."

"Thanks, I would like that."

Jim briefly looked up from the notes he was writing and said, "I'm good, thanks," before he had even been invited to join them. He was focused on drafting questions to ask the laboratory staff.

"He's the sensitive one," Kathleen said, rolling her eyes in an exaggerated gesture which brought a smile to Teri's face.

Kathleen and Teri walked about a block and a half away to an outdoor café. The spring morning was wonderful. There was a breeze of damp, cool air that could only be found in Washington, DC in springtime. Doves paced back and forth on the sidewalk, watching for a handout. The only clouds in the blue sky were long streaks of white. Teri and Kathleen sat down on white chairs around a small round table draped with a white tablecloth.

"This is wonderful," Teri said as she stroked her hand across the cloth on the table. "I didn't even know this place was here. It reminds me of France. It's funny what you never notice when you are focused on other things."

They each ordered a large Cappuccino. An elderly couple strolled past the table, walking slowly arm in arm. Teri's eyes followed as they passed. They seemed so contented on their morning walk. After a moment, the waiter brought two thick china mugs, frothy coffee with nutmeg and cocoa sprinkled on the top. Lost in the pleasure of momentary relaxation, each sipped their coffee.

"So, tell me about Kathleen Jackson," Teri chatted.

"Oh, not much to tell. I've been with the department two years."

"I know that much," Teri said as she leaned forward in her chair. "Two years with the department and you have a Ph.D."

"Getting," Kathleen interrupted. "I am getting my Ph.D. I don't have it yet."

"OK, almost a Ph.D., but there's more to you than that," Teri queried. "So have you always lived in DC?"

"No, small town, USA," Kathleen chuckled. "Born and raised in Burke, South Dakota. Population 800 and I think they had to count some of the pets to get the number that high."

"What a small world! My grandmother is Oglala Sioux. I bet it was nice growing up there," Teri said longingly. "I was a Navy brat, never a home, just a Base."

"I guess so," Kathleen pondered. "You know how small towns are, everybody knows everybody's business but you could play in the street for hours without a car ever passing by, you walked to the store to get your groceries and a whistle sounded at six o'clock to let the kids know it was time to go home for dinner."

"A whistle?" Teri asked.

"Yeah, an actual whistle at city hall which they blew at seven in the morning, noon and six. It sounded like a factory whistle. You could hear it where ever you were in town," Kathleen said, enjoying the memory.

"Do your parents still live there?" Teri continued.

"It was just my Mom and she died years ago," Kathleen explained. "When I was young, I couldn't wait to get out of that town. On my nineteenth birthday, I was packed and ready to see the world, too impatient to even wait for the good-bye breakfast my Mom was cooking for me."

"Have you ever gone back? Seen your old house?"

"Only for the funeral."

"That's too bad. How long ago did your Mom die?" Teri asked.

"She died when I was nineteen," Kathleen said quietly, longing for one of those wonderful breakfasts her mother used to cook.

Teri had not intended the conversation to take such a sudden turn toward a sad topic. She changed the subject. "God, you must love your job."

"Actually, no," Kathleen replied, happy the subject had changed.

Teri looked at her with disbelief and questioning eyes.

Kathleen continued, "I mean in theory, I think I would love my job but actually, I don't. I'm not very good at it. It's hard to explain, but when you're not good at something, it's hard to love it. Maybe if I were younger it would be different, but I'm OLD," Kathleen said with a laugh.

"Hey, that hurts," Teri chuckled. "You're my age."

"I know but I'm almost thirty-five. I just feel kind of old for where I am in life. Funny, it's what I have spent my whole life trying to be, a crime scene investigator. It's what my thesis was all about, but in academia, it's all so easy. You read about the crimes; you see how they are solved and then you critique how well everyone did. You present papers on how effective one strategy was or how ineffective another strategy was and everyone goes home knowing how the crime was solved," Kathleen said, reflecting on what she had said.

"It's not like that on the street when you are actually working a case. I never seem to have a strategy. I'm always trying to grab the pieces to the puzzle and trying to fit them together. My only goal is to just figure things out. And, it's HARD!" Kathleen said, taking a sip of her coffee. "You know, I was really hoping your lab director was the guilty guy," she confessed.

"What?" Teri said, genuinely surprised. "If you knew Mike, you would know it could never be him."

"He would be the perfect suspect. He had the access and the knowledge. It would all fit together so cleanly. Motive could have been political advancement or payoffs. We haul him in, make an arrest, and we all go home happy. Why couldn't it have just gone down that way?"

"That's funny. That scenario would never happen. But, sometimes, I look at the job you have with envy," Teri said.

"What?" Kathleen asked, confused. "After all I just said, did I hear you correctly?"

"I would love to be a detective."

"Did they put something in your coffee?" Kathleen said looking over at Teri's coffee, feigning concern. "A couple shots of something other than espresso? I mean, come on, you are a forensic scientist. Who doesn't want to be a forensic scientist?"

"I know forensics is important, and I am very good at what I do. I know I should be more appreciative of having a job where my work is the fair and objective voice in criminal cases, sometimes the only truth that can be relied upon. But, it's not like it is on television. Our objectivity comes at a price. We never know the full details to the case, not even in the major cases. We don't know the people involved. I analyze a DNA case and issue a report. I never learn what happens in the case. While you are filling in all the holes, all the details, I'm working the next case. Our laboratory worked 10,000 cases last year; a 1000 of those were DNA cases. There are five of us in the section. You do the math."

Teri glanced at Kathleen and took a sip of coffee. "Sometimes, I would just like to know what my work is doing. Is it freeing an innocent man or putting away a criminal? Is someone sleeping better at night because of me or are they spending their nights in jail?"

Kathleen and Teri looked at each other and smiled.

"We want it all, don't we?" Kathleen chuckled and shook her head.

Kathleen watched as the elderly couple made their way to their apartment building, a beautiful stone building at the end of the tree lined street.

"Don't worry, you'll find your way," Kathleen whispered.

"What?" Teri asked.

"It was something Jim said to me the other day, 'Don't worry, you'll find your way.'" Kathleen repeated.

"Jim's always the philosopher, ready to give advice at the drop of a hat, but he's usually right," Teri admitted. "At least he is usually right about things like that. So, I guess you shouldn't worry; it's all going to work out."

"Have you known Jim long?" Kathleen asked.

"Oh, about 10 years now, I had just started at the crime lab as a trainee, and he had just joined the Crime Scene Bureau," Teri said, thinking back to the first time she met Jim Jarred. "His hair was quite a bit fuller and wild. He brought a comb everywhere, always trying to keep his hair from standing up or sticking out. Other than that, he looks about the same. Well not exactly the same. Back then, he always had a smile or a twinkle in his eye, so that when you looked at him, he looked happy; and it made you feel happy, too. I miss that about him. He doesn't smile or laugh like he used to."

"It sounds like you knew him pretty well," Kathleen said, unable to picture her partner ever looking happy.

"I don't think we knew each other really well," Teri answered with a shrug of her shoulders. "I mean, we met on major case reviews. We always knew to show up at Stone's if they had questions on evidence or wanted to talk after hours."

"I don't think I know Jim very well either," Kathleen said, shaking her head as she gazed down the street. At the corner was a small local bank.

She watched as people went in and out of the bank, all focused on their daily jobs. Probably some of them loved their jobs and some of them hated their jobs, Kathleen thought. Kathleen noticed the building's beautiful sandstone, the arched plate glass windows, and bank tower that supported an out of place black digital clock.

"Ten twenty-eight!" Kathleen said abruptly, "Oh, my gosh! I have to go. I need to be back for Jack Johnson's questioning."

"Go on without me," Teri said, waving her hand. "I have nowhere to go and nothing to do. I think I'll just sit here and enjoy the day. Waiter," she said as she turned toward the doorway of the café, "another Cappuccino, please."

Teri turned back to Kathleen. "Go on, I'll be fine. Go catch some bad guys."

Kathleen rushed back to the District Headquarters and was told that the interviews would be done in one of the basement interrogation rooms.

"Well, so much for following the Laboratory Director's recommendation," she said as she headed toward the stairs.

Kathleen got down to the interrogation room late, and could see that Jack Johnson was already sitting at a small table. Standing with one foot resting on the seat of a chair, was her partner. Captain Freeman was in the viewing area, a concealed room that looked into the interrogation room. From the hallway, Kathleen could see the captain with his hands on his hips watching intently. In the interrogation room, no words were being spoken. Jim stared at Jack. Jack alternated between looking at Jim and looking around the room.

Breathlessly, Kathleen entered the room. Jim acknowledged her arrival with a nod and said brusquely, "I guess we can start."

"Jack, you're probably wondering why we asked you to come over here. There are some things we think are going on at the crime lab that have us a little concerned," he started in a pleasant and friendly tone. "There's some evidence that is missing. There have been some reports that may have been incorrect and samples which were mixed up. It was probably just a few unintentional screw-ups, but since it involves criminal cases, we are looking into it. We would hate for the wrong person to go to jail based on incorrect lab results or bad evidence. Wouldn't you?"

Jim stood over Jack, obviously dominating the situation, as Jack remained seated. Jim carefully watched Jack's expressions, his gestures. Jack sat solidly in his chair. The expression on his face never changed, and his hands never moved. He sat firmly in the chair, staring blankly back at Jim, saying nothing.

"Do you have any thoughts on how evidence might get mixed up or miss-labeled?" Jim continued.

"You have no right to question me," Jack snarled. He got up from his chair. "I know my rights. This questioning is over, or do I need to explain to you my rights?"

"Sit down," Jim said, still maintaining his pleasant facade as he stepped in front, pushing him back down in his chair. "We're doing a favor for your lab director, helping him work out some problems in his lab. The only right you have is to be unemployed if you don't cooperate."

Jack glared back at Jim but remained silent.

"That's it, Jack? You're just going to sit there?" Jim said, leaning in toward Jack.

"I don't really understand your question," Jack responded in a matter of fact manner.

"My question is *'Do you know anything about the evidence that has been compromised?'*" Jim said more loudly than before.

"No," Jack replied simply.

"No?" Jim asked back. "You don't know anything about any of the problems occurring in the lab? Missing evidence? Tampered with evidence? You know nothing?"

"That is correct," Jack said.

"Do you have any ideas of who might have done these things?" Jim continued.

"No," Jack replied.

The questioning continued with Jack giving up no information and Jim becoming increasingly frustrated. With each question, Jim's voice became a little more terse and tense, but Jack's responses had no emotion as his answers droned.

"Did you ever see anyone acting suspiciously?"

"No."

"Is it possible you mistakenly mixed up samples?"

"No."

"Do you know of anyone who might have tried to cover up a mistake?
"No."

"Has anyone ever asked you to help them cover up a mistake?"

"No."

"Did you do anything to the evidence in the Victoria Young case?"

"No."

"Did you touch the tubes of blood in the Victoria Young case?"

"I don't recall."

"Give it some thought," Jim said, trying to tone down the anger in his
voice.

"I can't remember," Jack said, shrugging his shoulders, again.

"Did you falsify lab results?"

"No."

"Did someone pay you to falsify lab results?"

"No."

"Will you take a polygraph?"

"No."

Jack's voice never wavered. The expression on Jack's face never
changed. Jack sat staring Jim in the eyes answering each question in a
dull monotone. Jim stared back, looking for a slight change or subtle
movement to know that he had struck a chord. There was none.

"Kathleen, why don't you get Jack a glass of water? He looks a little
thirsty," Jim said, trying to sound considerate.

Kathleen nodded, understanding what Jim wanted. From a cabinet,
she pulled out a glass and went to the water fountain and filled it, but
when she placed it in front of Jack, he slowly slid the glass away with
the tips of his fingers.

"I'm not thirsty," Jack said condescendingly.

Jim tried again. "Give it up, Jack. If you have done something to the
evidence, we're going to find it out. It will go down a lot better if you are
up front with us now. If you keep hiding it, covering up, it's just going
to get worse. It is going to grow into something you can't control. Then,
very bad things are going to happen. Come on, Jack, tell us what you

know. We know about the blood mix up, the bullet switch," Jim's words caused Jack to switch his gaze from Jim to Kathleen then back to Jim again.

Jim knew he had touched on something. "You did those switches, didn't you?" Jim leaned forward, glaring hard into Jack's eyes hoping to provoke him. Nevertheless, Jack, without a change in expression, came back with the same dull, monotone, "No."

Disappointed that he could not bait Jack into a confrontation, Jim continued. "We're going to track it down, Jack. You have to know that. You certainly did not doctor up all that evidence for yourself. Someone had to pay you. We are going to put it together. You're going to be under a microscope, Jack. We'll be checking your bank accounts, your purchases. Your life is going to be an open book after we finish our investigation. It's not pleasant. You could save yourself a lot of embarrassment. Jack, this is your chance to talk to me. Talk. Come on, Jack, do the right thing," Jim ended in such a sympathetic voice that Kathleen thought she would have told him anything he wanted to know. Jack, however, sat in his chair unchanged.

Jim stood staring at Jack. The only sound that could be heard was the muted ticking of the clock on the wall. Jack's eyes were the only things that moved, as though he were studying the room for future reference. Minutes ticked by, five minutes, then ten. Jim still stood intently staring at Jack, like a fisherman waiting for a bite.

After fifteen minutes, Jack said with complete arrogance, "Do you have any more questions?"

Kathleen responded with a curt, "Do you have any answers other than No?"

"No," Jack said flatly, raising his eyebrows toward Kathleen.

"Get out of here," Jim said, equally annoyed.

Jack slowly moved his chair back from the table and stood. He nodded toward Kathleen then Jim, and then in an exaggerated slowness, to let them know he was in charge, Jack walked out of the room.

"I think he knows something. I think he's involved," Kathleen commented.

"You bet he's involved, right up to his eyeballs. If there is one thing I am going to do, I am going to TAKE THAT JERK DOWN," Jim said as he emphasized the last four words of his statement with his fist hitting the table. "I wish he would have taken a sip of that water. We could have gotten a DNA sample. I bet he's the father of that baby."

Teri savored the time she spent at the outdoor café. She enjoyed watching the people walk by, some bustling toward an unknown destination and some strolling casually as they waved and said good morning. Before long, she decided she should go back to the lab and talk to Mike about her suspension. She hoped he might reconsider once she talked to him. Teri paid the waiter and walked the few blocks to her car. She felt fairly confident she could convince Mike to drop the suspension, so she enjoyed the casual walk to her car, knowing she would probably not have another one like it for a long time.

Turning the corner to her car, she stopped in disgust. "Could my day get any worse?" Teri thought as she walked over to her car looking at the rear passenger side tire which was flat. Teri dug through her purse for her cell phone. Not finding it, she set her purse on the car and began removing items for a more thorough search; then she remembered she had put the phone on its charger the night before and had forgotten to return it to her purse.

"Damn it," she said. "Now, what am I going to do?"

Teri looked up and down the street for possible alternatives. She chose a nearby antique shop, and as she opened the door to the old storefront, a little bell affixed to the top of the door rang to alert the owner. A frail, elderly man poked his head through the back doorway of the store.

"Hello. Can I help you?" the man in the back said.

The store was dark and cluttered with hundreds of porcelain knickknacks and statues. Every flat surface of the antique furniture was covered with something breakable. Teri looked toward the man. He was short with thick glasses and only a fringe of hair around his head. A vintage-style vest over a clean white shirt made his appearance perfect for the owner for the shop.

"I need to use a phone, if possible," Teri asked.

"Fine, fine," the man gestured. "The phone is back here. Come on back."

"Easier said than done," Teri muttered as she held her jacket close to her body and maneuvered toward the back. There were no clear aisles. A curving labyrinth of antiques, fragile china plates, antique wine glasses and statuettes cluttered the only pathway. Teri inched her way through the store.

"The way my day has been going, I will be lucky to get out of here without breaking a thousand dollars worth of stuff," she muttered.

"Sorry, dear. I didn't hear you. You have to speak up," the elderly man hollered.

"I said, 'Beautiful stuff.'" Teri yelled back.

When Teri made it to the back of the store, she was directed to an old black rotary phone.

"How cute," Teri couldn't help but say as she dialed the crime lab.

One of their new clerical staff, Maggie, answered the phone. Teri explained her predicament, and Maggie assured her that they would send someone out to help. With a sigh of relief, Teri hung up the phone, thanked the owner, and slowly made her way out of the store.

"Maybe my day is improving," she said to an empty sidewalk as she walked back to her car.

Teri's ears perked up at the sound of a man's angry voice.

"This is not my problem, this is *your* problem. If you want me to continue to do my job, you better do *your* job," the voice said. Just as the voice stopped, the man turned the corner, snapping his cell phone shut. It was Jack Johnson. Teri quickly pretended she had not seen him nor heard his conversation.

Teri focused on her flat tire. Then she heard Jack's voice behind her.

"Hi, Teri, what are you doing here?" Jack asked.

"Oh, hi, Jack, what are *you* doing here?" she asked as she turned around, feigning surprise.

"Oh, some stupid witch hunt. I think the boys at the PD have gone loco on us. Have they talked to you?" Jack asked smoothly.

"No, no. Not yet, but I'm sure they will. What are they talking to us about?"

"You don't even want to know," Jack replied. It was the farthest thing from the truth. Teri was dying to know what they had asked him and how the interview had gone.

"It looks like you have a flat."

"Yes," said Teri in honest disgust.

"Give me the keys to your car. I'll get your spare out of the trunk and change it for you," Jack said helpfully.

"I have no spare," Teri said, annoyed. "Remember, the crime lab borrowed my spare last week to do the tire track identification training. They didn't want to spend money buying a bunch of tires, so a handful of us with full sized spares lent them to the lab."

"Oh, yeah," Jack said. "I remember carrying the tires into the lab. I think that training is still going on. Well, let me give you a ride back to the lab. We can pick up your tire and bring it back. My car is just up there, a couple cars down."

"Thanks, Jack, but I already called the lab. They're sending someone over."

"The people at the lab have a million things to do. They probably won't get over here for hours. Let me give you a ride. It will be a lot faster," Jack said, pulling on Teri's arm.

Suddenly, Teri felt an overwhelming sense that she should not go with Jack. She couldn't articulate it. It was just an instinct that told her getting in Jack's car was the worst idea ever. Teri looked at Jack, trying to rationalize her feeling. She had known him two years and he had always been a perfect gentleman. She knew there was no valid reason not to get into Jack's car. Jack worked for the crime lab. His background had been investigated. He was the most helpful guy in the crime lab.

There was no reason not to get a ride back to the lab with Jack, Teri thought to herself. I'm a scientist and the evidence was overwhelming. Jack was trying to do her a favor and I'm acting like a frightened, emotional woman, Teri shook her head, annoyed with herself.

"Sure, Jack," she smiled. "That would be great. I would love a ride back to the lab."

As they got into the car and Teri made herself comfortable in the seat, Jack flipped the doors locked with the automatic door lock switch. This brought a worried look from Teri.

"You know me," Jack said with a grin. "Always Mr. Safety. You better put on your seat belt. That's not to say that I'm a bad driver," Jack said with a smile.

As Teri put on her seatbelt, she felt a burning sensation in her left arm. She tried to turn her head to see what had burned her arm, but she could only move her head in slow motion.

Her thoughts were thick and blurred. As her gaze finally reached Jack, she realized he was pushing a silver tube against her arm. Teri tried to speak but could not open her mouth. Her head began to sway back and forth; she looked forward as her world darkened. She felt her head drop forward slowly and then complete darkness.

CHAPTER **EIGHT**

PATROLMAN SANCHEZ PULLED up to Teri's car. He checked up and down the street but saw no one. He got out of his patrol car and peered inside Teri's car. He walked down a few storefronts looking in the windows, then turned back and walked the other way. He walked over to Teri's car again and checked the doors. They were locked. He stood there totally perplexed.

"Are you looking for the woman with the flat tire?" an elderly voice asked.

"What?" Sanchez responded as he turned to see who was talking.

"Are you looking for the woman?" asked the elderly man again. He stood in the doorway of the antique shop.

"Uh, yes," Sanchez said, not certain if the old man was talking about Teri Sedgwick. "The crime lab called me. They did not have anyone available to come out and meet her. She had a flat tire and her spare is back at the crime lab. I was going to take her there," Sanchez said, not sure why he was explaining all this to the old man.

"Another man took her away;" the old man explained.

"Do you know what man?" questioned Sanchez.

"Nope. He was a big man, but she must have known him. They talked for a moment, then he helped her into his car. She must have been tired, though. She fell right to sleep."

"What do you mean, 'fell to sleep'?" Sanchez asked, knowing details were important.

"Well, she got in the car, put on her seatbelt and then just fell to sleep. You know, how your head kind of bobs forward and you fall to sleep. My wife does it all the time, but she usually waits until we have been driving for a little while."

"Could you show me exactly how she fell to sleep?" Officer Sanchez asked.

The man was noticeably pleased someone was interested in his story. He demonstrated to the officer what he saw.

"How long after she got into the car did she fall asleep?" Officer Sanchez continued.

"That was the strange thing. It was right away. She just put on her seat belt and she was out."

"Thank you for your assistance," Officer Sanchez said, concerned. "Someone might want to talk to you further in the near future. Please, go back to your shop. We'll contact you. Thank you again."

Sanchez waited until the old man had returned to his shop and then quickly grabbed the radio clipped to his shoulder.

"Command Center, Adam 8."

"Adam 8, go ahead," responded a voice.

"Command Center, we have a possible abduction of a crime lab staff." Sanchez was not certain he was doing the right thing.

"That's a roger. There is a possible abduction. Crime lab staff," repeated the voice. "Do you have a name?"

Sanchez breathed deeply. He had no real evidence that a crime lab person had been abducted. He had no real proof of anything. He only had the word of an old man saying a woman had fallen to sleep in a car.

"That's a roger. It is Teri Sedgwick." As the words left his lips, he had a sinking feeling is his stomach. He would be the butt of a lot of jokes if this turned out not to be true.

In less that a minute, a squad pulled up behind Officer Sanchez's car, with lights flashing. From the car stepped a somewhat overweight police sergeant. As he got out of the squad, the sergeant adjusted his belt so his nightstick and service revolver rested more comfortably.

"OK, Sanchy, tell me what da' ya' got?" The sergeant said, half-yelling as he walked toward Officer Sanchez. The elderly man had now returned to the scene, alerted by the siren and the possibility of excitement.

"Well, sir. I was on patrol when I got a call to assist a woman from the crime lab. She was stranded at this address and needed a ride back to the lab. The woman was a Ms. Teri Sedgwick. When I arrived, there was no one present at the car. I ran the plates. This is Ms. Sedgwick's car. The elderly man who owns the shop several doors down…" Officer Sanchez's voice began to fade as he took a long gulp of air. The jump from the flat tire story to a woman's abduction was going to be rough, but he continued. "The elderly man said the woman was driven off by a different man. And, the, uh, woman, believed to be Ms. Sedgwick, fell asleep in the car."

"Fell asleep? That's what ya' got? A woman fell to sleep in a car! You called in a possible abduction based on that!" the sergeant yelled, and with a flap of his hand, he showed how ridiculous he thought the story was.

"Sanchy, Sanchy, you rookies, you act like a bunch of idiots," the sergeant said again, waving his hand in disgust. "You know, if that's all it takes for abduction, my wife was abducted three times last weekend when I drove her to her sister's house for a visit. Do you even know if this woman was Sedgwick?"

"Hey, old man," the sergeant said, yelling to the shop owner who stood nearby. "Did this woman look like she willingly got into this man's car?"

"I guess so," the elderly man nodded.

"Did these two, look like they knew each other?" The sergeant asked impatiently.

"Yes," the elderly man nodded again. "He opened the door for her. It looked like they knew each other."

"Congratulations, Sanchez. Her boyfriend probably picked her up." The sergeant patted Officer Sanchez hard on the chest. "Good work, Sanchez. You called in two people on a date. What a rookie. Let's get out of here."

"Sir, don't you think we should at least get descriptions of these people?" Officer Sanchez persisted, not wanting to drop the case so quickly.

Officer Sanchez turned to the elderly man, "Could you describe the woman you saw get into the car?"

Just as Officer Sanchez asked the question, Kathleen and Jim turned the corner at full sprint. It caught the attention of Sanchez for a split second, but then his attention turned back nervously to the old man. Kathleen and Jim were the last people on earth he wanted to see. Officer Sanchez, with his slightly trembling hand, put pen to paper as he wrote down what the elderly man said.

As Kathleen and Jim reached the group, they heard the elderly man's description of Teri.

"She was beautiful, tall and exotic looking. When I was in the service, I met a girl like her, but this woman had eyes that were like pieces of sky. She had such a smile, too, warm as a summer's day." He was obvious enamored by the woman he described. "Her hair was long and dark but it glowed like a sunset when light touched it."

Officer Sanchez took notes quickly trying to keep up as the elderly man spoke as he looked nervously at Jim.

"Right," Sanchez said. "Like the sunset," as he wrote it in his notes. "And the man?"

"Him, I didn't see so good," the man said, shrugging his shoulders as if to tell the officer it was a very unimportant question.

"Can't you remember anything about him? His size? His shape? His hair color?"

"Maybe bald, I think," said the elderly man quickly. "I never really looked at him."

"Officer Sanchez, are you the one who called this in?" Jim said, still slightly out of breath from the run from District Headquarters.

"Yes, sir," Officer Sanchez said, acknowledging them for the fist time. Officer Sanchez started to feel sick to his stomach. He had hoped they would leave before he had to explain the details of his call. The thought of everyone in the department knowing about his ridiculous abduction call over the radio was not pleasant. Officer Sanchez hated that he had already failed once in front of Detective Jarred when he had not correctly identify a witness's description of a muzzle flash in the Victoria Young case. Now, he watched as Detective Jarred and his partner came running in a full court press into his next disaster.

"Sir, why are you here, sir?" Officer Sanchez asked, hoping the answer was not that they had heard about his screwed up report.

"We were over at District Headquarter. The dispatcher told us about your call on the abduction of Teri Sedgwick." Jim recognized Officer Sanchez's trepidation. Jim patted him on the shoulder reassuringly. "Now, what do you have here?"

"He ain't got nothing," the sergeant yelled over the roof of his car. "Sanchy, there, just got stood up for a date. The woman he was meeting found a better offer," he said with a chuckle as he switched off his flashing lights and got into his car. "Good luck with your investigation, I'm not wasting any more time on his hair-brained story. You screw up like this again and you're on report," he shouted out of his window as he drove off.

Jim and Kathleen's focus turned back to Officer Sanchez. Officer Sanchez went over the story again with Kathleen and Jim. The three walked over to Teri's car. A small hole had been made at the top of the outside wall of the tire. Jim used his thumbs to spread open the hole ever so slightly.

"We'll have to bring it to the crime lab to be certain, but this puncture looks like it was made intentionally. It's just at the right height for someone walking by with a sharp screw driver or narrow knife to make this puncture without being noticed," Jim nodded toward the elderly man. "What about the man, what exactly did he see?"

They walked back to the elderly man, who seemed apparently pleased he was once again the focus of so much attention.

"Sir," Officer Sanchez said to him. "Could you describe again how the woman acted once she got in the car?"

"Like I said before, she got in the car, put her seatbelt on and then just fell to sleep. You know, how your head kind of bobs forward and you fall to sleep," he said then turning to Jim and Kathleen, he added his same joke as he told to Sanchez. "My wife does it all the time, but she usually waits until we have been driving for a little while." He laughed again at his joke.

"I need you to show me. Can you do that?" Jim asked, ignoring the joke.

"Oh, sure I can."

The elderly man sat on the front bumper of Teri's car. "She got in the car, like this. Then she closed the door," he mimed closing a car door. "She put on her seat belt. And, then she does this." The elderly man looked slowly toward the driver, looked forward again and then limply dropped his head to his chest.

Both Kathleen and Jim came quickly to the same conclusion. Teri had been drugged. But why?

"Thank you, sir," he said to the elderly man. "This young officer is going to take your statement," Jim said, patting Officer Sanchez on the shoulder. Turning to Officer Sanchez, Jim said, "Nice work, Sanchez. You did well today. Take down everything this man says, OK? We're going to go back to the District Headquarters. We will be back with reinforcements to comb the area."

"Yes, sir," Officer Sanchez said with satisfaction in his voice.

As Kathleen and Jim hurried back to the District Headquarters, they tried to figure out the puzzle.

"Do you think it might have been Jack Johnson who abducted Teri?" Kathleen asked, realizing if it had been, what was going on at the crime lab was worse than they had thought.

"I don't know," Jim said, shaking his head. "I'm not certain of the timeline. Johnson might have been in our interview when this went down. *We* might be Johnson's alibi. We need to check the sign-in sheet. If we can compare the sign-in sheets at District Headquarters with the calls to the lab and the dispatcher, we'll know if he was at District Headquarters or not when this thing went down. If Johnson was even out the door one second before Officer Sanchez contacted the Command Center, I want an All Points Bulletin out on Johnson."

As Jim thought about the possibility of Jack Johnson abducting Teri, his steps became quicker, hitting the ground harder. With each step, the angrier he became, the faster he walked, and by the time the District Headquarters was in view, Kathleen had to jog occasionally to keep up with him.

They were both so intent on getting to the District Headquarters that neither noticed the black Crown Vic which followed them for over a block. When Jim finally noticed the car, it pulled forward quickly, driving in front of Jim and Kathleen to block their path on the sidewalk. Instinctively, Jim reached for his Beretta and trained it on the two large men in black suits who limberly jumped out of the front and back passenger doors of the car.

"Relax, Detective," one of the men said, holding up his hands. Both men pulled black wallets out of their pockets, flipped them open, and held them shoulder high.

"We are from the Department of Homeland Security," said the other man.

"They teach you to drive on sidewalk at Homeland Security training?" Jim asked. "Whatever you want, catch us later. We don't have time for anything now." Jim released the grip on his firearm as he took a couple steps forward to walk around the car.

"Sir, Ma'am, you need to get in the car," the first man said with a stern look toward Kathleen then Jim.

Jim stepped close to the man, un-intimidated by his size and said in a slow, intense voice. "If you want to meet with me, make an appointment. We are in the middle of an investigation. We are losing valuable time. If you do not let me by, I will throw you both in jail for obstruction of justice. Do I make myself clear?"

The man leaned over slightly so his face was even closer and said, "If you do not get in the car, we will place you in the car and take you to Federal prison. Do you understand your options?"

"Federal prison? On what charge?" Kathleen stepped in, angry that this would happen when their window to locate Teri might be rapidly closing.

"No charge, ma'am," the man said bluntly. "A threat to national security has been identified. You appear to be involved in some way. If you do not cooperate, you will be detained. You will remain detained until the threat has been removed, or you can get in that car and we'll bring you to a department official who will explain the issues to you. You need to choose what you want to do."

Jim and Kathleen echoed each other's words. "Threat to national security?" Disbelief resounded in their voices. They looked at each other in absolute confusion, not certain they could trust the men who stood in front of them.

"OK," Kathleen said in a somewhat lighthearted voice. "I think you have mistaken us for some other people. We are Washington, DC detectives." She tried to chuckle as if she just caught the humor of the situation. "We are not involved in anything to do with national security. We are working on a murder case, and now a possible kidnapping."

"Detective Jarred, Detective Jackson. Please, get in the car," said the larger of the two men. Slowly and reluctantly, Kathleen and Jim got in back seat of the car. It was going to be a very uncomfortable drive, wherever they were going.

The car drove to a recently renovated Federal building. Kathleen could see a newly mounted emblem on the front of the building which read DEPARTMENT OF HOMELAND SECURITY.

"What exactly do you do at the Department of Homeland Security?" Kathleen asked innocently. No one in the car acknowledged the question. One man got out of the car and waited until Kathleen and Jim exited before signaling to the driver to leave.

The three of them walked up the marble staircase at the front entrance and opened the huge 10-foot glass doors. The entrance served its purpose; Kathleen felt small and inconsequential in the backdrop of the massive granite, marble, and glass entrance.

From the entrance, they were escorted to a waiting room on the fourth floor where the man in the black suit left them. After a few minutes, a woman entered the room and announced, "The Executive Administrator for the Homeland Policing Authority will see you now," and gestured for them to follow her.

She walked them into an immense office, completely paneled in wood with massive portraits hanging on the wall which masked the height of the twenty-foot ceiling. At the far end of the room, a man sat behind an expansive cherry desk. He looked up from his reading nonchalantly, as if abducting people for a meeting with him was an every day occurrence.

"Welcome, I'm glad you had time to see me," he said.

"We were led to believe we did not have a choice," said Jim carefully, taking in every detail of the room.

"Indeed," the man said. "Well, that is unfortunate. You certainly had a choice. I have only the greatest respect for police officers. The agents from the Department of Homeland Security must have overreacted to my request for their services. However, this is of a rather urgent nature." The man's accent had a bit of southern twang, but not the same smooth, silky drawl Congressman Thatcher had used so effectively.

"Let me introduce myself. My name is Thomas Crowell. I'm the Executive Administrator of the Homeland Policing Authority," he said, obviously trying to impress and intimidate the two detectives. "Are you all familiar with the Homeland Policing Authority?" Crowell asked, making no effort to stand or shake the hands of his guests.

Jim did not respond. His eyes scanned the room for information. Kathleen stepped forward.

"Well, uh, actually I'm embarrassed to say that I do not know anything about the Homeland Policing Authority, but I hope you will remedy that," she said, trying to gain the man's good graces.

"I admire your candor and your interest," Crowell nodded to Kathleen. "Let me tell you about our department. Our role is to bring balance to the various state and local policing organizations. We are a little known department, born from the Patriot Act. Our function is to protect this great country of ours. We are a fledging organization, right now, and work under the umbrella of Homeland Security, but I am certain that is only until our funding is identified," Crowell continued. "We do not have many of the resources of other departments, mainly because we still do not have a sufficient number of properly trained agents. I assure you, this will not be the case for long."

"What exactly do you do?" Jim interrupted, his voice barely containing the anger he felt having to stand in this man's office making small talk while Teri was in such grave danger.

"As I was saying," Crowell continued slowly, "In the past, all the state and local police departments worked on their own, never communicating with another jurisdiction unless they thought they had a criminal case in common. There are a lot of jurisdictions in this country, all of them investigating crimes and all of them collecting evidence but never communicating with each other about them. What if all of those police agencies could be collecting all that information and continuously linking it together? What if all over the country, police agencies were communicating with each other? There might be some information so obscure that they are not even aware of its importance, but that evidence might be the key to solving a crime two thousand miles away.

"That is where the Homeland Policing Authority comes into the picture. We take all information collected by all the various police agencies and compile it, cross-reference it, study it. Our job is to make certain no vital bit of information is lost or ignored just because it was collected in Podunk, Kansas or Backroad, Alabama," Crowell chuckled as he stretched his chest, strutting across the room.

"To be completely successful, we need well-trained individuals. Training takes time, as I am sure you know, especially when their role is so specific and unique. Of course, we currently electronically monitor most of the major police agencies and crime laboratories, but there is nothing like a field agent to give you hands-on knowledge. It makes all the difference in the world, don't you see.

"That is why we are in the process of receiving approval to develop a training facility. We actually have acquisitioned the property. It is an old Drug Enforcement Administration training facility. It's not much, but it is a start. We are currently just waiting for the funding. Once that facility is refurbished, we can hire our own field agents. We will not have to rely on other departments. Then, we can begin to develop to our full potential."

Crowell smiled, feigning a pleasant demeanor and continued, "Eventually the CIA, FBI, NSC, DEA will all report to us." He laughed, at his misspoken words. "Excuse me, I meant to say, they will report information to us on the criminal cases they are investigating. Unlike Department of Homeland Security, who looks for threats around the world that might hurt our country, our job is to identify the threats from within, the criminals that jeopardize our way of life. We assess the danger and determine the appropriate course of action that will eradicate the threat."

"It's a good story," Jim interrupted, mocking Crowell as he twisted his head back and forth as if to work out a kink in his neck. "Are you saying you monitor the computers at the Washington, DC Police

Department because you believe the muggings, burglaries and homicides are a concern to national security?" No one could mistake the contempt in his voice. "You pulled me away from a case which has nothing to do with national security," he continued. "It has to do with a woman's life and if anything happens to that woman, I will come back and arrest you for obstruction of justice."

"Such drama, detectives. I'm impressed with your dedication, but I beg to differ with you, Detective Jarred. The case you are working on has everything to do with national security," Crowell continued. "It's a homicide case I do believe. Correct?"

"How did you know that?" Kathleen asked, surprised and slightly sickened with the thought that what he was saying might be true, and that some Federal authority was monitoring their computers.

"It is my job to know what is going on in this city," Crowell said dismissively. "In fact, I have been made aware of an interrogation you performed on an evidence technician earlier today."

Jim turned to Kathleen and raised his eyebrow, knowing the case had just changed direction.

"This evidence technician is an important resource to our department," Crowell said in clear, decisive words. "He is not to be further interrogated during your investigation."

"That's ridiculous," Kathleen blurted out. "At a minimum he is a key witness to crimes committed at the crime laboratory; at worst, he is a criminal, maybe even a murderer."

"A poor choice of words, detective, which I attribute to your inexperience," Crowell said, admonishing Kathleen. "He is one of our finest trained individuals."

Jim asked, "In what capacity does he work for you?"

"In every capacity," Crowell answered casually, as if everyone in the room should have known this fact. "He is employed by the Homeland Policing Authority."

"Is the crime lab aware he works for the Homeland Policing Authority?" Jim began his interrogation of Crowell.

"Well, I don't know if they were specifically told he was being employed by the Homeland Policing Authority, but you would have to be daft not to have figured it out," Crowell said sanctimoniously.

"How exactly would someone have figured it out?" Kathleen asked.

"Homeland Policing Authority funded the evidence technician programs. We are opening up to laboratories all over the country. We developed the programs, distributed funding, and provided the training. We gave the crime laboratories a list of qualified and highly trained individuals from which they could hire an experienced evidence technician. We told them whom to hire and paid their salary. You would have to be damn fools not to think the evidence technicians were not in someway a part of the Homeland Policing Authority." Crowell sneered at the absurdity of the question.

"Why would the Homeland Policing Authority provide evidence technicians to crime laboratories?" Kathleen asked as she looked directly at Crowell who was still sitting comfortably behind his desk. She hoped he would not give the answer she thought he would.

"So they could report things to you," Jim answered for Crowell.

"Excellent, Detective Jarred. I can't depend on the forensic laboratories to report all the important information. We have individuals training at some of the federal laboratories, of course, like the FBI. Some will receive that assignment, and others will be reassigned to local crime laboratories," Crowell explained, almost bragging. "New York, Los Angles, Miami, as well as the California state lab, Florida, I believe, and my fine home state of Texas will all receive evidence technicians through this program; but currently we only have a few out in the field. Of course, Washington, DC was high on our priority list."

"I don't understand," Kathleen said, shaking her head. "The crime laboratories would certainly give the Feds any information you wanted. All you would have to do is ask. Why in the world would you want to place someone there to spy on what is going on?"

"Not spy," Crowell corrected her shaking his head. "Oh no, not spy. Of course, the laboratories would give us any information if we asked. That was never the question, but the problem is we have to ask. Sometimes we might not *know* to ask. The evidence technician screens the evidence of cases coming into the laboratory. They are in the perfect position to let us know if there is anything worth our attention. It also allows us to access information in a timelier manner. If we rely on laboratories to tell us about the significant crimes going on in their jurisdiction, a year might go by before we hear about it. All the formalities that must occur, the paper work, the memos, the chain of command all being informed; it becomes ridiculous. Using an evidence technician is a nice, clean way of keeping track of the evil that is going on in our country."

"It's a nice clean way of keeping track of evil?" Kathleen said sarcastically. "Are you serious? Evil in this country? You mean you want to be above the law?"

"Nonsense, no one is above the law," Crowell said.

"Do you know what was done in the Victoria Young case?" Jim said abruptly.

"Of course, I do," Crowell responded. "A small indiscretion of a high ranking public official was removed from public scrutiny. That is all. Minor scandals from within our own family should not divert the attention of our country's officials. Our focus, our goal, is to keep our country safe. A scandal is neither healthy nor desired when protecting our country."

"Murder is not an indiscretion. Murder is a crime," Kathleen said, staring in disbelief.

"We didn't murder anybody, and we didn't cover up a murder," Crowell assured them. "That poor young girl was killed for some reason that I do not know. Maybe a mugging, maybe she was dating a gang member. I do not know why she was on the National Mall at one o'clock in the morning. I do not know who killed her or why she was killed. But, I do know the fact that she was pregnant need not be a concern of the general public. The mother is dead. The child is dead. Who would it help to let the public know who the father of this dead child was? It would help no one, it might hurt many – it was patriotic, shall we say, to keep it out of the news."

Crowell ended his sermon with their dismissal. "I really have no further time for this discussion. If you value your job or if you value ever being employed in the field of law enforcement, you better ensure that Prendergass is not interrogated, not investigated, not even touched. My influence is very far reaching. Do not rock my boat or you will be thrown in with the sharks. Do I make myself clear?"

Jim's body stiffened as he heard a name from his past. "What had they gotten themselves involved with?" he thought. In a weak breath, he tried to confirm his worst fears.

"Who?" The opening of the door and the entrance of a small, well-dressed woman interrupted his question. She carried a pile of papers which she laid on the desk next to the name plaque that read Executive Administrator Thomas Crowell. Kathleen noticed CONFIDENTIAL was marked on the files. The woman nodded to Crowell, indicating there was some importance to the papers she had placed on his desk.

"Thank you, Carol," Crowell said, acknowledging to the woman he understood her meaning. "Ah, yes. Prendergass," Crowell continued. "George was using an alternative name, wasn't he, Carol?" Crowell asked, turning to the woman. "Do you remember what name we used when he was training for the DC crime lab?"

The woman stopped and thought for a moment. "I believe he used the name Jack Johnson," she replied, looking around the room to see if there were further questions; when there were not, she unceremoniously left the room.

"Ah, yes, Jack Johnson," Crowell said, recalling the name. "Yes, Jack Johnson. We needed to use an alternative name. There were some confidential issues regarding his military record that made it, shall we say, more efficient to use an alternative name. But never the less, I want to make myself clear: Prendergass is not a suspect in any cases you are investigating. Prendergass is a highly trained member of the Homeland Policing Authority, and you are to ignore any coincidences, shall we say, of his involvement in the case. I do not think I can be any clearer than that."

"George Prendergass is the evidence technician at the crime laboratory?" Jim asked, ignoring Crowell's instruction.

"Yes, that's what he said. George Prendergass went by the name Jack Johnson, an alias," Kathleen explained, trying to clarify Jim's apparent lack of understanding, but when she turned to look at him, she recognized the stone cold face she had only seen when the topic of his wife or his partner was mentioned.

"I have trouble understanding how someone could rise so high in your police department without understanding Basic English. *George Prendergass* is an employee for the Homeland Policing Authority. The work he is doing at the Washington, DC crime lab is vital to the security of this country. His work is not to be impeded in any way," Crowell said, annoyed at having to repeat his instructions.

"Oh, my God," Jim said with a voice that was a mixture of fear and anger.

Kathleen turned to look at Jim. He stared through her, his eyes darting from point to point, not fixed on any object. His thoughts were racing, trying to assess the situation.

"What's wrong? Who's George Prendergass?"

Jim did not respond.

"Oh, my God. We have got to find Teri. She is in grave, grave danger," Jim said, abruptly running out of the office.

Kathleen could not keep up as Jim flew down four flights of steps. For a moment, Kathleen looked at the elevator and then back at the steps, wondering which might be faster for her to take. She chose the steps, knowing she had no chance to catch Jim; but still, she put every fiber in her body toward an attempt. When she reached the first floor, Jim was already heading down the outside stairs of the building. She ran across the lobby and, as she reached the outside air, she could see Jim at the curb, with his arm raised.

"What is going on?" she yelled to his back.

"Taxi!" Jim yelled.

Kathleen finally caught up to Jim. As she grabbed his raised arm, she asked, "What is going on?"

But Jim ignored her.

"What is going on?" she repeated, out of breath. "Damn it, Jim, talk to me."

"We have got to get to the crime lab," Jim's jaw clenched. "George Prendergass was in the Marines with Pete Stone. George Prendergass is a psychopath. Pete talked about him all the time. Prendergass is a guy you don't want to mess with."

CHAPTER **NINE**

TERI FELT A distant sting across the side of her face as she felt her head jerk onto her right shoulder, unable to control it. Her thoughts were slow and dull as she tried to open her eyes. She heard a muffled voice say, "Wake up." When she finally opened her eyes, she saw the out stretched palm of a hand striking her across her face again. The stinging was much less muted. Her cheek burned, and her head bounced against her shoulder.

Teri tried to move, but realized she was firmly attached to the chair where she sat. Her legs were tied at the ankles to the front legs of the chair, her waist was tied to the back of the chair, and hands were tied behind her back. Teri tried to wiggle out of the restraints, but the only part of her body she was able to move was her head.

"Wake up," the voice said loudly.

Teri opened her eyes to the face of Jack Johnson.

"What are you doing, Jack?" Teri moaned. Her tone was more of a parent talking to a child, admonishing him for having done something ridiculously stupid. Teri repeated, "What are you doing, Jack?"

"Shut up," Jack barked. "This time, I ask the questions and you give the answers. Got it?"

Jack paced slowly, back and forth, in front of Teri. She looked around the room. Things came in and out of focus. The room was empty except for the chair in which she sat. The floor and the walls were concrete. Teri's head throbbed as she closed her eyes for a moment to gain some composure. When she opened them again, her eyes better adjusted to the light, making things a little clearer. The light from the small, barred windows five feet above the floor brightened the room. There was no glass in the windows, so when Teri took a deep breath, the fresh air filled her lungs and cleared her head. She knew they were not in the city; there were no sounds of cars; no smell of diesel.

"What am I doing here?" Teri thought to herself. It was a question she often asked rhetorically to the ghosts of the victims in her cases. What were they doing there; the place where they died; a place where they should never have been. Why hadn't they listened to their instincts? Why hadn't she? Now, she was the one in the predicament and she wasn't certain how she had gotten there. She sensed Jack stepping close to her.

"Tell me what you know about the Victoria Young case," Jack yelled even though his face was less than a foot away from Teri's.

"That was not my case. The Young case is Aaron's," Teri said, trying to turn her gaze away from Jack.

Jack stood up straight and with an outstretched arm, slapped her hard across the face. "Wrong answer," he yelled.

"Aaron was assigned the Young case. Aaron did the analysis on that case," Teri said again, her mouth dry and the words coming slowly.

Jack grabbed Teri's hair, forcing her to look upward into his face.

"Are you stupid?" Jack said incredulously. "Of course, Aaron was assigned that case! I assigned him the case. That is who *I* wanted to analyze the case. I'm asking you, what do *you* know about the Victoria Young case?"

"I don't know anything. I don't know anything," Teri's voice weakened as she strained to gasp for air.

"Wrong answer!" Jack yelled as another slap went across Teri's face.

Teri felt the warm, salty taste of blood as it trickled down her mouth. She could feel her lip swelling from the blows to her face. Her eyes were only half open as she saw Jack staring back at her with a look she imagined predators might have when they look at their prey. At first it terrified her, but then she slowly resolved that she was not going to be the prey. She would not give up any information he wanted to hear nor any information he needed to know. If she were going to die, she would die with the satisfaction of knowing that she had not been prey to Jack Johnson.

"Tell me, what you know!" he yelled again.

"They asked me to look at the case file. That's all," Teri yelled. "They wondered if someone changed the results."

"And what did you tell them?" Jack said, now calmer but still intense.

"I told them I didn't think so but I couldn't tell!"

"Did you do any testing?" Jack asked.

"No," Teri lied.

Grabbing Teri's hair again and jerking her gaze upward, Jack again asked, "Did you do any testing on any of the samples?"

"NO!" Teri yelled back as the syllable echoed in the barren room. "Check my stats. You'll see I did the cases I was assigned. I wouldn't have had time to do work on the Young case. I couldn't slip another case into my rotation. Let alone re-work one of Aaron's cases. I would have no time to do any tests. I just was asked to look at the *FILE*!"

He let go of her hair. "Good girl."

Jack walked out of the room. Teri quickly scanned the room for anything she could use, but there was nothing. Concrete walls, concrete floors concrete ceiling. Her sitting in a chair was the only thing in the room. She struggled with her restraints as she stared at room. Looking at the depth of the barred windows, the walls looked thick, maybe a foot thick and the room was cool because of that. The room was certainly made for some purpose but Teri could not figure out what purpose it could be. Just outside the doorway, Teri could hear him dialing a phone number. Teri heard Jack say quietly, "It's George. We are all good here. They still don't have anything to go on but some hunches. Jarred was just trying to bait me. They got nothing."

There was a pause as George listened on the phone, his heavy breath sounds told Teri he did not like what he was hearing.

"OK, I'll sit tight, but you had better figure out what we are going to do with this girl." There was another pause before Teri heard, "Of course she knows who I am, I've worked with her for the last two years."

As Jack walked back into the room, Teri pretended to be semi conscious.

"Wake up," Jack said, kicking Teri's foot with his boot.

Teri pulled her head upright and opened her eyes. Jack carried a large rifle with a huge barrel and a telescopic scope attached to the barrel's top. She recognized the M40A3 sniper rifle immediately. It was the weapon of choice for Marine snipers, preferred because of its extreme effective range. The small silencer attached to the front of the barrel was wholly insufficient for the power the rifle packed. Teri thought about the paper she and John Kragg had published together on silhouettes of the rifles most likely to be used by terrorist snipers. The M40A3 Teri knew the feel of first hand. It was longer and heavier than most rifles, but with only a 5-round magazine capacity, it was not standard issue.

Teri's heart sank as she thought about how her life would end, knowing a point blank shot by a high power rifle was worthy of a journal publication. It would probably be a joint paper between the Medical Examiner and John Kragg. They would publish the article describing her interesting but tragic death in measurements and trajectory analysis, a small cardboard ruler resting on her head to show the size of the wound. She shuttered.

"So, now you're going to kill me," Teri said. It was more of a statement than a question.

Jack grunted as he paced the length of the room. Leaning his rifle against the wall of the room, Jack squatted a few feet from Teri. "I didn't get approval to kill you."

"But, I'm a witness. I know you. I can identify you. Why wouldn't you kill me?" Even as she said this, she realized the stupidity of listing the reasons why her abductor should kill her but the scientist in her compelled her to outline the logic.

"Do you want me to kill you?" Jack smiled.

Teri quickly shook her head.

"Then I guess we all agree I'm not going to kill you, right this minute"

Jack said with a voice that scared Teri as much as the thought of her death. "Maybe we'll just ruin your credibility. Make certain everyone knows everything you say is a lie. You made this whole thing up."

"That would never happen. My reputation is impeccable," Teri struggled against her bonds. "There's no way anything you say about me would be believed."

"So you're back to wanting me to kill you," Jack said with a smug smile as he reached for his rifle and stood up.

"No," Teri said quickly, trying to calm Jack down. "I know you have your orders, you wouldn't want to ruin your career. We should just wait to see what they want you to do."

"Damn straight," Jack snapped as he took a few steps closer to her. "You know if we wanted to, we could ruin your career. You forensic scientists never want to admit that your precious reputation is no more than one case away from being ruined. When I saw you snooping around with those detectives, I know I had to get rid of you one way or another so I already screwed up some of your cases. I screwed them up real bad; your work is going to convict some innocent men. Those forensic friends of yours will be more like a school of piranhas," Jack laughed. "Once they start investigating your work, they won't know if you're lying when you say your name is Teri Sedgwick. Or maybe that's how they'll remember you after your suicide, distraught over being such a terrible forensic scientist."

Jack rubbed the smooth stock of his rifle as he checked the scope attachment and nodded approvingly, he added, "I like that," pondering the idea of a suicide. "You know how I knew you were involved with Jim and Kathleen? It was when they came to the lab with that cock and bull story about reviewing an old case. I knew there were no outstanding old cases," Jack continued, pleased that he finally had an audience to listen to his intellectual prowess. "I reviewed all the case files. Jim had nothing outstanding. That's when I knew. You're too willing to work with Captain America and his flunky over there at the Crime Scene Bureau."

Teri shook her head. "Jack, I think you need some serious help because, you are absolutely *crazy*," but her statement only got the cold metal of the rifle barrel pressed hard against her neck as her voice fell silent.

When Jim and Kathleen arrived at the crime lab, the evidence counter was busy. One of the forensic scientists filled in for the absent evidence tech, and things were not going smoothly. The line of officers waiting to submit evidence extended to the hallway. Jim grabbed one of the DC Police officers at the evidence counter and asked him to radio for someone to bring his car to the lab.

"Now, we need to see the laboratory director, Mike Marino," Jim said as he grabbed Kathleen's elbow, prodding her to move more quickly.

Mike Marino was in his office looking through several dozen videotapes on his desk. He had rolled several televisions and VCRs into his office. The usually impeccable Mike looked more disheveled than Jim had ever seen him.

"Jim, Kathleen, I am glad you are here. I have been going through these surveillance tapes ever since I got back from our meeting today. I think I have found something very interesting."

"Before we go over what you've found, can I make a phone call?" Jim asked, his urgency apparent as he reached for the phone.

"Sure." Mike moved his phone so it was easier for Jim to dial.

"Yes, hi, this is Detective Jarred. I need to have military records faxed to me at laboratory director Michael Marino's office." Jim waited for a moment before speaking again. "Yes, the name is Prendergass. That's Pacific-Romeo-Echo-November-Delta-Echo-Romeo-George-Adam-Sierra-Sierra, first name George, common spelling. Marines. Entrance date, 1984 or 85. I also need his home address and any contacts he has. Also give me all known prior addresses. Then, see if there is anything you have on Jack Johnson." There was a pause as the voice on the phone repeated the information Jim had given her.

"Yes, that is a roger. Fax it to the lab director's office not the clerical office. Got that? Great. We need this fast, Jodi. It's a possible kidnapping. I know you will," he said thankfully, then hung up the phone.

"What was that all about? Jack Johnson? Did something come up from the interview? I assumed you would have called me if you found something," Mike asked, wondering, if that call was so important, why they were doing in his office.

"It's a long story. Let's wait to discuss it until we get the fax," Jim replied. "Now, what did you find that was so interesting?"

"As I told you, I've been reviewing the last year of surveillance tapes. I've been looking for any tapes where the date stamp is missing. You know, like the tape Teri showed me. I found some, and it was Jack Johnson who wrote the outer label with the date on all of them," Mike explained.

"What about prior to a year ago?" Kathleen asked.

"Well," Mike said rubbing his chin, "we only keep these tapes onsite for one year. After a year, we place them in long-term storage. It's going to take some time to look through the rest."

"There is one more thing you might be interested in," Mike said, walking toward the television. "I was just reviewing this before you got here."

Mike slid the first tape without the date stamp into the VCR. He fast-forwarded the tape to 10:51p.m., then pressed PLAY. "Look at this upper screen," Mike said as he pointed to the view of the front entryway which revealed the parking lot and the street in front of the building. Look at this," Mike said. "At 10:52 pm, a blue Volkswagen Beetle drives past. Now watch this," Mike's finger dropped to the bottom of the frame and followed a cat walking past the front door. Mike paused the tape. "Now, here is the interesting part."

Mike turned on the other television and pressed PLAY. The tape had already been forwarded to 10:51p.m. Jim and Kathleen watched as the time stamp changed to 10:52pm. Then in the upper left corner of the screen, they watched a blue Volkswagen Beetle come into view. Both Jim and Kathleen looked down at the bottom of the display. A moment later a cat walked past the doorway.

Jim got up and randomly pulled another videotape from the pile on Mike Marino's desk. He placed it in the third VCR. All three watched the VW Beetle pass by the upper corner of the screen and then the cat walk past the lower part of the frame. As Jim paused the tape, all three television sets had the same view -- a cat, as it passed by the doorway.

"So, all the tapes are the same," Jim said, taking a deep breath. "How many tapes did you say there were?"

"There are 27 tapes," Mike said soberly, once again considering the breach of security that had occurred in his laboratory. Jim could see the emotion in his face as Mike thought about a rogue intruder roaming free in the halls of his laboratory, after hours, with no one watching.

"We used this system to insure digital segments could not be inserted. We never considered the whole tape being a fraud," Mike sighed, shaking his head.

"Mike," Jim said, trying to pull Mike's thoughts back to the present, "Who is this Jack Johnson? What do you know about him? Why did you hire him?"

Mike did not respond to the question for several seconds, then as if jarred awake, he said, "Jack Johnson was hired through a Federal grant program, a crime lab initiative. I think it was to reduce backlog in certain of the high crime cities; although some heavily populated state labs also got funding."

"Do you know who administered the program?" Kathleen wondered if Mike was at all suspicious of the source of the funding.

"No, I would have to look at the file. My administrative assistant, Mary handles the files on grants," he explained. "She's exceptionally good at that sort of thing. You know, filing for grants. We apply for so many. We couldn't possibly survive without the grant monies that we get. CODIS is from grant money, so is our entire digital imaging section. Interns, validation studies, new equipment all are funded with grants from the federal or private sector. Do you want me to pull our grant file?"

"Please. I think we need to see the file," Jim nodded.

Mike leaned over to his intercom button. "Mary, could you please come to my office and bring our grant file."

In less than a minute, Mary was in Mike's office with a four-inch accordion-fold file stuffed with papers.

"Mary, do you remember what grant money Johnson was hired under?"

"No, sir, I would have to check." Mary thumbed through the papers in the file. "Here it is. Crime Laboratory Initiative -- Backlog Reduction Program."

Mike took the paper and reviewed it. "This was one of our larger grant projects. It was more than just hiring an Evidence Technician. They paid for the remodeling of our evidence-receiving area so one person could manage it and gave us a computerized evidence tracking system and funds to hire a trained evidence technician. We were offered a trained evidence technician from the FBI lab. Wasn't that it, Mary?"

"Yes, according to his file."

"Who funded that program?" Jim asked, suspecting the answer.

Mike flipped to the second page of the form. "It looks like the Homeland Policing Authority. Um, I'm not certain I know that department. Must be new."

"Did you do a background check on Jack Johnson before he started?" Kathleen asked.

"Nothing extensive," Mike answered, surprised at the question. "The FBI usually does a thorough background check before anyone's hired there. Since he was coming from the FBI, we assumed his background was good."

"You're right, the FBI doesn't let anyone into their system without a full background check, even if they're just there a day." Jim moved over to the phone and dialed, leaving it on speakerphone. "But, something doesn't add up."

"FBI, Agent Carter," came a man's voice over the phone.

"Hi, Carter, it's Jim. Do you mind if I leave you on speakerphone? I have Lab Director Marino and Detective Jackson here."

"Jim Jarred! Well, it's been a while since we talked. We missed you at the last barbeque. Speaker's fine. What's up?"

"Do you remember an employee with the FBI, an evidence tech named Jack Johnson?"

"Well, he was assigned here few years ago but only for a few months, if I'm thinking of the right guy."

"A few months!" Mike interrupted. "His file said he was FBI trained."

"Well, I can ask around. Jack Johnson is probably a pretty common name," the man admitted. "Maybe there was another Jack Johnson."

"Tell us about the one you knew," Jim asked.

"I wouldn't say I knew him," Carter explained. "He was brought into the FBI to learn basic evidence receiving, but Homeland Security had a fit when we tried to print him for a background check. They sent over files with a bunch of printouts of backgrounds completed at Homeland Security but, of course, FBI does their own backgrounds. We don't accept others."

"So did you do a background check?" Kathleen leaned forward, eager for the answer.

"No, we never did," Carter continued. "We kept going back and forth with someone over at Homeland Security and eventually he was given a visitor level access pass, but was never allowed unescorted in the building. He never had independent access to anything for the three or four months he worked here."

Jim glanced at Mike who was slowly shaking his head. "Thanks, Carter." Jim said. "I'll give you a call later, maybe we can do that barbeque sometime this summer," he added before clicking off the speaker.

There was a moment of silence as each thought how this new information impacted the lab, the case and their friend. The silence ended as Mike's office fax rang and began to print out the military records of George Prendergass followed by the Department of Motor Vehicle report. When it finished, Jim stepped between Kathleen and the laboratory director so they could all read the pages.

"Wow!" Mike said, reading down the page. "Look at this guy, Prendergass. What a piece of work. Enlisted in the Marines in 1984. He was also up on a battery charge in 1984. Charge was dropped – unsubstantiated, then an assault charge again in 1984 -- dropped. 1985 - Threatening an officer -- charge dropped. Two more assaults in 1987 - - one charge unsubstantiated -- one charge dropped. In 1988 conduct unbecoming a Marine -- charge withdrawn. I think Prendergass must have known someone. No one gets this many charges dropped without the hand of someone pretty high up!"

As he read farther into the details of Prendergass' career, a startled look appeared on his face. "Prendergass received sniper training in 1989. Why would you train a guy with a record like this to be a sniper? In 1991, service in Iraq, WOW, look at this," Mike said as he moved his finger to the last notation on the paper. "Sixty-eight sniper targets during Operation Desert Storm, sixty-eight confirmed kills. At least we know this guy can hit a target. I guess they found something this guy was good at. This guy is a walking cannon."

"This guy is Jack Johnson," Jim said soberly.

"What?" The blood drained from Mike's face.

"What's worse is we think he kidnapped Teri Sedgwick," Kathleen added.

Mike threw a sharp look at Jim. "What! How could this happen? How could Jack Johnson be George Prendergass?"

"We need to know all you know about Jack Johnson," Jim said somberly. "If he kidnapped Teri Sedgwick, we need to find her."

"Do you have patrols out looking for her?" Mike asked, concerned that they were not doing more to find Teri.

"No," Jim said.

"Are you crazy?" Mike said. "If this Johnson is the man you think he is, Teri could be in serious trouble!"

"We know that," Kathleen said somberly. "I don't think Johnson or Prendergass is going to hurt Teri, at least not just yet. As absurd as it sounds, I think he believes he is acting as a Marine. Marines kill on orders or when trapped or assaulted. If we put on an all out manhunt and they find him, then I believe Teri *will* be in trouble. We have to find him, and we can't go in with a hundred backups, guns blazing. We need to find him and talk to him."

"That's ridiculous," Mike said. "Look at the man's record. That's no plan."

"It's a strategy," Kathleen corrected. "Crowell said the Homeland Policing Authority was developing a training facility that used to belong to the DEA. Do you have any ideas where the site might be?"

"I know where that training facility is," Mike quickly answered. "It closed down about a year and a half ago. Why in the world would you think that is where Johnson is?" he asked as he looked through his desk drawer for a map of the area.

"Johnson is acting on the belief he is an important asset for the Homeland Policing Authority. That site is empty and belongs to Homeland Policing," Kathleen answered, confident she was right. "He can't bring Teri to one of their offices in the Department of Homeland Security building. The training facility has to be where he is. It's the only place he can go. I know it."

Mike unfolded the map of the area and circled where the old training DEA facility stood.

By late afternoon, Jim and Kathleen arrived at the location Mike had circled on the map. The sun was still bright and warm, stretching shadows far into the yard but the starkness of the place gave the buildings in the yard a menacing quality. Jim and Kathleen got out of their car and took in the layout of the training facility. The ground was a dusty, red clay. Kathleen noticed the gentle wind stir up a cloud of dirt which circled around an occasional clump of grass growing freely, indicating the neglect of the premises. It was definitely a military-type facility, surrounded by chain link fences and razor wire, the yard was approximately 600 meters long, and half that wide with several buildings silhouetted in the afternoon light.

"These buildings do seem to be abandoned," Kathleen said quietly.

Jim nodded in agreement.

A heavy, thick chain fastened the gate, keeping unwanted visitors out of the yard.

"I think I can pick this lock," Kathleen said, sliding a small L-shaped tool from her pocket as Jim walked farther down the fence. "The lock is a little rusty so it's going to need some finesse," she said, pulling on the loop of the lock. "I think I almost have it. It just seems like it is stuck." Her voice strained as she tried pulling harder. She turned to see if Jim would lend a hand, but, to her amazement, he watched her from inside the fence.

Not wanting to ask how he got there, Kathleen just stared at him, waiting for him to tell her the answer.

He smiled. "Walk a little farther down the fence. There's a smaller gate for people to walk through. Wasn't locked."

As Kathleen ran to catch up, Jim surveyed the yard. The major structure at the distant corner was a three-story storage building with smooth windowless walls, the perfect tool needed to train individuals to rappel down buildings. Large arms swung off the roof of the building with ropes still attached. The few windows at the top were small narrow slots cut into the top floor. Bars without glass guarded the windows from intruders.

"Looks deserted," Jim said. "Are you certain Johnson's here?" Jim realized that, for the first time, he was asking Kathleen for direction.

"Positive," Kathleen said as she met him on the other side of the fence. "It's classic behavior. There are a dozen books written on this type of situation and behavior."

"Then let's do it." Turning to the building, he cupped his hands around his mouth like a megaphone and shouted, "Jack! We'd like to talk to you!"

Teri could not imagine a more beautiful sound than the echoing of Jim's voice from the ground below. Teri closed her eyes for a moment as she drew the deepest breath she could manage, then tried to gain her composure. Before Jack could muffle her voice, Teri yelled with all her remaining strength, "We are up here. Jack has a gun."

"Shut up!" Jack hit her across the face. "The next word you say will be your last."

"Hey, remember, you don't have approval to kill anyone," Teri reminded him.

"Shut up! How did they find me here?" Jack muttered, checking the yard from the window. "Boy, I have always wanted to frag that Jarred guy. He has been a pain in my ass the whole time I've been at that lab and now he walks right into my world."

Grabbing his rifle, Jack peered out the window again. Crouching slightly, to keep his head low, he could see the two people at the far end of the yard through his scope.

"They're up there," Jim whispered, pointing to the tower. Shouting, Jim repeated, "Jack, we just want to talk."

A gunshot rang out. Jim felt the wind of the bullet as it flew past his head. The distance and the light breeze were enough to cause Jack to miss his target on his first attempt. He would never miss on his second try.

"Get cover!" Jim yelled as he pulled Kathleen behind a long one-story building just to his right. "Keep moving." He ran along the backside of the building.

Kathleen followed, wondering if it wouldn't be smarter to get back to their car and radio for backup.

She could feel the pulse of her heart reverberating in her hands as she drew her service revolver for the first time outside the shooting range. She focused to control her hand's tremor as she grasped her Beretta Cougar firmly. She watched Jim as he slid to the side of the building, searching for the shot's source. Only a small sliver of his head twisted out to find his objective.

"Come on, Jack, you don't want to do this," Jim yelled, but only silence was returned. "Or should I say George?"

Finally, a voice came from the tower, "What is it with you guys? Why are you constantly interfering with me doing my job?"

"I don't know what you mean," Jim yelled back as Kathleen moved low to the ground, peering out slightly in the direction of the voice. She could see nothing.

"You and your partner have been the biggest pain in my ass since I started this job."

Jim turned to Kathleen "Listen to me. This is what I want you to do." He surveyed the back of the building, a long structure spanning about half the length of the fence. "When I give you the go, you run to the far end of this building and draw his fire."

"Draw his fire," she repeated. "OK, that sounds safe. That is exactly the plan I would have thought up except I would have had you draw his fire."

"I want you to be safe," Jim said, ignoring her sarcasm. "Don't stick your head out. Use something else, flap your coat, find a stick, anything you can wave that will draw his attention to you. He will fix on the movement. If you hear any gunfire that passes too close or you think he has a bead on your position, go to the other end of the building. Draw his attention to that side. Understand?"

"Hey!" the voice came again. "Did you hear me? My job is important and all you and that idiot partner of yours have ever done is to jeopardize the safety of our country."

"Let's leave Kathleen out of this," Jim yelled, stalling for time.

The voice from the tower continued. "Not *that* idiot partner, your *other* idiot partner…Stone."

Jim and Kathleen were so involved in their own conversation that it took a minute to register what Jack had said.

Kathleen stared at Jim. "I just want to clarify this. You want me to run 250 yards in that direction. Draw his fire, knowing he is a trained sniper, then run another 250 yards, the equivalent of three football fields to draw his fire toward me over there."

"Don't exaggerate, it's barely two and a half football fields." Jim added, "He *is* a trained sniper so don't stick your head out. If you're a target for more than a second, your head will be sticking to the back fence… in pieces."

Jim waited for an acknowledgement. Kathleen's tremors had expanded to her whole body, including her head, which Jim read as a nod yes. Giving her a thumbs-up sign, he whispered, "Good luck."

"Thanks," she said as she watched Jim run toward the building opposite the tower. "This is really swell. What a great profession where people try and kill you," Kathleen's heart racing madly, she reviewed what she had been taught at the Academy. She repeated them out loud. "Don't go to the same place twice. Go low, then go high; low then high. Draw his attention to my movement but don't give him a target."

Jack trained his rifle on the building where he thought the detectives had ducked for cover. "Hey! You listening? See, Jim, first it was your partner, Stone. What a screw up he was."

Jim fought his way to the far side of the building. "Yeah, but he knew you were George Prendergass," Jim yelled back.

"Very good, Jarred," Jack yelled, still searching for a target, scanning the grounds with his riflescope. "He saw me, you know."

"Saw you where?" Jim asked as he slid behind some 55-gallon drums. A shot hit one of the barrels. Some kind of fluid leaked onto the ground. "Thank heavens that wasn't gasoline," Jim whispered.

Jack followed the edge of the building with his scope, desperate for any kind of movement.

"He never trusted me," Jack explained. He jerked his rifle downward, reacting to the movement of a bird, then looked up at something at the closest building. He fired off two shots quickly.

Kathleen could feel splinters hit her face as bullets grazed the building. Then two bullets hit the ground behind her. There was hardly any sound to the shots, only a small noise like the slap of a clapping hand.

Jim stopped for a moment and hollered back, "Why do you say that?"

"He knew who I was," Jack shouted, trying to draw Jim out into the open.

"That night he died, he drove past the lab. Saw me leaving. He knew an evidence tech had no business there late at night. That was when I saw it in his eyes. He knew exactly who I was. He sped off. I jumped in my car. I only wanted to talk to him, but you know how he was."

"How was he?" Jim yelled, trying to keep Jack talking, distracted from his movements.

Jack noticed Jim's voice was coming from a different direction and turned his attentions toward the far side of the yard, carefully spanning. "Stone was an arrogant, self-righteous idiot. I tried to catch up to him. He never slowed down. He was getting on the highway. I just touched his bumper."

Again Jack scanned the yard methodically, his eye squinted through the telescopic lens. "I wanted to slow him down, make him pull over, but that SUV he was driving started tumbling over. Man, that thing just started rolling, end over end,"

Jack continued trying to get a rise out of Jim, trying to bait him into the open. Just one mistake from Jim, and he knew he would have him. "I knew there would be an investigation. My cover would have been blown," Jack caught a movement and swerved back to the building below.

His shot ripped the jacket from Kathleen's hand. Jack quickly reloaded his weapon. "I had to divert the attention away from me."

"Do you know," Jack obsessed with his story as he yelled into the yard, "Ten micro liters of pure ethanol in a 10-milliliter tube of blood gives a blood alcohol concentration at the legal limit for driving?" Jack saw something, set his aim and fired.

Kathleen clung to the side of the building, taking a minute to catch her breath. Then she slowly peeked out, hoping to determine where the shots had come from. The afternoon sunlight gave her a slight advantage. A quick reflection on the metal of the rifle gave her a location.

Jack knew how to bait Jim, he knew emotions would get the better of Jim, and emotions caused mistakes. Jack shouted, "Twenty micro liters, and the blood sample is twice the legal limit. When Stone's blood sample came into the laboratory, I thought I'd make him nice and drunk, three times the legal limit, just to be on the safe side. Stone always looked like a drinker to me."

"Now, your wife," Jack said, elevating the stakes another notch. "I added just enough ethanol to your wife's blood sample to let everyone think she was a drunk, too." He knew this would drive Jim over the edge. Jack waited for his prey to surface as he slowly scanned up and down the perimeter. He saw a flash of light and shot instinctively at a phantom.

Kathleen pulled the shiny piece of metal she had found on the ground back to her chest, which was heaving, trying to catch her breath.

"It's a sad thing," Jack said, wondering why Jim did not leap into action. "Your wife. What was her name? Was it Jennifer? It's a sad thing about all those rumors about Stone and Jennifer. I would have thought you might have stood up for her reputation a little better. Why didn't we ever hear anything from you when your wife's name was being dragged through the gutter? It's a sad thing that the last thing anyone will remember about Jennifer Jarred was that she was a…"

The door to the room flew open with such force that it shattered the doorknob as it hit the wall. Jim's foot came down hard on the concrete floor. Teri was terrified as Jim's hand rose to fire. She had never seen such anger in a person's eyes.

Jack tried to turn toward the doorway but the long barrel of his M40A3 caught on the bars of the window. Like a blast of thunder unleashed into the room, Jim emptied the eight rounds in his Beretta Cougar into the chest of Jack Johnson.

George Prendergass was dead before he hit the floor.

CHAPTER TEN

KATHLEEN HEARD THE shots and moved into action. She looked out quickly, and detecting no reaction from the tower, ran out into the yard at full speed. She did not stop until she got to the base of the tower. She took a quick look into the hallway of the buildings, spotted the stairwell and dashed up the three flights of stairs. At the top, she saw only one room. She pressed her back against the wall, next to the doorway. Her breath was so labored she thought it could be heard by the people inside the room. Silently, she counted to three. Weapon drawn, she leaped into the doorway.

A brilliant pool of blood sparkled in the afternoon sunlight, and the sun's rays formed a spotlight on the dead Jack Johnson. The size of the pool slowly expanded as Kathleen's eyes rose to Jim standing over the body, weapon still drawn. She spotted Teri tied to a chair and rushed over to her, untying her bindings. "Thank god, you're safe," she said as she released Teri's hands and a flood of tears began to stream down Teri's face. Kathleen looked over at Jim standing in the agony of revenge and said softly, "I need to go call for some backup."

Kathleen went down the steps slowly, trying to process everything that had happened in the last fifteen minutes. She knew she would be questioned by internal affairs for the shooting. She began to jog toward the car as the details became a blur.

She was surprised to see that police cars had already arrived. Obviously, reports of the shooting had come into the zone command. As she walked toward the officers, she pulled out her badge. "The area is secured," Kathleen yelled to the officers. "It is an officer shooting. The victim," she hesitated and then corrected herself, "the *suspect* is down. Detective Jarred and a forensic scientist are in the tower."

Reports were taken at the scene and the area was taped off. It seemed to take forever, Kathleen thought, desperately wanting to leave.

Jim stood in the yard with Teri and Kathleen, waiting for confirmation that Captain Freeman had been told about the shooting.

Just as the officer in charge cleared them to go, Teri finished her phone conversation with the crime laboratory director.

"Mike would like a full report tomorrow," Teri said, trying to think of the right words to say to Jim. "Uh, I didn't mention the evidence tampering to Mike. We can work through that with him tomorrow."

Jim simply stared off into the distance, his thoughts still on Jack Johnson's last words.

"Jim, why don't we go somewhere and get a drink?" Teri asked softly.

"No."

"Come on, Jim, I know we could all use a drink. Maybe talk about things, a debriefing so to speak," Kathleen added as she put her hand on his shoulder.

"No," Jim snapped. He rubbed the sweat off his temple and forehead. "Dave has a ball game tonight. I said I would be there." He silently walked to his car and drove away, leaving Kathleen and Teri to find a patrol car to drive them back.

When Kathleen got into work the next morning, Jim was at his desk. It appeared as though he had been there for hours. As she stepped to her desk, Jim asked brusquely, "Where have you been?"

"Well, I thought I might get a few hours sleep," Kathleen quipped, instantly regretting her tone.

Both Kathleen and Jim's nerves were on edge, each dealing with the stresses of the previous day. For the first time, Kathleen had truly real-ized her job could cost her her life. She could still hear the bullets flying past her head, but she also knew that it was nothing compared to what Jim must be feeling.

"The Johnson shooting made the morning paper," Jim said, ignoring her sarcasm. "I want to get over to Johnson's apartment before anyone else has a chance to move things around or take things out. If the people at the Homeland Policing Authority hold true to pattern, there will be some covering up." There was an unmistakable contempt in Jim's voice as he added, "I want to get these guys."

"Jim, you don't know if the whole Homeland Policing Authority is corrupt. It may have just been Johnson."

"They knew what Johnson was doing. They planted him in the crime lab. What do you think for?" Jim said with anger seething out of every word.

"Jim, it's not your fault."

"What! It's not my fault that my wife and partner were murdered and I did *nothing*," Jim said, pushing away the newspaper. "I just accepted those lab reports like everyone else!"

"You didn't know. It wasn't your case. You didn't review the evidence. You didn't do the investigation. You didn't know what they found."

Jim sat silently, staring at the papers on his desk. Finally he said, "I knew my wife! I knew my partner! I should have known something was wrong with that evidence. I just didn't want to look too closely because I was afraid of what I would find, that maybe I didn't know them at all."

Kathleen searched for the right words. She wanted to say something comforting. She wanted to say something wise, but the only words she could say were, "I know."

Jack Johnson's apartment was within walking distance of the Capital. Normally, it would have been suspicious that an evidence technician could have afforded an apartment in such an exclusive area, but having been listed as retired from the FBI, most thought his pension was covering the costs.

The facility manager let them into the small two-bedroom apartment. It was neatly kept, but very stark. In the living room was a weight machine, a sofa and a large television.

"I guess he didn't have much company," Kathleen observed.

Jim glanced through the videotapes stored under the television. "We'll have someone go through the tapes and review them, but it looks like a bunch of junk, mostly sports games."

The kitchen was very neat with a small table and half-empty cabinets. The bedroom was the same. There was a bed, one chair and a dresser. The clothes in Johnson's closet were neatly pressed.

"He must have taken most of his stuff out to be cleaned. This all looks like it was done by a laundry," Jim noticed as he flipped over one of the laundry tags still pinned to the shirt. Jim bent to examine the shoes on the closet floor.

"There's not much here, and I don't think anyone has tampered with the place. It looks like he barely lived here," Kathleen said as they left the main bedroom and headed toward the second bedroom.

When Kathleen opened the door, the covert life of Jack Johnson opened before them. There were shelves of binders with names of cases. There was video surveillance equipment and a rack that stored a number of firearms and high-powered rifles.

As Jim walked into the room, he turned to Kathleen, "Get gloves on." She took out the small white gloves she always had in her pocket and put them on. Her hands always felt strange when she wore them.

Jim was quick to note a familiar name on a binder sitting on the metal bookcase. It was titled… YOUNG. As he flipped through the pages, he read the details of the Young case as seen through the eyes of a psychopath. He found a list of the evidence that had been submitted to the crime lab and the computer printout of the evidence inventory that was generated by the lab computer. Next to each listed item was a hand written note as to whether the evidence was transferred directly to a forensic scientist or was altered first. In the back of the binder was an envelope. Jim slid the contents into his gloved hand. It was a bullet fragment, which looked to be from a rifle. He flipped through the pages of the file. Everything was noted in fine detail.

"Why in the world would someone keep these kinds of notes in such detail? Why would someone make notes of how he was breaking the law?" Kathleen wondered aloud.

"You said it yourself...the man never thought he was breaking the law. He never thought he was doing anything wrong," Jim answered. Kathleen watched over Jim's shoulder as he flipped through the paperwork.

"He has everything here, every day documented, every action listed. What a psychopath. Why would a government agency hire him? Then, try to conceal his past? It makes no sense. Someone had to know what he was," Kathleen murmured.

Jim put the binder back on the shelf, then scanned through the other binders. Meyer, Holtzburg, Sullivan, Taylor, Bonavia, Carlson. Were all these files the cases where the outcome was changed and the truth denied, the facts erased? Jim slowly read the labels until he came to one named "STONE".

His hand slowly ran down the spine of the binder. Jim wanted to look inside the file, but did not want to know what information it contained. He wanted to know the truth, but he did not think he could bear to read what he already knew.

"Let's get some back up here. We need to secure the location and then take these files to the crime lab," Jim said, replacing the 'STONE" binder."

They left the task of securing the apartment to the arriving officers as they loaded up the binders and transported them to the crime laboratory. When they arrived, the laboratory director paced outside. He had been briefed before their arrival and the look on Mike's face needed no words.

"Hi, Mike," Jim said soberly as he opened the trunk.

"What do you have for me?" Mike said. It was obvious he was infuriated that someone from his laboratory, someone he trusted, had falsified evidence on his watch. The reputation that he had spent thirty years building could all be gone in a puff of smoke. The anger Mike Marino felt toward Jack Johnson at this moment was seething and apparent. Jack Johnson had not only placed Mike's career in jeopardy by his actions but also the work of every forensic scientist in his lab. Jim knew the thoughts going through Mike's mind. The only consolation Jim could offer were the binders holding the information of what had been done.

"Mike, we have what we believe are all the records." Jim lifted out the boxed binders. "Let's sit down and go through them, then we can see where we are."

Mike nodded. He held open the front door so Jim and Kathleen could carry the binders into the laboratory.

In the conference room, Jim and Kathleen set the boxes of binders on the table. Mike went through the names, writing them on a sheet of paper. When Mike got to Peter Stone's binder, his eyes darted across the table to Jim. Jim looked back at him, but neither said a word.

Mike wrote down eight of the ten names on the file. Using the intercom, he asked his administrative assistant to come to the conference room.

"Mary, I need these case files pulled ASAP," Mike said as Mary glanced at the two boxes of white binders, noting their names. Mary's forehead wrinkled a bit as she silently questioned if there was a problem with the cases. She had seen many problems in her 20 years at the laboratory, some small, some major. None as serious, though, as the look on Mike's face indicated.

"I will be back as soon as I can," she assured Mike.

"Teri told me about these last two this morning," Mike explained after Mary left, as he drew two binders from the box. "Teri and I went over the case files all morning. We found a lot of issues. They're going to have to be reworked. I don't think we can trust any of the data. It looks like controls were removed. Data was definitely altered. We don't want to try and make a determination of all the things wrong with the case until we see what the original results were. I have already notified each officer involved."

Mike sat in one of the chairs, resigned to what they were about to discover. "The consequences for a forensic scientist making a mistake are huge," Mike said, shaking his head in disbelief that this was happening in his lab.

"Where's Teri?" Kathleen asked, thinking Teri might want to help them go through the binders.

"The cases won't be reworked by Teri. She's on suspension. I have not changed my mind on that," Mike said with a deep sigh. "I already sent her home. She is not part of this investigation. She is a scientist not a police officer. She knew the rules and she chose to break them."

"She helped us find the truth. She helped us stop Jack Johnson," Kathleen insisted.

Mike preferred to focus on the case rather than answer Kathleen. "He played me for a chump. If he wasn't already dead, I think I would kill him."

"I know exactly how you feel," Jim agreed.

For a moment, everyone's thoughts were on Jack Johnson and everything he had taken from them: Pete's life, Mike's career, Jim's wife and a life he could never reclaim.

Kathleen looked at the binders, knowing that everyone in those binders had also had their lives changed forever.

Mary broke the silence was broken by returning with an armload of files. She put the files on the table and began to leave. "Mary, stay," Mike said, putting his hand on her arm. "We're going to have to go through these files. We need to take notes on any discrepancies we find so we can put some kind of report together for the mayor. I need you to take notes."

Grabbing a pen and a pad of notebook paper, Mary sat down in a chair.

"Let's do this chronologically," Mike said as he flipped through the case numbers. Since the case numbers were assigned by date, it was easy to put the cases in order quickly.

"OK, first case is Meyer. He was arrested for DUI," Mike said as he flipped through the case file. "I remember this case. Meyer was a DEA agent. He was young, just a few years out of training. The case history states he was driving the wrong way down the interstate, hit a car and there were some injuries, but no fatalities. The officer noted a strong smell of alcohol on Meyer's breath. Meyer failed the field sobriety test. Lab tests results showed no alcohol, no drugs detected. No charges were filed, but as I recall, he was forced to resign from the DEA. What does Johnson's file say?" Mike asked Jim.

Jim opened the binder. "DEA agent. Terminated for conduct unbecoming a DEA agent. It looks like there was quite a bit of evidence submitted to the laboratory. The air bag was submitted to Trace, along with the front bumpers of both cars. The blood and urine were submitted. Johnson has made a notation next to Meyer's blood and Meyer's urine. It reads '10 mL blank blood, 35 mL blank urine.' I assume that is what he used to replace Meyer's samples."

"Mary, take down the submission dates of these cases. I want to see if they correlate to the dates we have on those doctored security videotapes of the lab, the one's on my desk without the date stamp," Mike said as he slid the first case file to Mary. "I'm certain they will correlate, but I want to clean up any loose ends."

"Second case is Bobby Carlson," Mike said opening up another case file. "Carlson is the son of a U.S. Senator. Carlson was 17 years old at the time of this case. He apparently was joy riding with a friend, hit one mailbox, nicked the side of a parked car breaking a headlight, then hit several cans of garbage, causing several thousand dollars of property damage. The friend never admitted to seeing anything, although he failed a polygraph. The evidence was submitted, but the lab could make no link to the car or the damaged property. Headlamp and plastic from the turn signal light found at the scene could not be physically matched to the car, either. Other than the friend, there were no witnesses. The charges were dropped. I do think his Dad, the Senator, did pay for the repairs. I guess as a good citizen gesture."

"And, Johnson's involvement," Jim said as he opened the binder. "He removed the transferred paint from the car and removed it from mailbox submitted. Transferred paint removed from garbage cans, and transferred paint removed from parked car door submitted. Plastic and glass found at the scene of the crime replaced with glass and plastic of same make and model car. Source of glass and plastic -- Junkyard. Can you believe this?" Jim said as he turned the binder toward Kathleen to read. "The guy submitted a reimbursement slip to the Homeland Policing Authority for payment he made for one glass head lamp and one turn signal cover. He put a copy of the request in the file. What a joke. It cost him $11.79 to conceal a crime and Johnson wanted to be reimbursed for it."

"Next case is Bonavia," Mike said grabbing the laboratory case file. "I don't even need to open this case file."

"Wasn't he the U. S. Representative who left because of that big scandal about 18 months ago?" Kathleen said remembering the front-page news.

"Yes," Mike said, looking up from the pages of the file. "Representative Bonavia was involved in a car accident where he was driving a young intern home late at night. The intern was a very young woman. That kind of stuff always breeds scandal in this town. Bonavia always insisted he had fallen asleep at the wheel and that was what caused the accident. At the scene, Bonavia refused to do any field sobriety tests. He said it would be undignified. He did agree to have blood drawn for an alcohol and drug test. The intern also had her blood drawn. The lab found high levels of cocaine and alcohol in both blood samples."

"The congressman was outraged," Kathleen added with a roll of her eyes in disgust. "I remember reading about it. He insisted the samples be re-tested at a private laboratory. He said he was being framed because of the work he had been doing on campaign reform."

"Yes, he did get the samples retested," Mike remembered. "We sent the samples, at the request of his defense attorney, to a private lab he chose. The only stipulation was the laboratory had an accreditation equivalent to ASCLD-LAB standards. The lab found exactly the same results we found, cocaine and a 0.160 gm% ethanol in their blood."

"What's an ass-clad lab?" Kathleen asked. "That doesn't sound very good."

"It stands for the American Society of Crime Laboratory Directors, Laboratory Accreditations Board. They are an accreditations board for crime labs," Mike explained. "If you are a good crime laboratory, you have that kind of accreditation."

"Did both the congressman's and the intern's sample contain the same amount of cocaine and alcohol?" Jim asked, knowing the answer would be yes.

"Yes, they both had the same ethanol 0.160 gm%," Mike said, skimming through the notes of the case file. "And, they both had the same cocaine level 550 micro grams per liter."

"Well, Jack," Jim said into the air, "I guess you didn't have much of an imagination."

"It cost Bonavia his career in politics. He always insisted he was innocent," Kathleen said. She was sorry she had believed Congressman

Bonavia was guilty and just making a fuss to cover up what he had done.

"Not too many in the House were sad to see Bonavia go," Jim commented. "From what I understand, the guy was really independent, with a capital I." Jim leaned over to Kathleen to explain, "Among politicians, independent is a bad word. It means unpredictable, uncontrollable, and unreliable. Someone you can't count on when you need a vote."

"So what do we have listed on Johnson's chart," Mike asked, knowing the information would just add to the disaster slowly unfolding before his eyes.

"Let's see. Johnson has listed that he added 20 micro liters pure ethanol to each of the ten milliliter vials of blood. He also added 5 micro liters of a stock standard of cocaine to each of the tubes of blood."

Mike calculated the numbers as he muttered, "Twenty micro liters times 0.789 density. Ten milliliters... convert micrograms to grams.... micro liters to percent by weight. That calculates to 0.160 grams % ethanol in a 10 mil tube."

"So I guess he was innocent," Mike said in a softer voice.

"He was innocent of drugs and alcohol in his system. He never did explain why the intern was in his car so late at night," Jim said with a smirk.

Kathleen whacked Jim's shoulder with the back of her hand.

"What?" Jim said, surprised.

"That is exactly the type of insinuation that DC gobbles up like fact. Was Bonavia convicted of driving under the influence of drugs?"

"No," Mike answered. "If I remember correctly, the case was SOL, that's Suspension of Litigation. The charges are still on file. Bonavia went back to New York. It all just went away after awhile. They could still prosecute him, but with this new information, I would think the charges would be dropped."

Mike pulled the next case file toward him. "Pete Stone and Jennifer Jarred," he read then looked toward Jim. "We don't have to do this one now."

"It's alright, Mike," Jim said, resigned. "I already know what's in it. Jack Johnson had the courtesy of informing me yesterday. He put 30 micro liters of ethanol in the tubes of blood of both my wife and Pete."

Mike opened the case file and began. "It looked like a pretty straight forward driving under the influence case. The police also submitted the rear right fender which they thought had some suspicious markings. Nothing was found by the lab."

"It looks like Jack removed transfer paint from the fender and changed the shape a bit to conceal him having tapped the rear right side of the car," Jim said, reviewing Johnson's binder, "and 30 micro liters of ethanol added to each blood tube."

The day seemed to grow longer and longer as Mike's nightmare of falsified evidence grew with every case.

The next file was marked HOLTZBURG. "Holtzburg was a trial lawyer who had filed a lawsuit against the FBI for some of the covert surveillance they had been doing on a governmental official, Jacobs was the name, I think. The case was scheduled to be heard by the Supreme Court later in the year; however, Holtzburg had to step out of the case when his fingerprints were linked to the death of a prostitute." Mike glanced up at them. "Ironically, Holtzburg had gotten a court order to inspect the FBI facilities. The FBI granted a limited inspection with the stipulation Holtzburg had a background check for any prior arrests. To do this, Holtzburg gladly allowed the FBI to take a 10-print card of his fingerprints, which the FBI ran through their automated fingerprint identification system. Holtzburg's background check came out negative, but his prints soon showed up on the murder weapon of a young Asian prostitute. The knife that slit her throat had been left at the scene of the crime. Holtzburg was convicted of the murder. The case is on appeal."

"How do you think Johnson pulled that one off?" Kathleen asked. "How could Holtzburg's prints be placed on a murder weapon?"

"I don't think Holtzburg's prints were actually placed on the murder weapon," Mike said.

"Well, how then— That makes no sense," Kathleen questioned.

Mike went on to explain. "Latent print examiners visualize the print and then take photographs of the print. Most of our latent print examiners will work off the picture they have taken of the evidence. If anyone had someone's 10-print card on their computer, they could print it onto a transparency, then they could lay the print anywhere on an item. Once they took a picture, it would be very difficult to tell if it was a visualized print or a picture from a 10-print card." Mike winced to think this case would be coming back to haunt both him and his staff's standard operating procedures. "Johnson did a lot of the photography. It helped out the latent print examiners." Mike rubbed his head, trying to massage away an ever-growing headache. "I'm going to have to call a staff meeting. I need to go over this stuff before they read it in the paper or hear it on the news. The next few months are going to be hell for this lab."

"Nothing's easy today, is it?" Mike said, getting up from his chair.

"The pattern seems apparent," Jim began. "They started out with a couple small cases to work out the kinks. He changes the results on a drunk DEA agent. Maybe it was a friend. It doesn't work out. A kid's joy ride – he's getting better. Then they start targeting people, not helping them after they screwed up but changing their lives – or ending them. Can we look at the Young case? That may be the one case here we can close."

Mike pushed the binder toward Jim.

"Everything in Johnson's notes matches what we know. The fetal blood was replaced with a mixture of Syrus Sandman and Victoria Young. The two Glock bullets were added to the case. Ethanol and cocaine were added to Victoria's blood," Jim said as he fingered the small manila envelope snapped into the rings of the binder. "There is a notation at the top of this page. It reads 'T- a go for 1a.m.'"

"I wonder what that means," Kathleen asked, leaning over to see the notation.

"What time was Victoria killed?" Jim asked Mike to confirm his suspicions.

"Um," Mike looked through the file, "estimated time of death was 1 a.m."

"I'm thinking Jack Johnson shot Victoria Young and his note is a notation that he received the approval to shoot her." Jim talked while he ripped the envelope containing a bullet fragment from the binder. "I think this was a trophy. Mike, we need the fragment compared to the bullets recovered from Johnson's rifle. Do you have the rifle?"

"An officer submitted the bullets fired at the crime scene and the Marine sniper rifle this morning. We can go to the firearms section and see if they have done any testing yet."

Kathleen, Jim, and Mike went to the firearms section where John Kragg was sitting at a stereo microscope, looking through the eyepieces. John Kragg had been in the firearms section as long as anyone could remember. He was someone who loved firearms, loved looking at firearms, loved their smooth feel, delighted in taking them apart and putting them back together. John should have retired many years ago, but his love of the work held him to the bench where he worked. Mike was glad that John had been in the section during his career as laboratory director, because John had made things easy. When Mike needed a favor or a rush case, there was nothing he would turn down; no job was too hard or time frame too restrictive.

"Hello, John," Mike said as he walked through the doorway.

John Kragg peered over his glasses.

"Mike, how nice of you to come visit our fine firearms section," John said somewhat jokingly as he stood. "Oh, and Jim Jarred. It is nice to see you, too. Since we started using an evidence technician, I hardly get a chance to talk with you," John stretched out his arm to shake Jim's hand. "How are the kids?"

"Fine," Jim said.

"John, we need you to take a look at this bullet. We want you to compare it to the case that just came in under my name."

"Under Mike's name?" Kathleen said, questioning why Jack Johnson's shooting would be submitted under the laboratory director's name.

"Usually cases involving a police officer are submitted under the lab director's name. The staff only knows it by its case number," Jim explained to Kathleen. "That way, the staff doesn't inadvertently release information to the officer being investigated. If it has the lab director's name on the file, everyone knows not to discuss it with anyone, especially chatty officers who give them a call. Once all the evidence has been tested, then the results are reported and the names are added to the case file."

Kathleen looked dumbly at Jim. "Aren't *you* the officer being investigated in this case?"

Jim rolled his eyes. "The guy was trying to kill me with a high powered rifle and a target scope. I think it is going to be determined a justifiable shooting. I'm not worried about the verdict."

John Kragg pulled some bullets out of an evidence bag that was sitting on the counter. "I have the bullets from yesterday's shooting right here," he said, holding up several badly damaged bullets.

"Here's the fragment," Jim said as he handed John the envelope.

John took the fragment out of the envelope and placed it on one platform of the stereoscope. He then put one of the bullets which had been submitted that morning on the other platform. Through the eyepieces on the stereoscope, he viewed a split image. Half of his view was of the fragment and half of his view was of the bullet. After several minutes of turning each of the bullets slowly into the correct position, John said, "They're a match. Both of these bullets were shot from the same rifle."

"That's it?" Kathleen asked, surprised that the whole analysis took only a few minutes. "Don't you have any instrumentation? Don't you have more tests to run?"

"I'm going to have to make some standard test fires to get more pristine bullets. I have to document everything with photographs, take a lot of notes, and write up a report," John explained. "My work will have to be verified. All the paperwork will be proofed by another examiner, and that's going to take several days; but this isn't DNA. Qualified examiners are the important instrumentation in the firearms section," John said with pride. "I make the determinations, not a piece of equipment. After 37 years of practice, I am telling you both these bullets were fired from the same gun. In two days, I will have the documentation to support that opinion."

"Thanks John, you are the best examiner I know. I don't need anyone else to check your work. Your word is good enough for me," Jim said as he grabbed Kathleen's arm. "Let's go. We have our answer."

CHAPTER ELEVEN

"WHAT ANSWER DID we get?" Kathleen asked as Jim accelerated out of the parking lot.

"Who killed Victoria Young, and why," Jim answered.

Kathleen didn't want to ask any more questions. She sat quietly trying to figure out why Victoria Young had been killed. She knew Jack Johnson was probably the murderer. Why would someone in the Homeland Policing Authority want Victoria Young killed? All the cover-ups involved changing the evidence. Now, they knew that the bullets that shot Victoria Young came from the same gun that Jack Johnson had used to try to kill them. That wasn't much help in telling her why the killing had taken place.

Kathleen soon relented and asked where they were going.

"Representative Thatcher's office. It's time he told us what he really knows."

"Aren't we supposed to clear that with the Deputy Director?" Kathleen asked. "You know she demanded to approve any further questioning of him. I think her exact words were 'If you do feel the need to contact the congressman, please clear it with me first along with the questions which you intend on asking him.'"

"Wow, I never noticed what a good memory you have," Jim said, truly impressed. "If there's one thing I need to teach you, it is to know when to follow the rules and when to ignore them."

"Could we be in any more trouble? Ah, yes. I guess we can. Let's just break all the rules," Kathleen quipped.

"Trust me on this one, I know what I'm doing," Jim assured her.

"You always do."

Jim and Kathleen walked in to Representative Thatcher's outer office with a look of determination. "We are here to see Representative Thatcher," Jim said to the secretary.

"What is this in regard to?" the secretary said as she jumped out of her seat, trying unsuccessfully to block their way.

"Murder," Jim replied, opening the door to the Representative's office.

"You two again!" Thatcher said, rising angrily from his chair at his desk. "I believe someone has already contacted your Deputy Director. What is her name? Catherine O'Connell. Did she not inform you that you are *not* to be harassing me any more? I am a United States Congressman and I will not have you treating me like a street thug," Thatcher bellowed.

"We aren't here to harass you, Congressman," Jim said in an equally confrontational tone. "We are here to ascertain your involvement in the murder of Victoria Young."

"I have answered all the questions I intend to, regarding that unfortunate tragedy," Thatcher said, glaring at Jim.

"Yeah, well, things have changed since we got back the lab results saying you were the father of Victoria Young's baby." Jim had played his trump card.

The secretary gasped slightly and backed out of the office, closing the door quietly behind her.

"That is impossible," Thatcher said as he slammed his pen on the table. "There are no such results."

"I'm afraid there are," Jim said bluntly as his eyes narrowed, trying to read the congressman.

"That is the most ridiculous thing I have ever heard. Your results are wrong. There is no possibility I was the father of that young woman's child. Victoria Young was a very beautiful woman, bewitching you might say. She cast her spell on many men. I, of course, am a man of sterner character than that. I have never surrendered myself to her, ever! It is out of the question to even imply I had any type of relations with Miss Young," Thatcher said as he waved his hand dismissively. "Get out of my office."

"The lab results tell us different. The lab results say your DNA made up half of Victoria's baby's genetic make-up," Jim lied, but his confident dismissal of the congressman's denial made Kathleen almost believe what Jim was saying was true.

"There is no way you could link me to that child. That child's father was a gang member who was known to commit a series of offensive crimes," Thatcher argued almost as convincingly. As Congressman Thatcher spoke, his silky southern accent became more pronounced. "How could I be linked to that child? You do not even have a sample of my blood. You do not have my DNA in your databases. There is no way you could make any comparison of me to any person. You may think me a backward southern fool, but I assure you, I am well-versed in the ways of science."

"Yes, Congressman, I'm sure you are well-versed in the ways of science. I suspect you have a keen interest in how DNA testing works. That knowledge would be in your own best interest, considering your interest in crime lab results," Jim was now playing a game of cat and mouse. "I am just not certain how up-to-date your knowledge is. The lab no longer needs a blood sample. DNA can be detected from a cigarette butt."

"I don't smoke," Thatcher responded smugly.

"That's not the only place someone's DNA can be casually left; piece of gum, a postage stamp or from the rim of a drinking glass," Jim smiled as if he had a secret to hide. "Have you noticed you're missing the glass you used the last time we were here? Don't worry, it will be returned to you."

Thatcher flopped down in his chair as if he had been shot through the heart. He turned white as the blood rushed from his face.

Kathleen could not help herself. The congressman's thoughts, his apprehensions were clearly apparent. Kathleen thought of the young woman who had been so casually disposed of. This time *she* was outraged by the congressman who chose to so dismissively deny his involvement, to blame the victim for her charm. To slither out of responsibility like a snake from its skin. Kathleen blurted, "That *woman* was smart and talented, and you had her shot through the head to protect your career?"

The moment gave Thatcher time to gain his composure. "Nothing you are saying is true. What you are even implying is an outrage; you're making up stories to trap me in your lies, but I will find out the truth in this matter. I do have certain contacts in the crime laboratory who can corroborate my innocence."

"Did you read the paper this morning?" Jim asked.

"I do not bother with that partisan banter," Thatcher replied.

"Jack Johnson is dead," Jim said bluntly. "He was shot while resisting arrest during a kidnapping. The firearm he used in the kidnapping matches the one used to kill Victoria Young. Now, why would Jack Johnson kill Victoria Young?"

Thatcher swallowed nervously. "I am sure I do not know. Perhaps he was the one of those bewitched by Miss Young's charm, but resisted her temptation in a violent, unfortunate manner."

"Oh, I agree, it was a violent and unfortunate manner," Jim interrupted, "but, it was not because of Ms. Young's charm. I doubt if Johnson even knew Victoria Young. To him, she was just another sniper target."

Jim was now sizing up his prey. "Jack Johnson took impeccable notes on all the cases where he changed results or destroyed evidence. Jack was a professional. Ruining people's lives was just a job to him. Jack Johnson's impeccable notes will be your downfall. 'T- A go 1a.m.' You are T. T for Thatcher. You gave him the go ahead to kill Victoria Young at 1 am."

"You can never prove that," Thatcher said with fury in his voice. "It is absolutely untrue!"

Jim was like ice. "I can prove it," he said with a slow grin growing across his face. "It may take some time to go through all the pieces.

We'll check your phone calls. We'll see when you called Victoria. Did you call her to ask her for the 1 a.m. meeting? We'll check your credit cards to see what you bought her, what you paid for. We'll check witnesses to see where and when you met with Victoria Young. The evidence is always there. By the end of this investigation, your life will be an open book. But, in politics, you don't really need a lot of proof. In politics, innuendo seems to be sufficient to end a career." Jim was now gloating. "Victoria Young deserved better than you. I will make certain she is remembered in the way she lived. You think Victoria has no voice to defend herself, and that's where you are wrong. I'm her voice."

As Kathleen and Jim left Thatcher's office, Jim whispered, "Walk slowly."

When they reached the doorway to the hall, they heard a loud, angry southern voice from the intercom on the secretary's desk. "Get me Crowell on the phone immediately!"

As they entered the hallway, Jim nodded with satisfaction "That's what I wanted to hear."

"Jim, there were no lab results linking Thatcher to Victoria Young's baby."

"No," Jim replied, "but there will be. Thatcher had Victoria killed because he got her pregnant, and he couldn't afford the scandal. Just think about it, a white Alabama congressman fathering a child with a black woman."

"So it was all a bluff? There is no evidence that proves Thatcher was the father of Victoria Young's baby?"

"It was a prediction," he shrugged. "The evidence is there. It just has to be exposed. Thatcher's DNA is not going to change. We will get a court order for a DNA sample based on the evidence we have."

"What evidence? We don't have any evidence," Kathleen said, throwing her hands in the air. "The man adamantly denied he had any involvement and he sounded pretty believable. You're forgetting he's a U.S. Congressman. Last time I looked, hit men ranked pretty low in popularity polls. It would be career suicide," she said as she grabbed Jim by the arm, forcing him to stop walking. She looked into his eyes trying to understand. The whole time she had known Jim, he had never leaped to conclusions. He had never tried to guess what the evidence would say.

Jim could see her struggle to understand his actions and after a moment, he turned to look off in the distance before he added quietly, "This case is personal."

Jim and Kathleen spent the next day writing reference notes on everything that had happened in the last several days, so they could evaluate what evidence they had; but the further they got into the details, the more twists, turns, untruths and lies seemed to be revealed. To convince a judge to sign a court order for a congressman's DNA, they knew their argument must be tight.

Kathleen leaned back in her chair thinking about the last few days. She was exhausted, both mentally and physically. Before she took this job, she thought it would be easy. She thought it would be satisfying. They would find the bad guy and put him in jail. She would rid the streets of one more unsavory character and the city would be grateful. She wanted to find the bad guys and arrest them, but they seemed as elusive as a shadow. Was Representative Thatcher the bad guy? Something about his proclamation of innocence seemed so believable to her.

As Kathleen sat at her desk immersed in her thoughts, her attention was drawn to a very well dressed man talking to one of the detectives standing at the office doorway. The detective turned and pointed toward Kathleen. As the detective moved to the side, Kathleen got a clear view of the man.

"Congressman Thatcher!" Her chair wobbled unsteadily as she moved it to stand, stunned the congressman had come to their office.

Jim looked up from his notes, "What?"

Kathleen pointed to the entrance. "I believe Congressman Thatcher is paying us a visit."

Jim glanced at the doorway and leaned back in his chair to assess the situation. "This should be interesting," he said, turning to Kathleen.

Thatcher walked to the edge of their desks. "Good morning, Detectives," Thatcher said in his syrupy southern style. "I am here on this beautiful morning to offer you a sample of my DNA," he said, his demeanor obviously changed from the previous day.

Jim scratched the side of his head. "What are you talking about?"

"I believe the tests the crime laboratory ran falsely identified me as a father to a baby. I am here to set the record straight. I want a genuine sample taken of my DNA. I do not want these vicious rumors about me to circulate any farther then they already have," Congressman Thatcher said. "The crime laboratory, I believe, has made a mistake. Although it may have been an honest mistake, an oversight perhaps, it is hopefully something easily corrected. I want to ensure they have a proper sample of my DNA and not something picked off a glass from my office or a Kleenex in my garbage."

Jim and Kathleen looked at each other in disbelief.

"We don't actually take DNA samples in the office," Kathleen explained.

"I want a sample taken of my DNA," Thatcher insisted.

"We'll take a sample," Jim said, trying to appease the congressman.

"How are we going to take a DNA sample?" Kathleen turned to Jim with eyebrow raised, waiting for his solution.

Jim got up from his desk and walked into the small office area Teri had used the week before to collect a sample of the fetal tissue. On the table in the corner were a couple unused test tubes with red rubber stoppers and a half dozen Q-tip-like wooden applicator sticks.

"We will take a buccal swab," Kathleen started to explain, playing along with Jim's actions. "Buccal swabs are the standard way DNA is collected, now. That will give the laboratory a sufficient sample of your DNA to compare with the standard they have."

"Could you please open your mouth?" Jim said matter-of-factly, as he held up one of the wooden applicators to the congressman's mouth.

Jim rubbed the inside of Thatcher's mouth with the cotton end of the stick, twisting it to cover all sides, then placed the wooden applicator in one of the test tubes, breaking off the portion of the stick he was holding so the applicator would comfortably fit in tube. Jim sealed the tube with the red rubber stopper.

"Congressman Thatcher, thank you for your cooperation," Jim said as he wrote the date and time on the test tube label. "If there has been a mistake, I would like to extend my deepest apologies. I will get this sample to the laboratory as soon as possible."

Congressman Thatcher shook hands with both Jim and Kathleen, smiling the whole time and thanking them for their assistance. As if a large weight had been lifted from his shoulders, Thatcher left with a noticeable lightness to his step, whistling down the hall.

"That evidence is no good," Kathleen said, perplexed Jim would have even taken the time to collect it. "Applicators have to be sterile. The one you used has been sitting out on that table for a week. Who knows what bacteria and cells it has collected. You know, Marcacci eats lunch in there. Any results we get from that swab won't stand up in any courtroom," Kathleen nodded her head before refuting her own statement. "I know. I know. You don't need a court of law in politics. But honestly, Jim, we should a least *try* and test good evidence."

"Oh, please," Jim snapped. "The guy believed the whole drinking glass story. He must consider this swab a 100 times more reliable. Besides, we're not having this swab tested," he added, dismissing Kathleen's statement as ridiculous as he emphatically threw the test tube in the garbage.

"You just told a U.S. Representative you were going to have that sample tested," Kathleen questioned.

"He wouldn't be here demanding to give a sample if he were guilty."

"Or," Kathleen said dramatically, "he thinks that if he makes you think he is innocent, you won't have the sample tested and his name will be cleared for lack of evidence."

"Did you come up with that idea yourself?" Jim said with a glimmer of a smile. "I just want to make certain everyone involved gets credit for the dumbest idea of the year. In October, the department has an awards ceremony, and this one is definitely in the running for the DI award."

Kathleen could only roll her eyes before Jim went back to the business of the case.

"Let's summarize what we know. We know Thatcher is involved in some way because he knew the father of the child was white, so he is somehow involved in this case, but not involved the way we thought," Jim began thinking through the sequence of events. "What we need to know is how the last person Thatcher spoke with yesterday is involved."

"Crowell?" Kathleen asked.

"Crowell," Jim said in agreement.

As they walked into the Homeland Security Building, Kathleen headed toward the elevator but a quick shake of Jim's head told her they were not there to question Crowell. Jim walked through the doors marked with the name Charles Mueller, the regional director of Homeland Security, passing the receptionist without even an acknowledgement. Kathleen quickly followed behind, waving to the woman with an apologetic smile as they walked through the second set of doors.

The man behind the desk looked up quickly to assess the situation, noticing the badge clipped to Jim's belt and the standard issue firearm, the man subtly gestured to his receptionist, letting her know she could return to her desk, but he did not acknowledge Jim or Kathleen until he completed his business with the man standing before him.

"So, these are the new terrorist task force identity cards," he said holding a three by five inch laminated card up to the light to get a better view. "I like the bigger picture; you can see the individual's face."

"Yes, sir," a much younger man in front of his desk answered, taking notes as he spoke. "This is a two by three inch photo."

"That's a good size and the emblem is a holograph?" he said, twisting the card to get a better view.

"Yes, sir, we have the US emblem in the upper right coroner which is a holograph. We also have a smart card wafered in the laminate."

"Once the perimeter is set up, satellites will track the global positioning unit in these cards.

"Hey, that's cool," Kathleen said, walking over to get a better view. "How does that work?"

"Fiber optics in the laminate with a light emitting diode in the center," the young man said proudly. "It took us forever to work out."

"And when the terrorist shoots the agent in the head and takes his card?" Jim said dryly as he paced in the back of the room. The comment silenced everyone for a moment.

The large man behind the desk cleared his throat to draw back the younger man's attention. "Can we get these to everyone on the teams within six months?"

"Or less," the man added before closing up his notebook and leaving the office.

"Now," the man behind the desk said, standing to offer Kathleen and Jim a seat but never taking his eyes off Jim. "Why have police detectives come to pay me a visit?"

The man was quite tall, with a round barrel chest and white wavy hair. The white hair was deceptive because, when Kathleen looked more carefully, she could see the man was much younger than his hair implied. Broad shoulders and massive arms told her that he lifted weights.

"Murder, kidnapping, obstruction of justice," Jim said, staring down the large man before him, un-intimidated. "We have a lot to talk about. Were you aware that one of your agents kidnapped and attempted to murder a forensic scientist? He was shot and killed during the kidnapping."

A loud laugh broke the tension, as the man leaned across the desk with his hand out.

"That's one hell of a story. I didn't get your names, detectives. Charles Mueller, regional director," he said, his hand still outreached toward Jim who gave no reaction for several seconds as he sized up the man before him.

"Jim Jarred," he finally relinquished as he shook the man's hand. "This is my partner, Kathleen Jackson."

"Well," Mueller said, gesturing them to be seated. "I've been at the Vermont office working on some immigration security issues but I'm pretty sure if one of my agents were killed, it would have been in my briefings, or at least a phone call," he chuckled. "Either someone has given you a wild tale or you have some facts mixed up. Either way let's get to the bottom of this."

He reached over to the intercom on the phone and said, "Debbie would you hold my calls and get me a cup of coffee. Oh, and Debbie, I just want to make certain none of our agents have been shot lately…can you check?" he added, smiling at his joke.

Within five seconds, his receptionist came running into his office, coffee cup in hand. The worried look on her face gave away her secret.

"Mr. Crowell said he spoke with you," she said, spilling some of the coffee over the rim as she hurried to his desk. "He said he spoke to you and you agreed to keep this off the radar."

"Off the radar?" Mueller snapped as the smile on his face evaporated. "What the hell does that mean? We don't keep anything off the radar. What exactly happened while I was gone?"

"It's Mr. Crowell's assistant, he had some kind of nervous breakdown. He kidnapped a woman he worked with, no one really knows why. He was always a little on the strange side, you know a bit high strung. He took her out to that old DEA site where there was a shoot out with police."

Kathleen whispered to Jim. "And I thought our department had communication problems."

"You're talking about that Prendergass fellow?" Mueller asked, confused.

"Yeah, George Prendergass," Jim interrupted. "Maybe you can enlighten us on exactly his role in this department and why the Department of Homeland Security is interfering with a police investigation. Obstruction of justice is a pretty serious crime, even if you are a regional director."

"Obstruction of justice?" Mueller said, waving to his administrative assistant. "Debbie, get your pad. I'm going to need you to take notes at this meeting," he added before turning to Jim. "Prendergass has no role in this department."

"What?" Kathleen interrupted, trying to process how this new information worked into the crime.

"What about Thomas Crowell?" Jim asked, leaning over to see what the woman taking notes was writing.

"Thomas Crowell has friends in very high places. I'm not exactly sure who, but I know they were pressuring the President to appoint him to a position in our office. I had concerns about appointing him to anything important. That's why we created the office he has. It's harmless; somewhere to put him."

"Executive Administrator for the Homeland Policing Authority! You call that harmless?" Kathleen said sharply.

"Well, the title sounds impressive, a title Crowell thought up, I might add, but the position heads a program that cross-links databases," Mueller said, taking a sip of his coffee. "They aren't even new databases.

They are ones that already exist. Crime laboratories download the information they find into various databases but the problem is they are written in different programs; they speak different languages. FBI programs can't talk to DEA. DEA programs can't talk to ATF. Crime labs don't talk to crime labs. Crowell is in charge of developing a Computerized Evidence Review and Tracking System; CERTS for short. When the program is fully functional, the information will be downloaded into one main database when the information is generated at the crime lab, but from what I understand, he's been having some troubles with the programming."

"Why would you need a DEA facility for that?" Kathleen questioned.

"You don't," Mueller replied with a shrug. "Crowell's been whining about having a facility of his own since the day he walked through my doors. I told him he could have the property if, and that's a big if, if he were able to identify funding and an approved agency expansion plan. He's never going to get that."

"How does Prendergass fit into this picture?" Jim asked.

"The evidence tech program," Mueller nodded. "That is actually the only good idea I think Crowell has ever had."

"Hiring a psychopath was a good idea?" Kathleen couldn't help resist the jab.

Mueller stared at Kathleen for a moment before continuing. His look, in combination with his size, was quite intimidating but Kathleen had been through too much to back down as she glared back at him.

"It was a pilot project," Mueller continued. "The idea was to train individuals on how to enter data into our system in a consistent manner, then send newly-trained evidence techs out to the crime lab, to enter into the database from the lab. It limits the amount of entry errors. Plus it would fund an extra headcount at the laboratory so they could better utilize their forensic scientists who often do this type of work. I agreed to try out the idea with a few contractual people. They were all hand picked by Crowell. Prendergass was one of the guys on his list, military career, I think," Mueller shrugged. "It's not like this is a field agent position or even a forensic scientist. They're glorified clerical crunching data on computers," Mueller said with a wave of his hand before adding, "But, until Crowell can get the CERTS program going, I'm not approving anymore than fifteen into this program."

"Fifteen!" Kathleen snapped.

"Fifteen is nothing. Do you realize how many crime labs are in this country? And, I'm not even talking about the private labs," Mueller said, looking like he was on the verge of becoming angry that his decision was being questioned.

"Did you happen to do a background check on Prendergass before you hired him?" Jim asked.

"Contractuals get a level two background check. It's fairly rigorous but mostly covers the basics, credit check, police records, that sort of thing," Mueller admitted. "Permanent employees would get a level one, where we would do interviews of neighbors, past employers. Level twos can all be done on computer searches."

"Who would do that check?" Kathleen asked.

"Crowell could have done it from his desk," Mueller said, rubbing his chin. "In fact, I think there was some problem with Prendergass' background check. The FBI called me about it. They didn't want him for some reason, so he ended up at the DC lab."

"The FBI never did a background check on Prendergass," Jim said soberly.

"Really?" Mueller said, surprised. "I didn't think the FBI let anyone into their facility without a background."

"So how did you leave it with the FBI?" Kathleen questioned.

"I told Crowell if someone couldn't pass the FBI check, we needed to let them go. Crowell told me everything had been some kind of confusion but it had all been taken care of. I never asked further. Prendergass was a contractual. I wasn't going to spend a lot of time worrying about him. Other than his first day, I don't think he spent any time in this facility. What exactly happened with Prendergass?"

"We're still working on the Prendergass case, sir," Jim said cautiously, looking over at Kathleen."

"Listen, if there is something going on with Crowell or Prendergass, you let me know," Mueller said, standing to shake their hands. "I will make certain it is investigated, otherwise, I will assume the man snapped and you can handle the investigation."

"One other thing," Jim said slowly. "Are your agents in the habit of threatening police officers?"

"Excuse me?" Mueller said, honestly surprised.

"During our investigation of the kidnapping, we were stopped by two of your agents and told we would be thrown in federal prison if we did not proceed to Crowell's office."

Mueller took a deep breath and rolled his eyes as he turned to Debbie who was vigorously taking notes, "Did Crowell request assistance from our agents?"

"Well," she said meekly as she cleared her throat. "I believe he requested assistance from Special Agents Darnell and Lockhart."

Before the words had left her mouth, Mueller was on the phone paging the two agents to his office. As they entered the room and saw Jim and Kathleen standing in front of their director, the change in their demeanor let everyone know they knew why they had been called down.

"I heard you were doing a little additional work for Mr. Crowell?" Mueller began.

Before he said anything further, Darnell began speaking. "Mr. Crowell asked us for a little drama. He thought they wouldn't willingly come with us immediately and there was apparently a time issue."

"Time issue!" Mueller bellowed. "The man is in data processing. What kind of time issue could he possibly have had?"

The loudness of the response, made both agents take a step back. Although both were large men, they were not even close to the size of the man yelling at them.

After a few moments, Darnell replied, "Sir, I don't know, sir."

"If I ever hear about either of you pulling this kind of stuff again, the only thing you will be doing is data input, is that clear?"

"Absolutely clear, sir," Darnell replied with an exhale.

"Consider this an oral reprimand," Mueller added, waving his hand to dismiss them.

"Yes, sir," they said as they glanced at Kathleen and Jim briefly, then left the room.

"I appreciate that, sir," Jim nodded. "If you have no objections, I think we are going to speak with Crowell."

"No objections. I will be speaking with Crowell myself but I will let you do your interview first. I don't want to be accused of impeding your investigation."

Leaving the office, Kathleen looked back to be sure no one had followed them out.

"What do you think?" she whispered.

"I don't know," Jim said showing an atypical lack of confidence. "Something about him makes me want to trust him but there is something going on. Mueller was pretty quick to cut all ties to Prendergass. He didn't even question what happened."

As they walked into the office of the Executive Administrator to the Homeland Policing Authority, Jim and Kathleen knew they were expected. As with any office, word travels fast when visitors are wandering about, causing trouble.

"Detectives," Crowell said, "I knew it would not be long before you graced my doorway. Please sit down."

"Mr. Crowell, everywhere we go lately people seem to be expecting us," Jim began. "Are you aware that Jack Johnson, the man also known as George Prendergass, was killed while resisting arrest during a kidnapping?"

"I'm aware that you shot him and as I am sure you're aware by now, he was my assistant."

Jim gave a quick nod but stood expressionless in front of Crowell waiting to see what the man would say.

"It must have been a nervous breakdown, don't you think. There is no other explanation for kidnapping that woman but you know I was a little surprised that you, Detective Jarred, were the one who shot him after I gave you specific instructions that Prendergass was *not* to be touched."

"Jack Johnson or George Prendergass, whatever you want to call him, was a criminal," Kathleen said, infuriated with the Crowell's tone. "He tampered with evidence. He got guilty people off by destroying evidence and innocent people convicted. Jack Johnson is not above the law and neither are you."

"I absolutely agree George's actions do need to be investigated and I assure you that we are in the process of addressing the issue," Crowell responded calmly. "If there was any misconduct, we'll find out about it."

Kathleen was talking faster now. "You don't need to investigate the issue. *We* are investigating the issue. We have a lot of evidence to go through and it's all in Jack Johnson's own handwriting. He left exceedingly detailed notes about everything he did. He noted all the cases, how he changed the evidence and when he destroyed it. He kept each case separated in perfectly documented binders."

"Ah, yes, the binders," Crowell said, apparently unruffled by the situation. "We will need those binders for our investigation. If you can have them brought to my office so I can conduct a full investigation, I would appreciate the cooperation."

"We aren't cooperating with you!" Kathleen said incredulously. "We are conducting the investigation."

"I've already made a few calls on this matter," Crowell said calmly. "My assistant was a Federal employee who was working under Federal orders at the time of his death. He was working on things of a confidential nature and his breakdown and death will need to be investigated by a Federal agency."

"He was a contractual employee," Jim broke in angrily. "The Feds have no jurisdiction in this case."

"It's you!" Kathleen said in astonishment.

"Excuse me?" Crowell said, turning his attention back to Kathleen.

"It's you! You were the one giving Prendergass his orders. You were the one who decided who would be innocent and who would be guilty."

"Very good, Detective Jackson," Crowell said, satisfied that his powers had finally been noticed.

"Last time we were here, you said your job is to identify the threats from within, the criminals that jeopardize our way of life. You want to eliminate scandals that allow people to lose focus of the direction you want them to see. Correct?" Kathleen asked.

"Exactly," Crowell said proudly.

"Then why go after Bonavia? That didn't eliminate a scandal. That made a scandal." Jim was quizzing him now.

"Bonavia was a fool. He was always causing trouble, looking into everybody's business, looking for some dirt," Crowell explained.

"Bonavia's demise was just a favor for a friend."

"What are you talking about?" Kathleen asked.

"Bonavia was framed," Jim stepped in, "because he found someone was doing something, maybe something illegal. Perhaps it was our good friend Representative Thatcher."

"Thatcher? Don't be silly; that man is a choir boy. He doesn't even litter, at least not since he became a congressman," Crowell said, enjoying that he had all the answers. "You would be surprised the friends I have," Crowell laughed. "Friends who thought it would be better to get Bonavia out of the House of Representatives," Crowell chuckled. "Now, Thatcher, on the other hand, owes me a lot. I made him the man he is today. From time to time, I ask him for assistance. Payment on the debts he owes; like, assistance from his staffers on this project I have been assigned."

"Like, Victoria Young," Jim said suddenly.

"Yes, Ms. Young. Ms. Young was a fine woman. It's a shame you never got to meet her," Crowell said.

"You're the father!" Kathleen said, amazed.

"I should have known Johnson would not have taken directions from a Representative," Jim said, angry he had made such a basic mistake.

"So you're the T that Jack meant when he wrote 'T- a go 1 a.m.'..." Suddenly Jim remembered his name was Thomas Crowell. "You had her killed because you wanted to conceal the fact that you were the father. It's that simple, isn't it?"

"That's a minor point but, I may have talked to her a little more than I should have about the confidential nature of my job. A fact you will never be able to prove, I'm afraid, not that or the pregnancy or the murder," Crowell said smugly.

"Why *are* you telling us all this information?" Jim asked suspiciously.

"I thought you would have a certain appreciation for the work I am doing. Even if you do not approve of my actions, surely you, who deal with cases on a daily basis, can appreciate the utter simplicity and yet complexity of the things I have done," Crowell explained.

"Are you going to kill us?" Kathleen asked nervously.

"Kill you? Don't be absurd. My dear, this isn't a James Bond movie," Crowell said dismissively. "Why would I kill you? Because you think you have an idea of the things I have done? *Prove it.* By the end of the day, I will have the notes, which I will obediently turn over to the Office of the Independent Counsel once an individual has been appointed to investigate the death of my assistant. Correct me if I'm wrong, but I believe that usually takes four to six months, doesn't it, detective? If you lay one finger on me before that investigation is concluded, I will have your badges and don't think I couldn't make one phone call and have that happen today."

"You're going to bury everything, aren't you?" Jim was disgusted he had to listen to this arrogant criminal flaunt the law in his face. "We're not stopping our investigation. We'll be back with a warrant for your arrest."

"Excuse me," Crowell leaned in toward Jim, cupping one ear with his hand. "Did I hear you say you are planning to interfere in a Federal investigation involving national security? I just want to make certain you did not say that. Talk like that could get you detained pending the outcome of the investigation. Do not mess with powers stronger than you." The arrogance in his voice infuriated both Kathleen and Jim.

"May we go?" Jim's face was like stone.

"By all means, Detective Jarred. Be my guest," Crowell said graciously, as he extended his arm toward the doorway.

CHAPTER TWELVE

KATHLEEN AND JIM left Crowell's office without another word, deep in their thoughts; frustrated, infuriated, they walked to their car.

"You know that man is crazy. He's as crazy as Prendergass. What are we going to do?" Kathleen asked. "Get a warrant?"

"I don't know," Jim answered honestly. Kathleen realized this might be the first time he really did not know what to do.

"We should talk to Captain Freeman. We need to go up our chain of command," Kathleen said, grasping at straws. "They can't shut down our investigation, can they?"

"If it turns into a Federal investigation, they can," Jim said crossly. "Our department steps out of the picture when the Feds take over."

"I say we go to Captain Freeman," Kathleen insisted. "Maybe he can argue for a joint investigation. At least that way we would still have some control over the evidence."

"OK, we can go to Freeman," Jim relented.

Kathleen marveled that the tough, all knowing Detective Jarred was taking her advice for a change but for some reason, it didn't make her feel good.

Captain Freeman did not look happy when Kathleen and Jim passed by the windows to his office. Before they could close the door behind them, Freeman began talking.

"I just got off the phone with Mueller," Captain Freeman said through gritted teeth. "Can you please tell me why a Senate subcommittee is being formed to investigate the death of a psycho evidence tech you shot?" he barked. "What the hell have you been doing? We have been completely shut down. How the hell could you have screwed this one up so badly that Homeland Security has requested everything be sent to the Office of the Independent Counsel? Could someone explain what is going on? He was an evidence tech at the crime lab, for Christ's sake."

The questions came too fast for either Kathleen or Jim to answer, each time starting to explain but having to wait until the next question was finished.

"Captain!" Jim finally yelled. "We believe Crowell orchestrated the crimes in the laboratory and will use his influence to guide the investigation to the wrong conclusions. We need back into this investigation."

"All the evidence points to Crowell," Kathleen added.

"According to the chairman of the Senate subcommittee, who also called me, you have no evidence!" Captain Freeman said sharply. "All you have are accusations concerning an administrator of a federal department. If you had something on Crowell, you should have given it to Mueller. He said you gave him squat."

"We know what the truth is." Kathleen hoped the truth would be enough to compel Captain Freeman into action.

"Listen," Captain Freeman said more calmly to Kathleen. "I have gotten four calls on this case in the last hour…from people who can make a lot of waves. The water is pretty rocky right now. Let's let things settle down. We have an officer shooting of a federal employee. You shot the man and now you want to go after his boss. In a month or two, if you think the federal investigation is coming short, we can make the request for involvement at that time. Until then, I suggest you show a little faith in our Federal Government. I do not want to see your names in the paper being quoted as a conspiracy theorist. Do I make myself clear? You will only make this department look bad."

"Let's go," Jim said as he turned to Kathleen, knowing this was a dead end.

"Listen," Captain Freeman said, trying to appease their concerns, "I will make some calls in a few days and see how the investigation is going."

"In a few days, nothing is going to be going on and that evidence will never make it out of Crowell's office. Thanks, Captain." Jim stood to leave, then looked around the room, frustrated. Then a slow smirk grew across Jim's face as he left the room.

"I know that look, Jarred," Freeman yelled as Jim left the room. "Don't you do anything stupid!"

Jim's muted voice from down the hallway floated into the room. "Never."

Kathleen remained behind, waiting for the captain to notice before she said, "Captain, could I talk to you for a second about something else?"

"Of course," Captain Freeman said, offering Kathleen a chair.

Jim sat in the car waiting for almost half an hour before Kathleen came into view.

"What was that all about?" he asked as she took the passenger seat. Jim could see her look and knew there was something important she wanted to discuss. Jim knew they had become partners. They had shared the fears, the excitement, the danger, anger and frustration of a hard case. He felt for the first time that Kathleen would become a good detective.

"I resigned from the Crime Scene Bureau," Kathleen said simply.

"What? You can't quit, not now. Don't let the frustrations of this one case make you do something you will regret," Jim argued, at a loss as to what to say. "I know I haven't been the best partner and I haven't been the mentor you had hoped for, but we worked so well together on this case. Don't give up."

"It's not you, Jim. It's not the case. Well, it is the case, I hate Crowell going free but it's also me. I'm no good at the job," Kathleen said, sharing her thoughts and feelings with Jim for the first time. "Jim, you walk into a room and you know exactly what is going on. You know who is lying to you and who is telling the truth. You weave a tale, spin a web, and trap the bad guys. You get the information you want and need by playing the players."

"You make me sound like a con artist."

"I don't think of you as a con artist," Kathleen said sincerely. She noticed that, for the first time, his smile was not the one she had become so accustomed to seeing. It was not that kind of smirking smile. It was the smile of a friend.

"I think of you as a good cop. You're getting better every day," Jim said sincerely. "Don't give up so quickly, Kathleen. Once you get to know this job, you will be good at it."

"Jim, have you even been paying attention these last six months? I'm bad, and I mean bad as in NOT GOOD, not bad as in wickedly good. I never know what's going on. Everyone is in on the game but me. If you weren't there to explain all the moves, I'd be a joke. I like to sit back and study things before I can figure them out. I like to give things careful thought. Read, then re-read the situation until I become a part of it. Only then can I can see the truth. I'm not like you. I can't step into a room and in five seconds figure everything out."

"You figure things out," Jim said, trying to make Kathleen remember all the positive things she had done. "You figured out that Thomas Crowell was the father of Victoria Young's child."

"Sure, I figure things out when the suspect stands in front of me and *spills his guts out.*"

"It's more than that and you know it. You read Jack Johnson pretty well. You knew where he was hiding. You knew how he would react in the situation."

"That was different. Jack was just following a predictable pattern." Kathleen signed.

"You've only given this six months! Give me one tangible fact of something you have done that proves you are not a good crime scene investigator," Jim argued.

Kathleen looked out the window trying to condense down all the little pieces of evidence into one fact. A family walked past the window of the car; a mother dragging a tired child behind her. The wind blew the mother's hair in her face as she brushed it away.

"The hair," Kathleen said softly.

"What hair?"

"The hair found on Victoria Young's body."

Jim recalled how Captain Freeman had removed the single strand of blonde hair so many days ago from Victoria Young's body, and how concerned they had been that he might collect it incorrectly. The thought that Captain Freeman might have jeopardized the evidence in this case made Jim laugh at the irony. Jim remembered that lab report had listed it as synthetic, probably from a wig.

"I will never get that hair out of my head," Kathleen confessed. "What was it doing there? What did it mean? How does it fit in the puzzle?"

"I don't know," Jim said honestly. "It could have blown there. Young could have had it on her body when she got to the Mall. Someone passing by might have dropped it on her clothing when she took the Metro. Not all the evidence we collect is going to mean something. You have to sift through the evidence. You have to find out what is important and what is unimportant. That's our job."

"I will always wonder," she said, "and, that's what makes this job so hard for me."

There was a truth to Kathleen's words that Jim understood. He thought for a moment trying to come up with an argument, any argument for Kathleen to stay.

"I want to resign. I know it's the right thing for me to do. Remember when you told me I would someday find my way? I am telling you, it is not here. It is not in this job."

Jim looked at his partner. "When will you leave?"

"I made arrangements with Captain Freeman to move over to the District Headquarters. I'm going to clean out my desk in the morning." The decision seemed to lift a weight from Kathleen's shoulders.

"Well, then," Jim said as he started the car. "You're still on the books and we still have one thing left to do."

Kathleen gave him a surprised look as he sped out of his parking spot. What could possible be left for them to do, she wondered, now that they had been taken off the case. "You're not going to get me into trouble on my last day, are you?"

"Nope," Jim grinned. "But, I did make copies of all the binders."

Jim dreaded work the next day. He had thought about calling in sick to avoid all the goodbyes, but he knew that was the cowardly thing to do. There was something about the thought of Kathleen leaving that was more painful than he expected it to be. Not seeing her every day was something Jim had never considered.

As Jim walked into the office, he saw Teri Sedgwick standing with Captain Freeman. Jim smiled warmly at her, noticing her bruises from the kidnapping were still readily visible. Teri smiled back, but Jim could see the pain from her swollen lip limited her smile.

Jim's smile disappeared when he saw Kathleen packing a box with her things from her desk.

"Well, Jim. I guess you know Kathleen will be leaving the Crime Scene Bureau," Captain Freeman said in a loud booming voice. Jim just nodded.

"Don't act so somber, Jim. No one died here," Captain Freeman said but then quickly added, "Oh, ah, that was a poor choice of words. What I mean to say is, we value Kathleen and we are not just going to throw her out on the street. This just wasn't a good fit. That's one of the problems we have when we select a person for a position rather than having them grow into it."

"I thought she was a good fit," Jim said truthfully.

"The department Psychologist noticed the work Kathleen did on the Johnson kidnapping when he was reviewing the case for the Shooting Review Board. She did some fine work, and he's been pushing for an assistant for years," the captain explained. "He has already spoken to the Deputy Director about creating the position for Kathleen. I don't know if that will go through, but it's one possibility."

"Psychology?" Jim said looking over at Kathleen. "I thought you were getting your Ph.D. in Forensic Investigation."

"I am," Kathleen said, pleased she finally had a small piece of information Jim did not know. "My Ph.D. is in Forensic Investigation, but if you remember I have a Master's Degree in Criminal Justice and an undergraduate degree in Psychology. A good mix don't you think?"

Jim noticed the contentment in Kathleen. She seemed happy and lighthearted, but Jim could not help but sigh with a heavy heart, as if the weight from Kathleen had been redistributed to him. He couldn't understand why Kathleen's leaving felt so uncomfortable.

"Jim," Captain Freeman's voice cut through Jim's thoughts. "I would like to introduce you to your new partner, Teri Sedgwick."

The astonishment on Jim's face was unmistakable and slow smile began to grow across Jim's face as he looked over to Teri.

"What is going on here?" Jim asked.

"Teri came to me yesterday, just before you visited me, asking if there might be a job for her with our Crime Scene Bureau," Captain Freeman explained. "I'm happy to say that we have put the paperwork through to hire her as an Inspector. It's not a detective, but she can work toward that under your supervision. Teri can work in the section and take the necessary classes to earn her detective badge."

"What?" Kathleen turned her head, for the first time interested in the conversation. "You can do that?"

"Sure," Jim nodded casually. "It's a civilian rank. She can't carry a firearm."

Kathleen thought back to all those difficult trials she had to endure in her days at the Academy. "Why didn't you make me an inspector?" she asked, turning toward Captain Freeman.

"Uh, well, Teri has more practical experience in law enforcement. You were just from academia you know, unproven, untested," Captain Freeman said, becoming more uncomfortable with each word he spoke. He knew he had the approval to hire Kathleen on as an inspector but wanted to test her resolve for the demanding life of a police officer.

Jim stepped in to assist the captain. "Teri's a natural. I think you will be great at this job," Jim took Teri's hand to welcome her to the department. In a move of unintentional emotion, Jim pulled her close and gave her a hug.

"Jim, you know my rule," Freeman added gruffly. "Partner's don't hug."

"You're quitting the lab? I thought you loved that job," Jim asked as he released her.

"I do love it, but I want something more, something different. I want these cases to be real. I mean, they are real. We always treat them like real cases. I guess it is hard to explain," Teri stumbled for the right words. There was so much involved in why she had asked for this transfer. Some of it was to get out of the lab, some of it was to work a case from start to finish, some of it was working with Jim. Teri knew Jim would be retiring soon, and she simply wanted to work with him.

"Teri's knowledge of the lab's capabilities are going to be very helpful to the Crime Scene Bureau. Collecting evidence, requesting tests," the captain said, pleased with his coup. "We are going to use the crime laboratory to its highest potential. I think Teri is going to be a huge asset." Freeman slapped Teri on the back harder than she expected. "Welcome on board."

"Captain!" An officer yelled from the hallway, "You'd better come see this."

Everyone looked out the office windows into the hallway. A large group had formed in the break area at the end of the hall, and seemed to be watching the television in the break area.

"What's going on?" the captain barked.

"There's a press conference," one of the officers yelled. "Someone's making a press release."

"It better not be anyone from this department," Captain Freeman shouted, his blood pressure rising.

"It's the director from the crime lab, Mike Marino," Teri said softly.

"What?" the captain said, spinning around from the television to Teri.

"Mike is calling a press conference to tell the public about the problems, or I guess you would call them the errors that the laboratory has been making," Teri explained. "Haven't you heard? The FBI is taking over the investigation of what happened in our lab. Homeland Security sent over boxes of stuff to the FBI late yesterday. The FBI came over to the lab and interviewed Mike until late last night. After they left, he called me. He called everyone involved to let us know."

"He's probably going to lose his job," Kathleen said soberly, her eyes were wide in wonderment.

"Feds against feds," he winked. "This ought to be interesting."

"I think he knows his job is on the line," Teri said, confused at Jim's statement. "He told me the only thing he wanted was to leave with his integrity intact. You know FBI investigations…they can take forever. Mike wanted to make certain those who were falsely convicted were aware there were problems. Who knows, politics are strange to say the least. Maybe the mayor will keep him on. At least he knows he's honest."

The captain and Teri moved toward the television to watch the announcement. Jim turned to see if Kathleen was coming. She had just finished emptying her desk into the box. As he looked at Kathleen, a sinking feeling came over him. He did not want her to go. He wanted to listen to her voice asking all those infernal questions and to watch her as she struggled to tell a lie.

As Kathleen headed for the door, "I wish you wouldn't go," he said quietly.

"I'm just taking this down to the car," Kathleen said, holding up the box she had filled. "I will be back to say goodbye."

Kathleen had to laugh. For a moment she felt like she was looking at small boy about to lose his best friend. "Jim, life goes on. It will be OK."

"I know," Jim said awkwardly. "I just thought maybe we could do something outside of work. Could you come to Mama's tomorrow? You know, it's Saturday. We *do* get weekends off, at least sometimes. Come to the Stone Soup Café, you'll enjoy yourself. My boys and I are going to make a payment on the conference room."

"Come to the Café tomorrow?" Kathleen asked as her thoughts quickly faded to the memory of that wonderful café and the garden. It had seemed like ages since they had been there sitting at a table looking out over the city, intoxicated by the fragrance of a stroll through a Monet painting. Kathleen imagined herself sitting in the courtyard, looking at the world through a gazing globe.

"It's Jenny's garden," Jim said softly, as if he were reading Kathleen's mind.

"What?"

"It's Jenny's garden. Jenny, my wife, planted it. When Pete and I worked late, Jenny stayed and worked on the garden. She thought we needed a tranquil place after a night of analyzing violent crimes. It was a place where we could escape from the world. Jenny loved to garden."

"It is a lovely garden," Kathleen said sincerely.

"Come tomorrow. I think the peonies are in bloom," Jim said as he took the box from Kathleen and walked her to her car. "What else do you have to do on a beautiful spring Saturday?"

"Not much," Kathleen smiled. "I'll be there."

"Great. Come in the morning. We'll have fun. Oh, and don't wear any good clothes," Jim said with a huge smile that warmed Kathleen. "Conference room payments are often very messy."

EPILOGUE

KATHLEEN ROUNDED THE corner to see the heartwarming sight of the Stone Soup Café. The sign waved in the light breeze. The neighborhood seemed to be a long lost friend. As she reached the entrance of the cafe, she could see a piece of paper in the window. Written in unsteady handwriting, it read CLOSED FOR REFRESHEN-ING. Kathleen jiggled the door, and it opened easily as the smell of fresh paint and home cooking filled foyer.

Stepping in, she could see Jim painting the trim on the far side of the dining room. Next to him was a boy, slightly taller than Jim, but with his face and light brown hair that was much drier than the last time Kathleen has seen him. Unlike his brother, Rob had the same slender build as Jim. Across the room was David, who waved as he scrambled up a ladder, his untamable mane bouncing with each step.

The tables were moved to one end of the room, and a painter's tarp draped over them. Tarps covered the floor. Cans of paint and several ladders were spread around the room. As Kathleen looked around, she noticed how "refreshed" the half-painted room looked.

Jim looked up from his painting and a huge smile came to his face when he caught sight of Kathleen. Jim stepped toward her, his arms out stretched to give a warm handshake or a friendly pat on the back. Starting to put his hand out, he realized it was covered in wet paint. With a shrug, Jim leaned in and kissed Kathleen on the cheek. "I'm glad you came."

Kathleen stepped back, surprised to get such an affectionate greeting. "I do realize," Jim said, recognizing her uneasiness, "that it is considered poor form to give a *friendly* greeting to one's partner, but I will point out that you are not my partner," he grinned as he turned toward his sons.

"I never got to introduce my boys at the game. May I introduce, my youngest son Dave, high atop the ladder," Jim said, gesturing like a ringmaster at a circus. "David, may I introduce Kathleen Jackson," gesturing grandly to Kathleen.

"Hello, Ms. Jackson," Dave said, waving a paint roller.

"Call me Kate."

"OK, hi, Kate," Dave said as he resumed rolling a fresh coat of paint on the upper walls of the restaurant.

"Kate?" Jim questioned with a confused look on his face. "You have always insisted at work everyone call you Kathleen. I think, in fact, the only one who gets away with calling you anything else is Captain Freeman. Is this some kind of new leaf you are turning?"

"I do realize," Kathleen said, trying to mimic Jim's voice and mannerism, "that I consider it poor form to call me anything other than Kathleen at work, but I will point out that we are not at work and my friends call me Kate."

Jim had to laugh at Kathleen's return of his humor.

Turning to the boy standing next to him, Jim said, "This strapping young man," as he slapped his hand covered with wet paint on the shoulder of his older son, "is Rob, my oldest."

"Dad!" Rob said moving away, trying to see the white handprint of wet paint on his back. "It's nice to meet you, Kate. As you can see, my Dad has no appreciation for fine clothes."

"Hey, I told you to wear painting clothes," Jim said, nudging Rob with his elbow. "But, Rob here is a little more concerned with impressing any cute girls who might walk past the window than dressing in tattered paint clothes."

"Hey, what can I say," Rob said with a grin. "The clothes make the man."

A voice from the back of the store turned everyone's head.

"Is that Kathleen I hear?" Mama said as she came through the kitchen doors. "Kathleen, it is wonderful to see you," Mama gave Kathleen a kiss on each cheek. "I so much want to thank you for being such a good partner to Jimmy."

"Well, I'm pretty certain I wasn't that good of a partner to Jim," Kathleen laughed thinking about the last six months, especially the last two weeks. "But if there is one thing you could say about Jim is that he did put up with me."

Mama waved her hand and head together as if to discredit Kathleen's last words. Mama's voice trembled a bit as she spoke. "You were a good partner to Jimmy. You were a good partner to Jimmy and to Peter," her eyes glistened with tears, but before anyone could say another word, Mama changed the subject.

"Before you start anything, you need a fresh cup of good Italian coffee. I will bring some out," Mama said as she turned back toward the kitchen.

Jim turned to Kathleen. "Listen, I know I wasn't a very good partner to you either. It was my fault that we didn't work together better. But, who knows, depending where you end up in the department, we may be working together from time to time. I just wanted you to know that I will do better. I promise."

"Working together?" Kathleen said surprised. "I thought you were retiring."

"Who has time to retire? I'm constantly breaking in new people at the Crime Scene Bureau," Jim said with a big smile. "They just can't live without me."

"Ah, yes, Teri," Kathleen smiled back. It was a good fit, Kathleen thought as she pictured them working together. Kathleen looked around the room. "Where is Teri?" she asked, surprised Teri was not there yet.

"Teri?" Jim said, surprised Kathleen would ask. "I suppose she's at home with her husband."

"Husband?" Kathleen said with even greater surprise. "I didn't know Teri was married."

"She's been married the whole time I've known her," Jim laughed. It was the laugh that always annoyed Kathleen because it always told her that she had once again missed the clues that told the story. But this time, Kathleen felt a curious contentment. She no longer had to compete with Jim's twenty years of experience of clue reading.

"You know, you may want to brush up on those observation skills before you go interview for that Assistant Police Psychologist job," Jim jabbed. "Somehow I think observations might be important. It is, of course, just a guess. I have never been an Assistant Police Psychologist. Actually, come to think of it, I don't think I have never even met an *Assistant* Police Psychologist."

"First," Kathleen said feigning irritation, "I will have you know that I am *very* observant. For example, I observed that Teri does not wear a wedding ring. Second, where is this fly-by-night husband of hers that doesn't show up or call? When she works all hours into the night, where is he? When she's kidnapped, no one even bothers to *tell* him. He never shows up anywhere, not even when she needs some help sleeping under her desk. Not a very close relationship, if you ask me. What exactly does he do? And, third," Kathleen said a little louder, "I AM an Assistant Police Psychologist. They called me this morning to offer me the job, thank you, very much."

Jim watched Kathleen's moment of immense satisfaction for a minute, before deflating it a little. "Well, forensic scientists seldom wear rings because they wash their hands so much and have to wear gloves. Teri's wedding ring is on a chain around her neck. And, her husband *is* a fly-by-night husband or at least a sail-by-night husband. He is a Commander in the Navy on the U.S.S. Atlantis. It's a nuclear submarine. He came in on shore leave last night. And, finally," Jim said loudly and slowly, clearly enunciating every word. "Congratulations on the job! You will be a natural."

"And, the best thing of all," Kathleen said, "is that the position has the rank of Lieutenant."

"Lieutenant! But, you do know that I'm not going to take orders from any Lieutenant who can't tell a good lie when they need to," Jim bent over close to Kathleen and whispered, "Here's your paint roller, Lieutenant. Conference rooms are expensive so you'd better get to work." Then, he turned to his sons and shouted, "Unless you guys want this to last all day, you'd better get painting. After that, we're going to polish the floors."

"Not until Kathleen has had some coffee," Mama said as she came out of the kitchen with a fresh pot.

Kathleen backed against the window with her coffee and listened to the stories of family that filled the room.

Rob reminisced about when his Dad and Pete brought a slab of beef into the back room because Pete was going to write a book on puncture wounds.

"He hadn't checked the slab," Rob laughed. "It was frozen solid. It took a week for that thing to thaw."

"Mama, didn't you eventually serve that to your customers?" Jim teased.

"I did no such thing, Jimmy. You know that," Mama said, smiling at the absurdity of having that hanging carcass in the back conference room for over a week.

"No, Dad, don't you remember, you brought that meat home once you had stabbed it a million times. We ate it for a month," Rob teased.

Dave told a story about how his Mom had planted a Ginkgo tree in her garden. When Jenny had planted the tree, she had described to everyone how in a few years its graceful fan-shaped leaves and a delicate trunk would give a beautiful accent to the courtyard, and that they should remember this planting day when that day came.

"Oh, yeah, it was beautiful," Rob added as he painted the trim around the window. "Until spring came and it had berries that stunk to high heaven."

"Boy, did that tree smell horrible," Jim added, thinking back to those pleasant times. "It smelled like a decaying body, drenched in pond scum."

"And, covered in honey," Dave added as he finished covering the upper wall in fresh paint.

"Oh, that smell had to go," Mama said as the room broke into laughter. "The customers complained so much."

"Yeah, we remembered the day we planted it and the day we pulled it out and threw it into the dumpster," added Rob.

"Dad, do you remember when you had the party for Captain Freeman's promotion?" Dave said, recalling the huge party Pete and Jim threw for their captain.

"The Captain Morgan Party," voices sang together.

Their voices faded into a medley of laughter as Kathleen's thoughts drifted. She closed her eyes as a symphony played upon her senses. Joy echoed off the high tin ceilings and the scent of Mama's food danced around the room like a Thanksgiving dinner from her childhood. Kathleen felt the beam of sunlight on her back as it shone through the huge plate glass window bathing everyone in its glow as she felt the warmth of the light and the people embrace her.

Kathleen took a sip of her coffee and looked around the room. Somehow, she knew she *would* find her way.

ABOUT THE AUTHOR

SUSAN CONNELL VONDRAK is a 24-year veteran of the Illinois State Police, in the forensic department. She started her career as a forensic toxicologist, and currently is the Director of Research and Development and the Statewide Training Program. Vondrak began writing police procedural novels to entertain her family, but with the public's current interest in forensics, she began to take the writing more seriously. NO EVIDENCE OF A CRIME is her first novel, and the first of a series of three novels.

Made in the USA
Lexington, KY
30 August 2011